CISKE the RAT

CISKE

Doubleday & Company, Inc., Garden City, New York
1958

the RAT

by Piet Bakker

TRANSLATED BY

CELINA WIENIEWSKA

AND

PETER JANSON-SMITH

All of the characters in this book are fictitious,
and any resemblance to actual persons, living or dead,
is purely coincidental.

LIBRARY OF CONGRESS CATALOG CARD NUMBER 58–6629

PRINTED IN THE UNITED STATES OF AMERICA
FIRST EDITION

CISKE the RAT

I CAN well remember the day Ciske came to our school.

"Today we are getting a boy who will make our lives a misery," said Maatsuyker, the headmaster, as we stood, some of us smoking cigars, in the corridor before classes began.

"A terrible type! And it is you, Bruis, who are privileged to have him in your class."

I tried to look as disinterested as possible, since Maatsuyker was apt to get rather excited and to become very overbearing on these occasions, especially where I was concerned as I was the junior member of his staff. He knew that the others had ceased to be impressed by him long ago.

"Whom am I getting in my class?"

Maatsuyker let the cigar ash fall onto his vest and became disagreeably animated. "A pearl, my dear fellow; one that they want to get rid of at the Catholic school and have turned over to us. Our new pupil is called Francis Aloysius Gerard Freimuth, but he is by no means as pious as his Christian names would imply. He is already not unknown to the police, in fact a typical juvenile delinquent. He apparently threw an inkwell at the head of his former class mistress."

Maatsuyker grinned at me unpleasantly, and then proceeded to give me a few hints on how to be a good schoolmaster. "If I may advise you, shove him straight into the corner. One can only deal with boys of this sort by being tough with them. The more firmly you handle him, the sooner he will come to respect you. The best thing of all would be to treat him immediately to a sound thrashing."

"That I have no intention of doing," I answered sullenly. "That would only show the boy at once that I was really afraid of him."

"A nice little job for Bruis," put in Tedema. "Our friend Bruis still has some ideals left. He will have quite a handful to educate."

I always rather liked Tedema. She was a typical sour schoolmarm, but she really cared about her charges, although she often cursed them. This was not surprising, though, considering that she had to cope with fifty years of age and fifty pupils. In addition she suffered from asthma.

Meerstra, whom I liked best of my colleagues, nodded at me encouragingly. "Yes, my dear Bruis, you may have quite a time of it, all things considered. I myself once had such a customer in my class, who used to pinch the chalk from under my very nose. One day he did not turn up and two weeks later I heard that they had put him in jail for blowing a safe!"

At the end of the corridor there now appeared a boy, whose head did not even reach to the children's coat pegs. A tiny slender fellow, who stood there tightly pressed against the wall.

"Ha! There he is!" exclaimed Maatsuyker and immediately went up to the boy, towering over him. It infuriated me to see that he gave the boy quite unnecessarily a clip over the ear. At the same time, we heard his rasping voice again: "Why don't you take off your cap? Hurry up—take your cap off!"

The fool! All the children run along the hall with their caps on.

The boy was completely taken aback, but as Maatsuyker was clearly getting ready to hit him again, he slipped under his arm and ran off. Verbeest, who always used to arrive a little later than the rest of us in the morning, because he had to take his little daughter to nursery school, caught him and carried him struggling back to Maatsuyker. "Here's the fugitive," he said, laughing.

By then I had had enough of this. Maatsuyker's stupid behavior did not fit in with the plan that had begun to form in my mind. I had decided to treat the new boy just like any other child in my class, but now Maatsuyker had completely spoiled this for me.

"I'll take him along to class!" I said firmly. "Come with me, my young friend."

The boy eyed me nervously. He had large eyes, full of expression. They were beautiful eyes and were particularly noticeable under their colorless brows in the pale face with its thin lips. All in all he seemed a forlorn bundle of misery. And yet that would have been true only if the eyes had been different. Those eyes, however, dominated everything.

What do you want from me? they seemed to say in hostile

defiance, and I suddenly remembered that this boy was known as "the Rat": Ciske, the Rat.

"Come along!" I said sharply, and Ciske meekly followed me.

I have always envied teachers like Meerstra and Jorissen, whom nature has endowed with the ability to find the right tone to use for all pupils. I myself certainly didn't possess it at that time. A few hundred pupils would have to be sacrificed as guinea pigs before I became a good teacher.

When I took "the Rat" into the classroom, the children were sitting apparently intent on their exercise books, but I could see that they all stole curious glances at the new boy. He had the expression of a man in the dock who has made up his mind to admit nothing.

"Now then, my boy, let's have your name," I said as naturally as I could.

But "the Rat" must have recognized something forced in my tone; he looked at me steadily but said nothing.

You don't take *me* in, said those eyes, the eyes of a wary, suspicious, wild animal.

"It's not very smart of you not to answer," I said quietly.

Ciske's eyes did not leave my face, but he still said nothing.

Then I made a mistake. "Perhaps you would rather tell the friendly gentleman outside what your name is?" I asked ironically.

I immediately realized that this was a stupid thing to do—to threaten the boy in this way. Ciske disdainfully shrugged his shoulders, not a trace of fear to be detected in his face.

I said sharply, "Well then, sit on the front bench, boy-without-a-name."

Drikus van den Berg, who was already sitting on the front bench, moved to one side, as if he now had a leper for a neighbor. I could foresee that that very afternoon there would be a note from his mama: "Dear Mr. Bruis, How can you expect my boy to sit next to this dreadful child? . . ."

"The Rat" remained unperturbed. And I suffered my first defeat. "Reading books out!" I barked to cover my irritation. In the hour ahead of me, I determined to observe Ciske secretly, without his noticing. When he had reached for his book I took it out of his hands. "You don't belong to us yet, since you haven't told us your name!" I whispered these words quite softly in his ear. He became a shade paler.

So, one can get some reaction from him, I said to myself; and then we began the reading lesson. As I called out each child's name, he or she would chant out the sentences in a monotone.

Small and thin, Ciske sat there at his desk. He was looking at the ceiling. I wondered what he was thinking. What kind of boy was he? He interested me more than the rest of the class put together. Lena Heinrink stubbornly read the same sentence incorrectly, over and over again. The class laughed, as they always do when somebody is so gloriously stupid. They were all waiting for my usual comment: "Well then, who would like to try to improve on this?" But I decided not to interrupt just yet because I noticed that Ciske was by now looking at Drikus's book. Suddenly I said to him, "*You* have a try now! Hmm . . . A pity I don't know your name. For you, Drikus, *you* have a name." The Rat blushed scarlet. So far so good!

Things went on like that all through the morning. The Rat was not really one of us and was terribly bored. A child who is forced to be idle is never happy.

But I have never been the sort of person to stand too much on my own pride, especially where children are concerned. They usually win, because their characters are not yet affected by any feelings of responsibility. A lot would have to happen before the Rat would come to me of his own free will and say, "Please, sir, my name is Francis Aloysius Gerard Freimuth."

Therefore I held Ciske back for a moment when I dismissed the class. I put a piece of paper in front of me and asked in a matter-of-fact tone, "When is your birthday?"

"August 8." That was the first time I heard his hoarse, expressionless voice. The rest followed quickly enough; with embarrassment he rattled off his Christian names.

"I am glad I know at long last what your name is," I said, much relieved. "Now I can include you in things and you don't need to just sit and watch."

Was he pleased to have been accepted into the community? I don't think he was. He looked at me coldly, but the hostility had disappeared from his eyes.

In the afternoon we tackled fractions. Ciske had no idea what they were. "Didn't you ever learn about them?" I asked him.

"I haven't got that far," he said, and was clearly not worried about it.

In the last half hour I told the class to draw what they liked. There is no better way of getting to know one's pupils. The Rat was a study in grim concentration and drew two airplanes firing at one another with their machine guns. Even the pilot who was shown bailing out of his burning machine was sketched with realism. The frightening light had appeared again in Ciske's eyes. His drawing had force and expression. Ciske was so absorbed by his work that when Drikus unintentionally jogged his arm he gave him a powerful dig in the ribs. I could not fail to see how professional that blow was and that Drikus was obviously very impressed. If he hadn't been a plucky lad, it would certainly have produced tears.

At four o'clock I met Ciske's mother. I took an instant dislike to that blowzy overdressed woman. She was wearing a little hat, overloaded with flowers, and a cheap yellowish fox fur. Her veil only partly covered her vulgar features, and I could plainly see an ugly mole on her face.

She had come to give me, as Ciske's new master, permission to thrash her son as often as I liked. Without having studied, she had reached the same conclusions as Maatsuyker regarding a teacher's duties; she obviously had a natural talent for this sort of thing.

Without trying very hard, I got quite a good idea of the Rat's home environment. Mrs. Freimuth was most free with her revelations, particularly when it came to blackening the character of "that fellow," Ciske's father, who did not care a damn about anything and only came home when he had no money left to buy gin. He had just walked out and left her to cope with four children! She had to earn her living as a barmaid—wasn't that awful? And to have a child like Ciske, a limb of Satan, didn't I agree? Of course she sometimes worried about her other children, but she could cope with them. Only the other day, when Ciske threw a plateful of food on the carpet, she had locked him up in the coal shed for the night. And it worked! That was the only way to manage when one was a mother on her own!

"But that Ciske"—her voice broke with excitement—"he is as wicked as sin, I can tell you, a thorough good-for-nothing. Although he is my own flesh and blood, I can say nothing for him. He is bad, bad, bad! It may seem silly, but I am often afraid of him. Sometimes in the middle of the night I wake up screaming because Ciske has been standing in front of me, with a big knife in his hand, wanting to murder me. In my dreams, of course. But he will help me to an early grave; me, his mother!"

Should I feel any sympathy for this witch? It would be a sheer waste of time.

"The brat has the devil under his skin," said Ciske's mother as an afterthought and then expressed her pleasure at being able to speak to an understanding person.

It was already dark in the hall by the time Mrs. Freimuth, swaying her hips, took her leave. I felt a lump in my throat. The atmosphere of the school did not help—it was at its worst—with its smell of damp clothes. Everything was bare and empty.

I went to wash and thought about Ciske's mother. Such a woman is one of the most pathetic specimens of the human race. But she certainly explained a lot about my Rat. Could one wonder that the boy was rebellious?

After school I went over to the street where Ciske lived. I found tall tenement houses, with only a glimpse of a gray sky between them, and a thin drizzle of rain falling into numberless dirty puddles.

Why must children grow up in such surroundings where there is not a trace of color? My God, even if their families live in a single room, can't they at least have a sister wearing a clean apron, and a smiling mother! What can we expect from a child that has none of these things?

Why is it that, on the whole, the children feel well and happy at school although it is a dreary building where the walls run with damp? It is because there is a warm human atmosphere there—if one forgets about the few teachers who are too free with the rod!

Because of this warm human atmosphere, I still like being a teacher.

AT THE end of Ciske's first week in my class he was still odd man out. He did his work, but avoided all contact with the other children. He was by no means stupid. He was the last to arrive in the morning and used to slip hurriedly into his place. There he would sit quite still, just waiting for the beginning of the lesson without displaying interest.

He was not shy, as became clear when Charlie Kerk, fussing as usual, wanted to take the Rat's exercise books during break. I saw Ciske's face harden. Before I could do anything to prevent it, Charlie got a skillfully aimed punch in the stomach. It was an effortless, almost professional blow: not a display of temper but a simple warning to Charlie not to interfere in Ciske's affairs. It made Charlie drop the exercise books and catch his breath.

I stood the Rat in the corner for half an hour. I might have left him there for two or even three hours for all the impression it made on him.

The other children didn't know what to make of the Rat, and so they left him alone. For his part, Ciske did not make any effort to get himself accepted into their circles. He would look arrogantly at his classmates and avoid them, but if they tried to come too near him he would immediately clench his grubby fists.

I began to wonder how to put an end to this unfriendly state of affairs.

An outsider like the Rat is bad for any community. A class is a class, even though it is a mixture of bright boys and girls and dunces, of well-behaved and troublesome children. In my class then I had a boy called Drikus, the one who sat next to the Rat—a perfectly ordinary, average pupil, not particularly stupid, not particularly bright, industrious and dull. If they had all been like Drikus, I would have been yawning all morning. One must have a sprinkling of "characters" in a class. Yes, even a prattler like Charlie Kerk, who had to be corrected three times an hour, could bring some color into the daily routine. Even the hopelessly silly Betty Van Gemert used to break the monotony with her monumental stupidity. And when it came to the taciturn Rat—he at least was a personality: sullen, complex, and touchy though he was, he had boundless vitality. I had grown fond of the Rat. But he had to stop being the outsider in our community. Somehow I had to achieve this. Once I could make Ciske understand that the whole world was not against him, I would make a start.

And yet there was someone who seemed to be fond of the Rat. It was a custom in the school for each master to take his class to the gate after lessons. One day, after Ciske had passed me without a greeting, as usual, I saw him leap down the stairs two at a time, nearly knocking down Charlie Kerk, fly across the road, narrowly avoiding an enormous truck, and run up to a man who slapped him heartily on the back. In high spirits, behaving for once like any normal boy, he then skipped along beside the man as he moved off.

Could the man be his father? I sincerely hoped so. A boy with such a mother needs a father whom he can love, even if that father is not very much in evidence.

In the afternoon the same man brought Ciske to school. Most children, I have noticed, are embarrassed when their parents put in an appearance, but the Rat took no notice of the others. He was chattering away merrily to the slim man in the well-cut blue suit, who listened, smiling, to the childish talk. The man struck me as a bit casual; in his deeply tanned face one could see from time to time the glint of sharp white teeth. He glanced at me, appeared to hesitate for a moment, and then swung unhurriedly and nonchalantly across the road toward me. When he had come up to me, I found myself looking into Ciske's eyes, except that these eyes were perhaps even more compelling and proud. They looked searchingly into my face; the heavy lids did not flicker.

The Rat looked angry; he did not like any unforeseen interference in his life. He was obviously wondering what I could want with his father.

I told Ciske to go on in to school.

I felt strangely nonplussed. What could I say to this silent man? "I would like to speak to you about your son"? No, I decided, that would be the wrong approach. Suddenly I made up my mind not to mince words. "Ciske is going to the dogs; do you realize that?"

The shot went home: the haughty indifference disappeared from the gray eyes, but in spite of this he had a ready answer. "Perhaps—but he's not the only one."

This hard-boiled fellow was clearly not a father in the ordinary sense of the word. Nevertheless I realized that I must win him over if I wanted to get anywhere with the Rat. "I thought you were fond of the boy, Freimuth! When I saw him run up to you this morning, I thought, So there *is* someone who cares for him—let me finish what I have to say. At home there seems to be no one who has a good word for him and therefore he hates everybody. The boy is a mass of distrust. I would like to help him, as I have become fond of him, but I cannot do it entirely on my own; I need your help. Everything depends on you, and it is you who are leaving him in the lurch. That's a pretty poor way to behave, in my opinion!"

(If Maatsuyker had heard me, he would certainly have said, "By the way, Bruis, do you think that is the proper way to address a pupil's father?")

Freimuth glared at me. For a moment I was afraid that I had been so blunt that he would turn on his heel with an unfriendly "Go to hell!" and leave me standing there. To my relief he only said, "You shouldn't talk rubbish, my dear sir! You know absolutely nothing about me or about my life. Do you imagine I enjoy leaving the boy with that woman? He is the only thing I care about, I can tell you."

Although this was said roughly, I could detect an undercurrent of genuine feeling. "Perhaps you could come back at four o'clock," I suggested. "Then we could talk more freely."

"All right," he said and sauntered dispiritedly away.

Maatsuyker advised me to be careful when later I foolishly told him that Freimuth was going to visit me after school. "By all accounts he is a tough customer. I am told that he has already been in jail for resisting arrest. I always believe that an apple does not fall far from the tree."

A typical example of Maatsuyker's poisonous philosophy.

When the classroom was empty just after four, Freimuth wandered in as if he were completely at home there. Yet his entrance had nothing provocative about it. He squatted rather than sat, in a somewhat studied pose, on the front bench. We each lit a cigar.

He was completely at ease and there wasn't the slightest trace of servility in his manner. He was clearly a man who had seen something of the world.

It was a straightforward story which Ciske's father told me, without any false shame, omitting all the more personal details. He'd been a stoker on a coal freighter, ten months at sea, one week at home, then back to sea again—a vagabond of the seas and ports. When he'd come home one day from Rio, one of the girls from the cheap night club that he used to frequent had led him to a cradle. The child was his, she said, and he—the stupid clod—had married her. In the course of the years three more children were born, but only with Ciske was it certain that he was his own flesh and blood.

Thus had fate stranded him high and dry one day, he explained. He was not the type for marriage. When a man has spent the better part of twenty years at sea, with never longer than one month ashore, he can't easily settle down to life in an apartment with a nagging wife. Ciske! Well, he was not exactly an angel; in fact, he was a little devil. It was quite possible that the boy did lead his mother a pretty dance, but did she deserve any better? What sort of mother was it, who lay all day long in bed and let her sister do the housework for her? Who squeezed her fat self in behind a bar every evening and made eyes at men? And who, at home, was always foul-mouthed and bitter? She was utterly worthless! And so, after fourteen days of married life he had grown tired of the whole setup and had taken himself off. And now he was a rolling stone; he worked at various odd jobs on the docks and waited for a chance to sign on a ship again.

"For the sea, Mr. Bruis, damn it, the sea is the only thing that one *can't* do without."

"And what about the boy? Suppose you took the boy with you?" I asked immediately.

"I? *I* take the boy?" he almost shouted.

"Yes, you! Who else? You would have some purpose in your life then and Ciske would be released from hell. Can't you rent an attic somewhere and care for your child? To talk about being fond of him is not enough. You must give some proof of your affection."

Freimuth burst out laughing and his laughter echoed around the empty classroom. "That's a good joke! *I* bring up a child! I might as well apply for the job of midwife on a battleship! No, Mr. Bruis, I'm sure you mean well, but you don't know anything about life."

Thus the talk with Ciske's father produced no practical results and I was too busy to let it worry me too much. For twenty-six hours in the week I had Ciske under my care, but in a week there are 168 hours altogether, and during school time I had forty-seven other children who needed looking after. Moreover, what was involved was not only Ciske's soul but his mind, which had to be trained and stuffed with fractions and historical dates. Ciske's acquired knowledge seemed to be nil. Even Betty Van Gemert, the stupidest child in my class, did not make such fantastic spelling mistakes. It obviously wouldn't be easy to push him into the fifth form. But I wanted to achieve this at all cost, otherwise he would fall the following year into the hands of Maatsuyker. And one thing was quite clear: it would be easier for a hippopotamus to repair a wrist watch than for that professional lion tamer Maatsuyker to tame the Rat!

Ciske was not stupid, but his education had been completely neglected. The red-haired schoolmistress at his old school had probably never given him a chance to learn, because she had not liked him. This was a great pity, because Ciske was not slow-witted. His math, for instance, was quite good by then. It seemed that he should be quite capable of competing with the best boy, Gerard Jonker, in this field.

While the others were trying to solve simple equations, I used to squat beside Ciske and try to explain fractions to him. He made quite good progress. At first he was anything but pleased, and would slowly edge his way to the other end of the bench, as if he thought that there was really no need for such close contact between us. Also, he seemed to take the view that one can sail quite happily through life without being able to add one-half and three-fourths.

I resorted to an undignified trick in order to get the Rat to cooperate. For quite a long time I had had the suspicion that Johnny Verkerk was Ciske's confirmed adversary, that there had been a mutual enmity at first sight. Johnny was of course jealous because he noticed that I gave more of my time to Ciske than to him.

"Well, Ciske," I said one day, "we will now wring the necks of these fractions. If you really try, you will soon know as much as Verkerk."

The Rat did not seem particularly interested, but Johnny himself proved to be of great assistance to me in my plan, as that was too much for his pride. "He will never do that!" he said. "He is much too stupid."

I should of course have rebuked him, but instead I turned to the Rat. "Did you hear that? Will you stand for it? Come and sit next to me and we'll show Verkerk how wrong he is!"

Grimly he slid closer to me, and we began diligently to cut apples in four and cakes into three parts. The Rat was a picture of concentration. After fifteen minutes, I left him to himself, but he continued to work away like mad, while I went around the class, praising the industrious and scolding the others.

Five minutes later, Ciske sat back—I thought he had given up already. "What now," I asked him, "are you taking a rest?"

He pushed his exercise book toward me without a word. He had finished!

"You see; it was quite simple really, Ciske."

"They weren't very difficult," said Johnny contemptuously, but I could see that he was mortified.

From then on the Rat worked doggedly at his fractions. I couldn't boast that I had solved the problem with any particular intelligence, but the result was satisfactory, and this seemed to me to be the important thing.

When it came to singing, the Rat was a dead loss. I could imagine the boy as almost anything—as the strangler of Johnny, as a burglar, as the best at math in the class—but not as somebody who could intone with feeling, "Softly rustles the wind . . ." When the class sang sentimental part songs, Ciske sat there with tightly compressed lips. He hardly ever spoke, so how could one expect him to sing? But I felt I must make him do it. Only when I'd got him to open his mouth and start singing with the others, no matter how badly he did it, would I have reached my second objective. Only then would he really become a boy like the others, an integral part of the class.

Once, before class began, I saw him staring, mouth wide open, at the goldfish bowl on the window sill, quite engrossed in the small world of water plants and goldfish and sticklebacks swimming here and there. He drew back as if he had been caught misbehaving when I came up beside him.

"You could clean the bowl if you felt like it," I said.

He looked at me with astonishment, then laughed rather shamefacedly. If I dared, I would stroke your fat head, I thought to myself. A child that could laugh so naturally could not be unreceptive to a little happiness. This miserable little Rat, who was kicked around by everybody, was capable of deriving pleasure from something beautiful. My God! How many blighted and crippled lives there are around us which can be made happy by some small trifle! Short moments of happiness can mean so much to a human being. Why must one always pursue some big goal, out of one's reach?

AND then the Rat stuck a knife into Johnny Verkerk! There was nothing to mitigate the deed. It happened during lunch break. Johnny came to see me, pale and excited, surrounded by some of the others. He had a large bandage on his left wrist. When he tried to begin his indictment, Cornel Verstaveren got in first.

"Sir, the Rat has cut him in the wrist!"

"With a knife, sir!" added Piet Steeman.

"He drew blood, sir!" supplemented Kart Baak. It was obviously the great news of the day.

Johnny Verkerk could only nod his head. With the importance of a special messenger, he handed me a slightly soiled note, whose sender, I assumed, must be his mother.

"Dear sir," I read, "I would like to advise you that our John was today wounded with a knife by another boy. I have just notified the police. . . ." Signed, Mrs. Verkerk.

The first thing I did was to get them all into the classroom, as I was afraid that Maatsuyker would appear at any moment and I had to get to the bottom of the matter without him. In the classroom, Johnny again put himself dead in front of me. With the expression of a Christian martyr on his face, he was obviously waiting for a word of sympathy.

"Is your wrist bad?" I asked finally.

"It is bleeding," he whined.

"Was it a big knife?"

"Yes, sir, as big as this!" He indicated the size of a large butcher's knife.

"And why did Freimuth do it?"

"I don't know, sir."

"Don't talk nonsense, Verkerk, you must know. Tell me, how did it happen?"

Johnny looked very hurt. He obviously considered the sternness of my tone to be most unfair. "He just did it like that, sir!"

"You are not telling the truth, Verkerk!"

I didn't press him further, because the other children began to come into the classroom. They immediately crowded around Johnny, who took his place at his desk, feeling most important because of his enormous suffering. His eyes rested tenderly on his bandaged wrist.

When the culprit came in, a hush fell over the classroom. Ciske was even paler and more sullen than usual. I was glad that the Rat had not decided to play truant that afternoon.

We were just about to start arithmetic, when Maatsuyker sailed in. "This is a nice story," he shouted. "Sticking a knife in a fellow pupil! I have never had such a case in all my experience!"

How he loves to dramatize everything! I thought to myself angrily, but aloud I said only, "Wouldn't you rather leave the matter to me? When I have completed my investigation, I shall report to you fully."

"I naturally expect you to get to the bottom of the matter. A case like this concerns the whole school," he replied icily. As he prepared to leave the room, he could not deny himself the satisfaction of hissing to the Rat as he passed him, "You will have to answer for this, my young friend!"

When he had finally disappeared, the Rat remained completely unconcerned. I had no intention of dismissing the matter as a trifle. It is a serious affair when schoolboys attack one another with knives; it is a great deal worse than ten bleeding noses or a few broken teeth.

"Give me the knife!" I shouted at Ciske.

From his trouser pocket he produced a miserable little penknife. It was really rather funny and I was vastly relieved that the knife was no bigger.

"Can't you use your bare hands when you have accounts to settle? Why did you use a knife on Verkerk?"

The Rat said nothing.

"Aren't you ashamed of yourself for attacking another boy with a knife?"

The Rat still remained silent. His face did not betray the slightest trace of contrition.

"Verkerk!"

Johnny came up to me with disconcerting speed.

"Tell me what happened at midday today. And don't leave half of it out! I want the whole truth!"

"Nothing happened at all, sir. The Rat stabbed me—just like that, sir."

He seemed determined to stick to his original story.

"Did anyone else see what happened?"

The hands of Piet Steeman, Cornel Verstaveren, and Sip Eisma shot up.

"Sip, you tell me what you were all up to."

"We were only playing together, sir."

Sip is a bad liar.

"What were you playing?"

"Oh, just playing, sir, and then Ciske suddenly lost his temper, sir."

"So there were four of you, were there, and you were playing jokes on Freimuth?"

"Yes, just a little, sir!"

"Please, sir!" Betty Van Gemert got up; she was very red in the face. "They threw the Rat's cap into the mud, sir, and then they chased him and tried to pull off some of his clothes. Verkerk was the worst, sir; he even hit Ciske in the back. They do it every break, sir."

Unfortunately I had to leave the class at that moment, because the police wanted to see me.

In the headmaster's office sat a fat man with a fair bristly moustache which was slightly singed under the nose. Clouds of smoke filled the small room and on Maatsuyker's desk lay several used matches.

"My name is Muysken," he said by way of introduction. "I'm from the police—juvenile branch." He stretched out a large flabby hand which felt like an overripe peach. Confronted by this genial giant, my initial apprehension began to fade.

"So you are the Rat's form master, are you?" he continued. "I know the boy quite well, but up to now he has not been guilty of knifing anyone!"

"The other boys provoked him, and I think he didn't quite know what to do," I volunteered.

"Was it a large knife?"

I handed him the little penknife, which looked like a toy in his large palm.

"This wouldn't be much good for attacking an elephant," said the policeman calmly, and looked up without enthusiasm as Maatsuyker entered the room.

"This is a deplorable case, gentlemen. You must take stern measures. If need be, we'll have to send the miserable brat to an institution."

This was typical of Maatsuyker. I would like to have slapped his stupid face.

The policeman gave him only a fleeting glance. "First of all, it is not my job to send him anywhere, and secondly we are in the middle of finding out exactly what happened."

"Shall I call the boy Verkerk?" asked Maatsuyker, who did not wish there to be any reflection on his authority as headmaster. He would have done better to keep his big mouth shut.

"When I require your help, sir, I will ask you to come in." The policeman cut the conversation short and pushed him gently toward the door. "For the moment I want to talk to this gentleman here."

Maatsuyker demurred, but he did not want to get on the wrong side of the police. "I had hoped I might be able to be of assistance to you," he said in a wounded tone.

In order not to offend him further, the policeman added, as an afterthought, "Well then, please, send me the pitiful victim of this dastardly attack." He pulled strongly on his cigar twice, but it had become quite cold and wet. "Well now, the Rat," he said, resuming our conversation. "He's a regular customer in our division. He's not a bad kid, but he's rather excitable and one day things may end badly for him!"

A very frightened Verkerk appeared in the doorway. Muysken's face twitched. "Sit down, my boy," he said kindly. "Here, in this armchair. You must be quite weak from loss of blood. Are you comfortable there? Well then, let me look at your wound. There's no need to cry. I must have a look at it. My goodness, but your mother must have sacrificed a sheet for the bandage!"

His thick fingers skillfully unwound the piece of linen from Johnny's wrist. He was the personification of sympathy. When the bandage was finally off, we saw a small cut about an inch long.

The policeman assumed an awestruck expression. "My word, this isn't a trifle! How could you stand it, my boy? Didn't they take you immediately to the hospital? Does it still hurt?"

"A little," peeped Johnny.

"What a dirty trick, to do something like this to you! And you did nothing to provoke the other boy? You were going quietly home and suddenly this monster rushed toward you and stuck a knife into your body—into your arm, I mean. That's what happened, isn't it?"

It suddenly dawned on Johnny that the policeman was pulling his leg. He squinted uncertainly at Muysken, who was playing absent-mindedly with the Rat's ridiculous little penknife.

I mentioned what Betty Van Gemert had told me.

"What's this I hear? You provoked him?" exclaimed Muysken in a shocked voice. "Oh, oh, oh, when the inspector hears this . . ."

Johnny began to cry noisily. He had fallen too suddenly from the heaven of martyrdom into the hell of ridicule. As he showed no sign of stopping crying, I indicated to Muysken that it would be best to leave him alone. After all, I wasn't quite blameless myself. Hadn't I played the jealous Johnny Verkerk off against the Rat? I didn't particularly want him to have to show himself tear-stained in class. Muysken put a small piece of adhesive on Johnny's wrist, and wound up the enormous bandage most carefully.

"Put this in your pocket and take it home to your mother. You can tell her that I took it off. And if you provoke the Rat again, you will have to answer to me."

Johnny looked so pathetic with the tiny piece of adhesive on that I felt sorry for him and gave him a drink of water.

"Ha, the Rat," said the policeman gaily as Ciske entered the room next. "So we meet again."

The boy threw back his head and showed a smile which—sour as it was—brightened his gloomy face. To my great amazement, he approached Muysken and held out his hand to him.

The policeman took the grubby paw in his for a moment and then said reflectively, "It isn't pleasant for me to have to go later to Mr. Van Loon and tell him that Ciske Freimuth has stuck a knife into a friend. You see that, don't you? I'd be very ashamed of myself if I were in your shoes."

The Rat blushed deeply and stammered, "He is not my friend. He has been annoying me every day, ever since I came to school here. I . . ."

Muysken then interrupted Ciske and I was sorry about this, as I would like to have heard the rest of his story. ". . . And when someone irritates you, you think that you can simply stick your knife into him, do you? Tomorrow, I suppose, you will use a revolver, and the day after—a machine gun?"

The Rat narrowed his eyes. I got the impression that his heart was not exactly torn by pangs of conscience. "If he ever touches me again, he will regret it," he said sharply.

"And you too," I interrupted, "or do you imagine that it is quite in order to do things like that at this school?"

My remark had interrupted the conversation of intimate friends. Ciske's face became like a mask. He did not answer me, and I felt a certain bitterness welling up in me. I envied Muysken the contact he had established with the boy. For the fat policeman, Ciske was nothing more than a naughty boy who had been up to mischief. But, even so, his paternal severity evidently made an impression. What a bad teacher I must be, I thought, if I can't find the way to this child's heart!

When later I returned to my class, the Rat was standing in a corner. The assistant teacher, who had taken over for me, had put him there.

Of course, I said to myself, how can one expect an assistant teacher earning thirty guilders a month to be a proper schoolmaster into the bargain?

"Writing books out!" I said sharply, leaving the Rat where he was, in the corner.

If I hadn't known it for myself, the eyes of the children would have told me: Something has upset you! . . . A class has a sixth sense for these things, and a class is never wrong.

I pulled myself together and, I believe, acted quite normally for the rest of the afternoon. Calligraphy is, moreover, one activity which requires the full attention of each pupil. They sat there calmly and filled their pages. I walked up and down and helped them from time to time. Otherwise I sat at my desk and corrected exercise books. It was usually a quiet half hour. But that afternoon the atmosphere was electric. Everyone was unnaturally quiet, and every now and then one or another of them shot a furtive glance at me. I was tired and depressed, and I longed to get to my own room, to my pipe and a cup of tea. I was oppressed by the thought that after school I would have to go over the whole disagreeable story once again. What was the use of talking when no one listened?

When most of the children had gone, I sent Johnny and Ciske into the hall. Only Piet, Cornel, and Sip, the direct participants, were told to stay. I said to them that it was unfair to fight four against one, and gave them extra homework as a punishment. Piet and Cornel stared at me blankly. Only Sip Eisma seemed to understand—at least there was understanding in his light blue eyes. That Sip was pure as gold. There are natures which are incapable of dishonesty and Sip was one of them—a thoroughly nice boy!

Verkerk looked as if he had been treated most unjustly. To be first wounded with a knife and then kept in was altogether too much! Was there no justice to be had in this world?

I told Johnny that it was extremely naughty of Ciske to stick a knife into him, but that he was not without guilt himself, because he had provoked him. He, too, would get extra homework as a punishment.

And next the Rat!

The conversation ended in a clear defeat for me. First of all, I was visibly nervous, which of course was stupid. With children one must in such cases look angry, but be in fact quite calm. Instead I was feeling sick at my helplessness where this boy was concerned. I shouted at him, while all the time I wanted to be calm and collected. I wanted to do an older-friend act and to bridge the gap between us, but the Rat's face expressed only one thing: I wish you would stop chattering! What was worse, there was a glitter of triumph in his eyes.

This almost brought my self-control to an abrupt end. I felt like grabbing the boy by the hair and dragging him from the room. Why? Because he always succeeded in slipping from me. You stupid fool, I said to myself, can't you see that the boy gets a lot of pleasure out of seeing that he can make you angry? Yes, I could see it all right; but the more I saw it, the angrier I became.

Ciske, meanwhile, stood quite still, staring at my desk and the inkstand on it. He was completely unmoved. He was the stronger of the two of us. He sat in a bombproof dugout and let the shells whistle overhead.

In the end I took him by the arm and pushed him out of the classroom."Get out of my sight!" I shouted. "I am sick of you!"

And that was how I suffered defeat at the hands of the Rat. I cannot forget the humiliation of it. And, to cap everything, just at that moment Maatsuyker appeared.

"Well, Bruis," he said good-humoredly. "As I was passing, I heard you talking to the Rat. That's more like the right tone! Such creatures must be made to understand that they just can't get away with it!"

It was an effort not to laugh in Maatsuyker's face.

When at last I went home, I made a firm resolution not to waste any more energy on the Rat. He was a hopeless case. There was no point in making myself a nervous wreck when the results were nil. I was a teacher, not a saver of souls. I would do my duty, but no more. I would teach Ciske fractions and the names of the tributaries of the River Maas, but I decided to keep out of it as far as everything else was concerned!

ONE day I confessed to Susan, the girl I was shortly going to marry, that she had a rival—Betty Van Gemert. Yes, really, I had grown very fond of that little girl. Betty was unbelievably stupid, but charmingly so. The funny thing was that her lack of sense was no handicap to her at all. She herself knew that she was not very intelligent and made no attempt to conceal it. When sometimes during a geography lesson I asked Betty to come forward —one had to do this from time to time—the whole class would begin to laugh. On one particular occasion I was just teaching them the geography of the South of Holland: Boskoop, Alblasserdam, Tiengemeten—names which an ordinary person forgets anyway when he leaves school. Up till then Betty had been looking around the class happily like a little mother. She had listened without envy when the others displayed their knowledge, but now she had to show me what *she* knew.

She looked at me sweetly with her blue doll's eyes. How funny that you have brought me out in front, she seemed to be thinking. . . . Well, if you insist, I'll have to do it, I suppose.

"Well, Betty," I began, "do you see the two large red dots on the map?"

"Yes." Betty nodded, pleased that she could give me some pleasure. She made the pointer wander over the North Sea. After a lot of circling, it stopped finally at Leyden.

"No, Betty, I mean the dot below that."

Betty did not understand: both dots were red. She looked at me questioningly, and I chivalrously helped her to find The Hague.

"What is the name of that city, Betty?" Again a wondering look. A city? Was that red dot a city? What was the teacher talking about? The class laughed.

Betty looked at me and smiled. Oh, teacher, said her blue eyes, I would like to do something for you so much, but I cannot do it. You know that as well as I do. And the most good-natured child in my class returned to her place, while all the others laughed without malice. Betty looked around very pleased with herself. How nice that she had been able to give the other children a moment's pleasure!

I had made Betty responsible for tidiness in the classroom, and for looking after the flowers on the window sill. Betty managed these things supremely well.

The domestic-science teacher had great hopes for Betty. "Tell me, Mr. Bruis, how is Betty Van Gemert doing in your class?" she had asked me once.

"Betty is the stupidest and most lovable child in the whole world," I had to admit.

". . . and with me she is the best of all."

The Almighty had thus endowed Betty with a kind heart, a pair of neat hands, and a sweet face. She will certainly get on all right. One's only concern was that she should not be hurt for life while at school. A school is after all an institution which should impart only a certain amount of knowledge. Whenever I made intellectual demands on Betty, she failed, and I should really at the end of the year have kept her back in the same class. That had already happened to her once. If it were to have happened again, she would have been two years older than her classmates, and moreover she would have fallen into the hands of Maatsuyker. That I wanted to avoid at any price.

EVENTUALLY the Rat began to settle down. This was no testimonial to my pedagogical skill; he had simply begun to thaw out once I stopped caring too much what happened to him. The class was taming the Rat. When one thinks about this, it is nothing unusual: children are natural educators of other children.

They form a solid defense against the world of grownups, who so rarely apply the right measure of understanding to the problems of childhood. The less we interfere, the less we risk laying ourselves open to ridicule.

I had sincerely wished to make the Rat feel at home in my class. From the moment when, in a fit of discouragement, I had decided to leave him to his fate, things had been going much better.

Betty Van Gemert had taken over my task and she had achieved ten times as much as her teacher. As I have mentioned, she was in charge of the flowers, while the Rat looked after the goldfish bowl. Through these pitiful specimens of nature in our shabby classroom, the two of them found one another. I noticed how Ciske used to carry the watering can and hand it to Betty. He would wait patiently while she watered an ailing geranium and then he would run and put the empty can away. Once in his zeal he spilled some water, and she told him off.

"Hey! Do you want to flood the classroom? Quickly, go and get a mop from the closet in the hall! Hurry up, slowpoke!"

She then saw that the Rat mopped up the puddle properly and I left the two of them to get on with it.

One never knows exactly what is really happening in a class. I don't believe it was accidental that there was, about this time, a slight change of heart in Johnny Verkerk's gang. Sip was, I believe, the first one to stop bullying the Rat.

And Ciske? He went around with much less constraint; he did not come into class so shyly, so much like a timid animal. And when I sat next to him on his bench, he did not move away from me so pointedly. He was making quite good progress. He showed himself to be much more intelligent than, for instance, the phlegmatic Drikus, who was as colorless as only a very average person can be. He always got the second-best grade for behavior—I never award the highest grade as a matter of principle.

I had noticed for some time that things were not going too well between Drikus and the Rat. They both sat within reach of me on the front bench and their furtive skirmishes didn't escape my notice. This is what would happen.

Ciske's arithmetic book would be lying a little to the wrong side of the middle of the desk. Immediately Drikus's passion for orderliness asserts itself, so he moves the offending book toward Ciske.

The Rat acknowledges this with a vicious blow under the desk, and Drikus's hand shoots into the air.

I would leave him for a while with his arm outstretched, until it began to get tired. Then I asked him with indifference, "What is it?"

"Freimuth has punched me, sir."

"Stop quarreling, you two, and get on with your work!"

Drikus falls silent, but he is clearly offended. The Rat's book has again found its way a little over to his side. Drikus, who is not certain now of my protection, dares not do anything about it. Moreover, he is a bit afraid of Ciske.

All these little games were quite significant. They were symptoms of normality and proved that Ciske did not feel he was an outsider any more. I first had to let him become an ordinary boy among others, then perhaps later he would stop being shy and distrustful where I was concerned. His opinion of me would then depend on what opinion of me the class had.

A class is very critical. It passes judgment just at those moments when one forgets for a while that one is a teacher. This happens when one looks out the window at a woman shaking her rug, or when one loosens one's tie or tries to pick one's teeth without being noticed. One cannot in those moments avoid being seen by at least someone in the class.

I don't know what that class thought of me. If they found me moody, as I presume they did, I cannot hold it against them. When I had sat up half the night over my French books and had once again no time to spare for Susan, then no doubt I did turn up sullen and irritable to face the children the next morning—and the little devils certainly sensed it at once. They would be quiet as mice and almost all of them as well behaved as Drikus always was. If there had been the slightest incident, they knew they would be punished. I don't know which irritated me more in such circumstances, my chastened class or myself. I wished I could have the detached superior manner Meerstra had. I used to wonder if I would ever achieve it.

THE inevitable clash between the Rat and Drikus had occurred. It might have been wiser for me to have separated these two and sat them at a distance from one another—such opposing natures should never be at too close quarters—and then it was too late.

The class was analyzing sentences which I had dictated. In the meanwhile I was going through their arithmetic exercise books and could give them only my divided attention. Suddenly I saw Drikus's hand go up into the air. Not slowly and haltingly, but quickly and with determination. His eyes were on Ciske who, the tip of his tongue between his teeth, was writing his exercise. The good Drikus obviously wanted to complain about Ciske again.

I waited at first to see what would win the upper hand—Drikus's wish to report or the tiredness. But the arm remained up in the air. He must consider it important.

"Anything the matter, Drikus?" I asked him finally.

"Yes, sir, Freimuth is copying from me."

"He is lying," interrupted the Rat.

"Oh," gasped the class; they were usually very careful about making such accusations in front of a teacher.

Ciske bent over his exercise book again.

"It is true, sir," Drikus assured me.

"Have you been copying from Drikus?" I asked Ciske. No answer. "You should be ashamed of yourself; it is such an easy exercise."

The boy shrugged his shoulders; he seemed not to wish to defend himself. Drikus, however, nodded vigorously and persistently. The Rat really had been copying from him.

I was in as much of a hurry as the children to go home, because I was coaching a child in French during the midday break. Quite a distance from the school I saw Ciske coming, chasing Drikus, with a crowd of boys at his heels: the Johnny Verkerk gang—Johnny, Sip, Cornel, and Piet. It was obvious that Ciske would catch Drikus, who tried to hide in a doorway. The Rat, however, jumped on him, seizing him by the scruff of the neck. What a wild animal he was! This is how a leopard jumps on his prey. I could not quite follow what happened next, because the others had formed a circle around Ciske and Drikus, but I could hear stifled screams and encouraging shouts.

Without hurrying, I steered my course toward the group. The boys were so engrossed in the fight that they did not even notice me. Drikus was lying on the ground and the Rat was sitting on top of him. Ciske's small fists were belaboring his victim systematically, while Drikus was helplessly sobbing.

"Go on, Rat. Give him the works," encouraged the onlookers.

I was shocked by Ciske's face. This was not just a boy who could administer a healthy thrashing to another once in a while. In his eyes a dark light was burning; his lips were tightly pressed together, his face a cruel mask.

Quickly I took the Rat by the scruff of the neck and pulled him away from Drikus. The boys, frightened, dispersed, but Ciske did not run away. Now Drikus clambered to his feet, lightly bleeding from the nose and lip where one of his teeth had bitten into it. How plump and helpless he looked next to the wiry little Rat!

The circle closed again. A few passers-by had been attracted by the commotion. Under no circumstances could this be allowed to degenerate into a public performance! I had to restore order and quickly! The rest could be done at school.

"Have you had enough now, or will you carry on as soon as my back is turned?" I asked the Rat. His face relaxed a little. The revengeful fire disappeared from his eyes.

"Well then, forward march," I said lightly. "You in this direction and you in the other."

Drikus took himself off. Alone.

Johnny and the others went off with the Rat. Ciske had been accepted into their circle.

In the afternoon Drikus brought a letter from his mother. Having asked once already that her son not be seated next to Ciske

Freimuth, she now threatened to take him away from our school altogether.

What could I do? For safety's sake, I sought Maatsuyker's advice. He became terribly angry that there had been more trouble with Ciske. That boy was a blemish on his school's good name! He was not to be deflected from his line. Meerstra exchanged glances with me.

"When things happen outside the school boundaries, we cannot be held responsible for it," I said shortly. "I would only like to know whether I have to give in to the threats of Drikus's mother."

"I cannot interfere in this," said Maatsuyker icily. "You have always insisted very firmly that you were the master of your own class. As headmaster, my functions are purely administrative, aren't they? Well then . . . I must decline to give you advice."

"And to face a difficulty," I snapped back.

Angry, I returned to the classroom where Ciske and Drikus had been kept sitting. But I had no wish to preach or punish. Why should I? The boys had had a fight. What business was that of mine?

When I had looked through the exercise books, I sent them both home. In the hall I saw them chatting together, but whether they were exchanging pleasantries I did not know.

Meerstra caught up to walk home with me. "A pleasant customer, our Maatsuyker, isn't he?" he smiled. "D'you know what I would do in your place? I wouldn't do anything for a few days, then I would separate the kids. In this way you will not appear to have accepted the ultimatum, and yet will have solved the problem. We must, after all, handle our pupils carefully, since they are our most valuable working capital. . . ."

If in the first place I had put the Rat next to Sip and Gerard Jonker next to Drikus, there would have been no bleeding nose and no torn underlip. With a little wise forethought on my part, the peace would never have been disturbed, nor would Drikus's mother ever have issued an ultimatum; furthermore, I would have avoided an angry scene with Maatsuyker. On the other hand, the gang around Johnny Verkerk would then never have come to their senses.

Luckily Drikus was not vindictive. Since the Rat had been sitting next to Sip and had therefore stopped being a source of irritation to Drikus because of his proximity, peace had been restored. Life with us now became quite uneventful.

So the Rat sat next to Sip, who was a typical Dutch boy with healthy apple-red cheeks, pale yellow wiglike hair, and bright blue eyes. Six months before he had come from Freesland to Amsterdam, and the boys sometimes called him "the little peasant." At the beginning, because of his "funny" speech, he was often teased, but this didn't last long. Sip had once thrashed Cornel Verstaveren's urban hide according to all the rules of the game, and since then he had been accepted by all his classmates. What was more, Cornel had become his best friend.

Children are in many respects natural realists. The class knew, for instance, that Piet came from a well-to-do family, his father being chief of a branch post office, and that every year they went to Scheveningen for their vacation. But because Piet was a first-class rogue and never boasted, there was no one who despised him.

The face that the Rat made, when I made him change his place, was worth seeing. In spite of himself, he grinned with pleasure that he would now sit among the real boys of the class. To betray his joy too clearly would be to show too much appreciation for me, and after all we were not yet such good friends. He therefore pretended to be surprised.

"Don't you want to sit with Sip?" I asked while he was collecting his odds and ends.

Ciske answered once again with a shrug.

"And you, Sip, what is your view of your new neighbor?"

"Let him just come," said Sip very distinctly.

They all burst out laughing; even Ciske's mouth was twitching. I took him by the collar of his coat and led him, amid general laughter, to his new seat. This was the first time that I allowed myself such familiarity toward him, and he took it well.

Drikus, on the other hand, felt very honored that Gerard, the top boy, would now sit next to him. His mother's wishes had been respected after all, it seemed.

Betty looked upon the change-over with motherly solicitude. The Rat was now sitting in her immediate vicinity, separated from her only by the aisle. She would keep a watchful eye on him, the little clucking hen!

ANOTHER new boy had come to our class. In fact, he was an old acquaintance at school, but the boys had only a vague recollection of him. For eighteen months Dorus Keulemann had been unable to attend school. He had trouble with his glands—that is all the children knew. I, however, knew more. My colleague Jorissen, who had had him in his class previously, had told me that Dorus had been "given up" by the doctors. There was nothing medical science could do for him, and he was expected to live for two more years if things went well. In the intervening period he had been in the hospital, but had been discharged again and told he could attend school.

To find out a bit more, I went to see the doctor who had been treating Dorus. I wanted to be told officially what was wrong with him. I was also worried about the danger of infection for the rest of the class, for Dorus had t.b. of the bone and had been surgically treated. And after all, there was, God knows, a world of difference between getting a pupil who was at the beginning of his life and getting one who was coming to the end of it.

The doctor admitted that there was practically no hope for Dorus: it was difficult to say anything with certainty, but it would be almost a miracle if the boy's life could be prolonged beyond the period of puberty. The cavities were healed and it would be good for the boy to be in the company of other children again. Danger of infection? No, there was none; I need have no fears.

To be quite truthful, I was not at all enthusiastic about having Dorus come to our class. Why couldn't such an unfortunate child be left in peace? What was the use of an interlude at school when the child was doomed anyway? Weren't the people who sent Dorus into the midst of healthy children rather cruel, in spite of their good intentions?

The very next day I changed my opinion. I had Dorus in my class for five hours and saw how happy he was to be among other boys.

I couldn't quite understand why Maatsuyker hadn't sent him back to his old class. Of course, while he had been in the hospital, he had missed a lot, but was this so particularly important in his case? But Maatsuyker was a headmaster down to his toes. Even in a case like this, the regulations had to be strictly observed: the boy had to strive in order to pass into another class.

It was not much to Jorissen's credit that he, too, did not put himself out for his former pupil. But recently Jorissen had been letting things drift a little anyway. Perhaps he was pleased to have got rid of this difficult case.

Well, that may have been so. Anyway, Dorus was in my class. His mother brought him to school in a little wheel chair: a decent woman with a worried face and terribly sad eyes. I took Dorus out of the wheel chair and put him on my shoulder.

"Now then, old man," I said on the staircase, "you are going to ride upstairs. Tomorrow you had better bring your crop, so that you can make me trot better."

Good heavens! The little fellow was as light as a feather; one could hardly feel the weight of his delicate body. With great care I put him down on the front bench, so that he could stretch out his legs which were in braces.

Dorus had a fine face, wax pale and transparent. Dark eyes, old and wise, shone in it like velvet. His rather thick lips were stretched into a smile. It was almost as if he were amused by the rest of the class.

There is something to be said for liking somebody at first sight. I felt that way about Dorus, although of course sympathy with the child was also a factor. I felt the same about the Rat's freckled face, although it was so much less attractive.

I considered whom to make Dorus's neighbor. I would have liked best to put him next to Betty Van Gemert, who would mother him, but I didn't want to start by treating him as an exception in class by sitting him next to a girl.

Sip wouldn't have been too bad as a neighbor, but I couldn't very well separate him from the Rat now—it wouldn't be fair. Johnny Verkerk? No, he was not gentle enough. A perfectly ordinary boy should sit next to Dorus. After a little while I found him: Barend Hilligers! He made friends with everybody and had a pleasantly even temperament.

The children looked somewhat shyly at the new boy. Even the Rat displayed an embarrassing interest in him. Dorus became uneasy under the many inquiring glances, so I occupied the minds of the curious by giving them a very long sum to work out.

Barend took his seat next to Dorus, smiling benevolently, as if this were the most natural thing in the world. Then he calmly proceeded with his sums.

"Sir," exclaimed Betty, who worried about everything, except her equations, "the boys in his former class always carried Dorus upstairs. It worked very well."

"They were certainly very strong boys and not such weaklings as you," I joked.

"We're not weaklings, sir," protested the class unanimously and many boys playfully showed one another their bulging biceps. Dorus's arrival in class was made into a gay occasion. The new boy looked happily around.

Later, when we came to the reading lesson, I said to Dorus, "And now, you read first."

It was a boring piece that we were reading just then, but the sick boy read softly, in a thick voice, without stumbling once and with excellent accentuation. He was very much better at reading than any of the other children. Only a sensitive child with a good deal of imagination could have read as Dorus did.

"You have stuck your nose in a great many books, haven't you?" I asked him when he had finished.

"Oh, yes, sir," nodded Dorus, pleased with my indirect praise.

Of late I had made it a habit to stay at school during the lunch break in order to study French for an exam I intended to take myself. With a diploma in French, I hoped to be able to make a little more money, which, in turn, would enable me to get married. Dorus, who would have been too tired if he had had to go home and come back, had his lunch in the classroom and kept me company. We often had long conversations while we ate, and I came to know the unfortunate child much better.

Reading was his great passion, and best of all he liked adventure stories. He had devoured Shackleton's book about his expedition to the South Pole and many books about Africa. He read Jules Verne quickly, but with concentration.

Dorus had overthrown the top boy, Gerard Jonker, from his throne. Now Dorus came first, then for a very long while no one, then Gerard. But Gerard saw that Dorus was somehow in a class apart and did not feel discouraged.

I should really have tried to insist with Maatsuyker that the sick boy be taken into a higher form. Being fantastically well read and having a quick mind, he would have been all right in the top form, but Maatsuyker did not wish to hear anything about it and Jorissen was strangely disinterested. It had to be admitted that Dorus, considering his particular circumstances, was doing very well, so why should one uproot him and put him in strange surroundings? Moreover, he would have to make more of an effort in a higher form, and this could be harmful for his health.

It was Meerstra who found an answer to the problem. "Let's leave the decision to the boy himself," he suggested. And Maatsuyker agreed to this. Probably for the first time in the history of education in Holland, a pupil was going to decide in which form he would be. And lo and behold, the order of things at school was not shaken to its foundations!

On the next day we again sat together over our sandwiches, and I made sure that Dorus was eating his lunch, which consisted of four rounds of bread and cheese. This I had faithfully promised Mama Keulemann I would do.

"How do you like it here with us?" I asked guardedly.

"Very much, sir." Dorus's face shone.

"But the work we are doing is really too easy for you," I said.

"Oh, no, no!"

"Wouldn't you rather return to Mr. Jorissen's class? You would then be in your old form, and they are of course much more advanced than we are. If you wished, you could make the move this afternoon." I was rather tense. If Dorus said yes, I would be hard put to it to suppress a feeling of disappointment. "Of course, you would still be able to have your sandwiches at lunch time with me," I said encouragingly.

But Dorus looked at me in a panic. "I would much prefer to remain here, sir," he said without hesitation.

Against my better judgment, I tried to persuade him to change over to the higher form. I stopped doing so when I discovered real fright in Dorus's eyes. His normally pale face was highly flushed.

"Please, let me stay with you," he begged in his hoarse little voice. "You are always giving me extra essays to do, and I feel so well in this form."

To be quite honest, I was very pleased about this decision. Who knows whether Jorissen would lavish so much affection on the boy as I was ready to do? "Very well then, you can stay with us," I said, and we both took out our books, I a French textbook and he *Pieter Marits.*

I must have hit upon a difficult passage in my lesson and have groaned aloud, because Dorus asked with sympathy, "Must you also study still, sir?"

I told him that in a month's time I would have to pass an examination in French.

"Is French very difficult to learn?" Dorus wanted to know.

"No, not too bad. But in an examination everything is made to appear very complicated."

In his look there was a mute question which he dared not voice.

"Would you like to learn it too?" I ventured a guess.

Dorus laughed with embarrassment. Yes, he would like that!

"Tomorrow I'll bring a book for you," I promised. "From it you'll be able to learn something, and I'll help you as much as I can."

Poor Dorus! How pleasure lit up his sad little face! Weren't you thinking what use French would be to you, you small, dear boy? I felt a lump in my throat when my eyes glided from the expressive childish face to his little legs, in their braces, stretched out straight in front of him as if they did not belong to him.

Did Dorus guess my thoughts? I didn't know. I was trying to master my emotions and concentrate on my book. Suddenly I felt the child's hand on mine.

"It is so nice that I may stay with you, sir," he stammered.

"Well, I'm glad that you seem to like it with us," I countered with embarrassment.

"Oh, and how!" he exclaimed. "The boys are all so nice, Barend, Sip, and all!"

"And Betty too?" I tried to tease him.

But Dorus remained serious. "Yes, Betty too!"

"And whom do you find nicest of all?" This question was extremely foolish. One does not ask a child questions like this, particularly when one is a teacher.

To my great surprise Dorus answered, "Nicest of all? I think Ciske is the nicest of all."

"Ciske?"

I could not understand this at once. I had never observed any bond of sympathy between the two, and I usually pay a lot of attention to the way in which children behave toward one another.

"Why particularly Ciske?" I asked with curiosity.

"He comes every morning to get me. Then he pushes my wheel chair for my mother, and we sometimes laugh like mad when he does it. Also in the afternoon he takes me home very often. He's a really fine fellow!"

Could I believe my ears?

SHORTLY afterward a man called on me who had the unusual name of "Alarm." He sat facing me on the only chair in the empty classroom, while I crouched on the front bench.

"Yes," he said with circumspection, "I want to speak to you about our Francis."

For a moment I didn't really understand what he wanted with me. Only when he added, "I have come here in my capacity as welfare officer," did I have an inkling that he had the Rat in mind.

"Francis is at present working in the bar where his mother is. Afternoons and evenings!"

"What! Is the woman crazy?" I exclaimed. "But why do you come and tell me about it? Wouldn't it be much more appropriate for you to tell the magistrate of the juvenile court?"

Mr. Alarm was somewhat piqued. "Your remark is a little out of place, my dear sir," he said coldly. "I shall naturally report to Mr.

Van Loon, but I thought that you as his teacher should also be enlightened."

I pretended to bow ever so slightly.

"It might well be," continued Mr. Alarm, "that Francis's progress would be adversely affected by his working at night, and that you might unjustly make life difficult for him. I would like to prevent this. The boy must not suffer for it, don't you agree? Therefore I feel that cooperation between the welfare officer and the teacher can be rather useful."

"That depends entirely on the welfare officer," I would like to have said, because Mr. Alarm's pompous manner was rather irritating. I wondered how much this man would ever achieve with the Rat.

"In my practice I have rarely come across such a difficult child as this Francis," continued Mr. Alarm when I said nothing. "The boy is a mass of inferiority complexes. Don't you agree?"

I was hard put to it to retain my composure; this man, who should be concerned with seeing that the Rat should as soon as possible stop going to the bar, sat there and uttered big words about complexes! I am bored anyway when laymen talk about inhibitions and the like. Any upholsterer who has ever looked through an article on "psychology for everyman" will brandish with breathtaking assurance catchwords about inferiority complexes and so on, touching upon a field where even qualified specialists are groping their way along. It seems to me as likely to be effective as a watchmaker trying to tackle a precision job with an ordinary saw.

"No," I said somewhat rudely, "that is not so." Mr. Alarm now looked really alarmed. "I am only a schoolteacher and not a psychologist," I added.

"Not a psychologist?" he exclaimed. "How can you teach children, then, or try to educate them?"

"That's my worry, if you'll excuse my saying so," I answered curtly. Mr. Alarm had hit me on a bad day. I was tired and overwrought, as that morning I had sat for my written exam. My nerves are not made of steel, and this man and his pomposity irritated me beyond measure. After all, the good of a boy from my class was at stake. What had this very ordinary fool to do with it?

Mr. Alarm reached for his hat; he was trying very hard not to lose his temper and not to step out of his role. "I am sorry that I could establish so little contact with you. You seem not to appreciate the importance of my mission."

"May I ask you what you intend to do to stop Ciske's employment in the bar?" I asked him.

But my visitor was now on the defensive. "That, sir, is my concern. . . ."

All right, you clod! . . .

I could not get over the fact that the Rat was washing dishes in a broken-down bar. What a boy! No one would have guessed it. He did his homework as well as before and appeared every morning exactly on time. In the last few weeks, in fact, his homework had seemed rather more inspired, and I thought that this should be put down to Dorus's influence, as Dorus had confided to me that on the way to school they sometimes repeated their lessons. It would not be the first instance of a pupil learning more from a classmate than from his teacher. I decided not to lose sight of the matter. But meanwhile my head was swimming. If only I had had the wretched examination in French behind me!

I decided to make a call on Muysken, the friendly man from the juvenile police, and complain about the bone-headed welfare officer.

The next day I plodded on with my grammar and translation. I had stage fright like any of my pupils and was pleased when I was told, "Well, if you don't mess up your oral test, you will pass."

Susan, who was only waiting for me to pass the examination so that we could at last get married, wanted to celebrate already. And had it not been for the fact that my mother-in-law was terribly superstitious and convinced that one should never praise the day before the evening, I would have had to face that too.

Maatsuyker once again surpassed himself. My colleague Tedema told him about my exam. She was most movingly concerned about me, worrying about the rings under my eyes and about my lack of appetite. Immediately our headmaster became very vocal. He had no time for these supplementary examinations, he said. We all knew why, incidentally—it had once slipped out that he failed his English exam, but of course only because he had been trapped by a series of stupid questions. That I was now in the process of taking my French, he found particularly absurd and generally objectionable.

Tedema made an apposite remark about sour grapes, but Maatsuyker persisted. For him it was enough for a teacher to pass his basic exams. Why the extra trimmings? Who would there be left to teach in the primary schools if every teacher was highly qualified?

"People who have failed in English," said Tedema pointedly and turned around to go to her class.

Dorus was the only one of my pupils who knew anything about my examination worries. He looked at me questioningly and I gave him a reassuring nod.

I saw his eyes light up. Good, but this is what I expected of you, he seemed to be thinking.

"Ciske, stay in class at four o'clock; I want to talk to you."

The Rat darted a frightened look at Dorus. What do you say to that? his eyes said. I have done nothing wrong and yet I must stay behind, so we can't go home together.

He was waiting for me with a dejected face when I returned to the classroom again.

"This has nothing to do with punishment," I reassured him at once. "I only wanted to talk to you about the bar where you work at night. And that is no business of any of the other children."

He looked at me, taken aback. His whole face expressed amazement.

"Mr. Alarm, the family welfare officer, was here and told me that you are working in your mother's bar. Is that true?"

Ciske nodded.

"And how much do you earn there?"

"A rijskdaalder."

"How long must you work for it?"

"From five till six. And from seven till nine."

"Is it fun?"

The Rat shrugged. He obviously found my question idiotic, and I could not blame him for that. I took a seat beside him on the bench and looked at him more closely. The child did not look well. The shadows under his eyes had deepened. His thin face was even less childlike than before.

"Would you like to give up that job?" I asked him gently and put my hand under his chin.

"Yes, sir."

The answer came pat. Something glistened in Ciske's eyes. Had the little Rat some tears left? I had never yet seen him look so human. This was the first time that we had established contact. And if I had to shift the world from its axis, I would get the boy out of the filthy bar!

Should I wait until the unctuous Mr. Alarm made another appearance? A lot of time would pass before then. Perhaps I had better take the matter into my own hands. While putting on my coat, I told Ciske, "You can go to the bar now; don't say a word to anyone, but don't go there later in the evening or any more afterwards. You have too much homework to do and you are too young to have a job as well."

We left the school together. The Rat seemed undecided. Should he run along or walk with me?

"Well, Ciske," I said smiling, "will you walk a little way with me? You would have preferred to walk home with Dorus, wouldn't you?"

"Yes," said the Rat candidly.

"Dorus is your friend, isn't he?"

Ciske nodded, slightly embarrassed. It was not easy to make conversation with him, but this was not because of his shyness. As a rule children are completely nonplussed when you want to talk to them privately.

"Where is your father now?" I suddenly thought to ask.

"At sea," he answered. "He will be home again in two months. He is in Australia; I had a picture postcard from him last week."

God Almighty! How talkative the Rat could be!

"Is your mother at home, do you think?" I asked. But now Ciske seemed in a hurry to be off. He stammered a few muffled words, and I understood that he did not want me to come to his house.

"Good night, sir," he said and politely took off his cap. A well-bred little gentleman!

My appearance in the tenement house where the Freimuths lived produced a considerable commotion.

"Ciske's teacher," I heard a woman's voice say.

"What does he want here?" said another.

I climbed the dark staircase. There was an unpleasant smell there and the higher I got the thicker the air became: cheap face powder and cabbage. In this mixture of smells I could not thrive either bodily or spiritually. The nose, too, must be an organ of the soul. One can detect more with it than merely material things. I could smell the presence of an abominable woman.

Ciske's aunt asked me to come into the "best room." Her sister would be in presently. I shuddered inwardly at the sight of the many crocheted mats and the bright cushions on the sofa. The sideboard looked like a barrel organ. Behind the glass pane stood a number of decanters with spirits and liqueurs. From the golden lantern lamp in the middle of the room swung a hanging jumping jack. On the mantelpiece stood a large marble clock, leaving just enough room for two enormous china dogs, but between them a picture of the lady of the house was squeezed in. Everything was ugly and pretentious. The expensive super-radio set made me think of the Rat's worn-out shoes. Any wooden barrack had more decency than this room. And the milieu became quite complete when madame appeared, wearing a silk housecoat and bright orange lipstick.

I left her little time for polite greetings. I also declined coldly the invitation to make myself comfortable on the sofa.

"Ciske works in your bar, doesn't he?" I asked her abruptly.

The Freimuth woman blushed a deep red under the thick layer of powder and replied that one could hardly call it "working." It was much more a case of giving the boy something to do so as to keep him off the streets.

"So much the better," I said. "Then it won't be difficult to stop it at any time."

"How do you mean?" she said, perplexed.

"This is what I mean: if you make Ciske work tonight in the bar, you will have the police after you. It is forbidden by law to employ children. Both the landlord and you, as the mother, are committing an offense. And you probably know what that means?"

The friendliness of my hostess disappeared like a pale March sun behind a shower of hail. An outburst followed which did not leave anything to be desired as to its violence. Behind the orange-red painted lips the pale gums shone odiously. The eyes glinted meanly. The obscenities which were thrown at my head I could understand by their tone rather than their meaning. So I was in league with the Rat, was I, with that mean malicious villain who had denounced his own mother? And why? Because he was too lazy to work. That wretched child was able to earn a rijskdaalder, and this was thrown at her. What a fine thing to threaten a woman on her own with the police. But I should not imagine that I would get away with it! We could all go to hell. She, and only she, had the right to decide about her own flesh and blood.

At last the flood of words dried up and the lady collapsed onto the sofa which a few minutes before she had so graciously asked me to occupy.

At that moment the Rat came into the room.

He looked with fright at the sofa, then at me—a child who was thoroughly ashamed of his mother!

I would like to have stroked his hair and said, "Let her get it out of her system, Ciske, it will all pass," but I was not entitled to say this.

When the woman noticed the child, her strength seemed to come back to her. What she now said in accusations, and curses made everything I had heard so far seem like a mild preface. She completely let herself go in a flood of anger and rage.

Ciske stood motionless. Not a muscle twitched in his pale face. His eyes did not express fear, only boundless contempt. I would like to have pressed the child to me, to face the stream of invective together with him. What an unhappy creature this boy was! The father whom he loved was wandering around somewhere in the world and he was delivered defenseless to this slut of a woman who was his mother, in surroundings where there was no love. It was astonishing that things were not far worse with the child. This den of iniquity would provide mitigating circumstances for more than a petty theft or an attempt at arson.

"If you would allow me to put in one word," I interrupted finally, "I could tell you that it was not Ciske who told me anything. I learned about it from quite a different source."

"Aha, from the welfare fellow," she guessed at once. "That, too, is a filthy institution. And how do those gentlemen know about it, if I may ask?"

"Do you know that, Ciske?" I asked the boy.

"Yes! A gentleman came here and asked for me. Aunt Chris

told him that I was at the bar, working," said the Rat. He said that with a certain satisfaction. His mother could not blame him for that. And in fact Mrs. Freimuth's rage was now deflected in another direction.

"Chris," she shouted. "Chris, where are you hiding?" She continued screaming toward the kitchen. "Did you tell the man from family welfare where Ciske works?"

"Yes," came the answer in a drawl.

"You dirty fool," Mrs. Freimuth shouted, "now I'm really in trouble. I can never leave anything to you, you silly cow. Must I think of everything?"

"Should I have said nothing?" came the innocent question from the world of saucepans.

"You're a rotten bitch," screamed Ciske's mother.

"So you see that the boy is not guilty," I joined in again. "He has not talked to anyone, although he had more than the right to do so. A child should not work in a bar. He should not do anything for pay. I am warning you again: if you send Ciske to the café tonight, you will get into trouble."

Mrs. Freimuth was silent, visibly hurt. The Rat was hanging around as if undecided what to do.

"Go into the kitchen to your aunt, Ciske," I told him. Ciske looked at me understandingly, with his childish eyes with their grown-up expression, before leaving the room.

"You know now how I learned about all this. I am not interested in anything else but protecting the boy. He is still doing well at school, but I want to prevent him from coming to class tired. A boy like Ciske should have plenty of fresh air and not sit about in a bar. He will then be better behaved toward you. You just think it all over quietly, Mrs. Freimuth."

I had the feeling that all that sounded a bit like a sermon. Was I putting on an act? Not entirely; most teachers develop during their lifetime a proselytizing streak where the welfare of their children is concerned. No amount of acquired professional cynicism can prevent it. And yet I stopped, dismayed, in the middle of it, when I suddenly realized that I was preaching.

Yet I had not spoken in vain. Without warning, Mrs. Freimuth started to cry pitifully, but her sobs did not sound very genuine. I let her cry, but kept looking uncomfortably toward the door through which I would have dearly liked to disappear. I was no good at dealing with a woman in tears.

I was just beginning to feel the first twinges of sympathy, when Mrs. Freimuth began to stammer, "You want to protect *him*? To protect that boy? You should rather protect me! I, a woman, have to face all these difficulties alone. Who cares about me? And now I have to go without the money, too. Who will compensate me for that? Do you think I can produce money out of a hat to feed all these hungry mouths?"

I felt that I would suffocate in there. I wanted to get out in the fresh air, away from this unreasonable, selfish, complaining woman. Why was she howling anyway? Because of the money?

When I got out again into the street, my thoughts turned to the Rat. I was able to run away; he had to stay put. Tomorrow he would again sit in my class, but no one except myself would know what hell there was at home. He was a brave little good-for-nothing.

Next morning I saw Ciske happily pushing Dorus's wheel chair with Mrs. Keulemann walking beside it.

"May I join you?" I asked.

Mrs. Keulemann smiled at me and I fell in step beside her a few paces behind the two boys. I didn't quite know how to start a conversation.

"How are things with Dorus?" I asked eventually.

"Ah . . ." she sighed.

"Does he still like it at school?" I continued quickly, in order to take refuge in a happier subject.

She reacted immediately. Yes, school was everything to him! And now to learn French! I could not imagine how much pleasure the boy derived from it; he lay for hours on the sofa learning new words. She sometimes had to take the book away from him by force, so that he would not get overtired. And he never stopped telling her about school, about his teacher, about Betty and Sip. And also, of course, about Ciske, who had become his best friend.

"Ah, Ciske, what kind of boy is he really?" she wanted to know as we were talking about him. "There isn't much good to be said about his home, is there?"

I did not need to answer, for Mrs. Keulemann went on at once.

"He is a dear little boy. Every Wednesday and Saturday he comes to us to play. And I have to laugh when Dorus pretends to be the teacher. It is a wonderful change for my boy. Nobody has ever cared before about my boy outside class. Children never have any time for the sick."

And yet, despite her gratitude, I felt that Mrs. Keulemann did not quite know what to make of the Rat. I sympathized with her, for I too was rather puzzled by the child. But when I saw how the two of them, Ciske and Dorus, chattered away to each other, quite happily, I felt reassured. Dorus was not a boy to be attracted to bad friends. He was much too sensible and decent a boy for that.

Quite on her own, Mrs. Keulemann then started to talk about the medical reports on Dorus. All things considered, his health was not too bad; the doctor was not displeased, as the operation scars had healed almost completely now. But how was one to know that there would be no worsening of his condition? She and her husband were happy, anyway, that the boy has become so carefree now. They recalled with alarm the time when, prepared for the worst, they had stood beside his bed in the hospital. For a moment the sad overtones disappeared from Mrs. Keulemann's voice when she described her boy's good nature.

"The children are to make an excursion, I hear. But you must not think that Dorus is jealous, that he has ever complained about not being able to go with them. He has never seen the sea, yet he is pleased that Ciske and the others can go. He only wants Ciske to bring him a few shells, big ones, in which one can hear the murmur of the sea when one holds them to one's ear. The boy is an angel, Mr. Bruis. I know it is a sin to say such a thing. . . ."

I didn't know where the sin came in. . . .

Betty had now joined the two boys and Ciske was holding forth. He must have been telling them a funny story, because Dorus and Betty started laughing out loud. Three happy children walking in front of us: one marked by the inevitability of an early death, the second with a hellish home life, the third too stupid to absorb any book knowledge. Yet, on the whole, they seemed to be enjoying life.

In the school corridor I took the Rat to one side. "Did you have trouble last night?" I whispered to him.

"A little," he answered, laughing with embarrassment.

"The coal cellar?"

Surprised, Ciske looked at me. What's this? his eyes said clearly. So you know about that too? But he only shook his head.

". . . and did you go to the bar?"

"She has been there and has told them that I cannot come any more," he informed me.

So this much had been achieved at any rate, but I would like to have been able to do considerably more. If Ciske's father had not been at sea, I would have moved heaven and earth to try to convince him that he should have the boy with him. How could I take him away from that mother of his? Should I limit myself to teaching Ciske math? There were no real difficulties as far as his studies were concerned; he was making quite good progress, and I was now expecting each singing lesson to be the one in which he would begin to sing with the others. I had made up my mind that he must do it.

Ciske remained a little shy. Like Dorus Keulemann, he took little part in the normal life of the class. Perhaps the two had been attracted to each other because of this. Did they unconsciously feel they were outsiders? One, because of his physical disability, the other because of his background? Yet the class attracted them like a magnet—irresistibly.

And the class? They certainly showed a kind of respect for Dorus. He was so bright and yet one could not envy him. The Rat had also proved a number of times that he was all there, most of all when he beat up Drikus. If he continued to show some spirit, he would certainly be accepted by the class.

I felt again that there were many rewards for being a teacher.

CISKE had broken a window. I had come to his defense and had therefore almost become his accomplice. It was one of the windows of a police station.

In the morning a policeman came to the school, in order to question the Rat in Maatsuyker's presence. I was only asked in when the questioning was well under way. In the headmaster's study I found two angry men and a completely clamlike Rat.

"He has done it again," shouted the headmaster. "Your star pupil has broken a window!"

The policeman followed suit. "If this is education, I can do without it!"

I stupidly at once lost my temper. Were they crazy, to adopt such an attitude? "How would it be if you paid attention to police regulations while I looked after the education? Each man to his own job, in fact?"

"In the streets it is we who are responsible," the man retorted.

"Perhaps so, but now we are in school," I snapped back.

"Last night about eight o'clock this boy, together with some other boys, threw a stone through the window of the police station in Davis Street."

"I don't believe it!" I said firmly.

Both the policeman and Maatsuyker looked at me in amazement.

"No," I said, "that is just not possible. One cannot throw one stone together with a few other boys! Only one boy can do that. How do you know it was this boy?"

"That's just quibbling," said Maatsuyker crossly. "There is no doubt that Freimuth was the culprit. Everybody knows what kind of boy he is."

This was the limit. The man who should defend the school before the outside world took the other side without a scruple. I was angry about this betrayal and therefore did not mince my words. "Yes, gentlemen, I know just what sort of boy he is. I have had him in my class for six months now and I have only good to report about him. I know that every day he helps his sick friend. Why do you always accuse him? Simply because you are prejudiced!"

"I would like to question him, but I can't get a word out of him." The policeman stared at the ground under his feet. "This boy and a few others had been playing football on a public thoroughfare, which, as you know, is forbidden. He had done it more than once, and therefore I took the ball away from him. What does he do then? He comes to me and has the nerve to ask for the ball back. The ball belongs to a friend, he says, and he has to return it. I, of course, refuse to believe such a tale. I tell him to go home. Instead he begins to abuse me. Nobody can hold it against me that I slapped his face once or twice. But what do you know?—no sooner am I back in the station than—crash, the window is broken. One does not need to be a Sherlock Holmes to put two and two together and guess who did it."

Unfortunately I had to admit that the evidence seemed to point to the Rat as the culprit. "But you still have no proof of your opinion," I declared stubbornly.

Maatsuyker spoke up from his corner. "I cannot understand why you always set yourself up as a defender of this infamous brat."

"Because the brat happens to be my pupil. As long as his guilt is not proved, he has the right to my defense. I have as much right to ask you why you always act as his accuser."

Maatsuyker glared at me and said nothing. The policeman added only, "Could you now help me to get at the truth?"

"Certainly, officer," I said with suspicious haste. "We both wish to know the truth." What a hypocrite I was! I was of course completely convinced that the Rat was the culprit, but I wanted to help him all the same. First the policeman took his ball away, then he hit him, so a boy like Ciske had only one answer. Violence! A stone from the street! Why was I so eager to whitewash him? Only because I wanted to irritate Maatsuyker?

Sternly I now addressed Ciske. "Well then, did you break the window? Yes or no? Tell me at once!"

I would dearly have liked to wink at him, to tell him with my eyes, Don't be taken in by my maneuver! But this was completely superfluous. I was absolutely convinced that he would not say a word. That would be foolish indeed! If he were clever, he would keep his mouth shut and allow the storm to blow over. He looked at me as if he wanted to say, "Can't you see that I cannot say anything?"

The policeman turned his eyes to the ceiling and sighed. "Gentlemen, I unfortunately have other work to do, but I'll keep an eye on the boy."

"And I too!" added Maatsuyker.

And I too! I thought to myself.

I spoke roughly to Ciske, "Go on! Get back to your class!"

"Have you lost your ball?" I asked Dorus when, during the lunch break, we had our sandwiches together. This was, to use football language, a shot at an undefended goal. Poor Dorus blushed like a turkey. Ah . . . The shot had gone home. Dorus looked helplessly at me, and in less than a second I understood the whole situation. The Rat had borrowed the ball from Dorus. How did Dorus come to have a ball? Just so, to stroke it sometimes when he was in bed, to feel at least in his imagination fit as other boys. And the policeman had taken the ball away from the Rat, Dorus's ball! Ciske had told the story to his friend that morning, when he was pushing him in his wheel chair. Under the seal of the strictest secrecy, of course. Dorus felt in a pleasant way Ciske's accomplice.

And now the teacher had him in his clutches. What was he to do? Betray his friend? Never! Lie to his teacher? Yes, when nothing else could be done, of course.

But I gave Dorus no opportunity to do it. His flushed cheeks gave me warning that I could not put this sensitive boy into a real dilemma. Recently Dorus had again begun to look almost transparent. One could never tell what effect such an emotional conflict might have on him.

"You needn't blush," I said, laughing. "I've known about it all along. But don't be afraid, I will not let Ciske down in front of the police."

Dorus became even redder than before. Why didn't I keep my mouth shut, fool that I was! He crumbled his bread nervously and I decided to make a joke of the whole affair.

"A crazy fellow, this Ciske," I said. "He thought a police station is like a slot machine: that when he threw a stone through the window a policeman would come out the door! But we won't tell anyone. Otherwise we'll have, all three, to go to prison for a month and make paper bags. And I have no great wish to do that. . . ." Now Dorus laughed heartily. The teacher in a conspiracy with him! This was fun! The adventure had become even more colorful.

Ah! Goodness me, life is so short and the boy was so pleased. From the educator's point of view my attitude was, of course, deplorable. Yet I have repeatedly had the experience that a child is most happy when one can forget the more serious side of education for a short while.

We passed the rest of the midday break in the best understanding, almost as if we were colleagues. Dorus learned French grammar and I read a book on natural science.

It was a pleasure to watch Dorus's progress. He could now conjugate the irregular verbs fluently and sometimes surprised me with a sentence he had made up himself, such as, "*Monsieur, dois-je manger encore une tartine?*"

When Maatsuyker once overheard by chance that Dorus was learning French, he said pompously, "What use has such a boy for a foreign language?"

Meerstra answered for me. "To be a little happier and to forget about his illness."

Before class began I had a private word with the Rat. I waited for him in the hall and took him around to a quiet corner in another room.

"Listen, my boy," I began, putting my hand on his narrow shoulder, "you must not think that you can now do what you like with me. No, don't say anything now! I'll tell you what happened. You borrowed the ball from Dorus, and then the policeman took it away. You asked him politely to give the ball back to you, and instead you got your face slapped. Wait now! You thought to yourself, I won't let it go at that! And so you threw a stone through the window. Was that what happened or not?"

Ciske at first was not at all pleased at my interference. But I turned his head toward me and forced him to look into my eyes. When he noticed that my expression was not overstern, a pale smile passed across his face. "Yes, sir," he said simply.

In this short "Yes, sir" his confidence in me at last found expression. For the first time!

I looked at the boy with gratitude and then said like a typical schoolmaster, "In any case, I am glad that you have not lied to me. We both know very well now where we stand; you really deserve another thrashing but I think that the one you got was enough for you. I shall not tell Mr. Maatsuyker anything. But one thing cannot be avoided—Mr. Muysken of the juvenile police will be informed about the whole thing. He will be told what a good-for-nothing you are. And for me, you must copy out very neatly, as a punishment, the first page of your reading book. And remember, a boy from my class must behave properly in the street. Is that clear?"

Ciske blushed a deep red. Apparently he did not think I had been unfair.

In the afternoon the class was in a good mood for work. This happens sometimes. It seemed as if an epidemic of intelligence had suddenly broken out and spread from one child to another. Even Betty got only seven sums out of ten wrong, which was a record for her. She also got a good mark for it, because for Betty there were special scales of appreciation.

Everything would have been lovely and peaceful if it had not been for Maatsuyker, who came to see me after the end of lessons. His face forecast three days of rain! He cleared his throat and began to speak. "Bruis, I cannot really carry the responsibility much longer. After all, a school is not a shelter for criminally predisposed children. I have been thinking about it the whole afternoon. I am going to write today to the magistrate of the juvenile court. I shall inform him that we have had nothing but difficulties with Freimuth and request him to take appropriate measures."

"All right," I answered indifferently and went on tying up my pile of exercise books.

"Is that an answer, Bruis?" asked Maatsuyker angrily. "You don't seem to appreciate the seriousness of the matter."

I smoothed out the strap for holding the exercise books and replied, "I have just told the Rat that I am going to get in touch with the juvenile court."

Maatsuyker was obviously put out. "I must protest against such a step being undertaken without my knowledge. I, as head of the school, have . . . "

". . . when Mr. Bruis last asked for my advice, declined all responsibility. It was so, headmaster, you may remember. And I would not like to be exposed to a rebuke a second time."

Offended, he stumped off.

Between myself and Maatsuyker things would surely come to a head one of these days.

THAT man Muysken is a fine fellow. Without warning, I burst into his house. He received me in shirt sleeves in his aviary. He had a hobby—his canaries. The little birds hopped up and down in enormous cages. The room was full of sunshine, and Muysken presided like a god in this temple of song and light.

"We are just having a singing lesson," he whispered to me. "Come quietly and listen. These are the most wonderful notes that God Almighty has bestowed on us." He looked at me, his eyes shining. "Can you hear the trills? And the whistling? Pure as gold! The light yellow bird is the leader, the other ones have yet to learn to bring their voices to the pitch of perfection. I breed them all myself. I have studied the Mendelian Theory in my own way. And every time when I think I have penetrated the last secrets of nature, I see that I know nothing. There, this vulgar market crier will be sold later today. He spoils my ensemble with his silly shrieks. But here I am, chattering away, and I am sure you have come about the Rat."

I told him about Ciske's latest exploit.

Muysken was amused. "Such a little villain," he said, not unkindly. "At the slightest obstacle in his way, he gives you tit for tat! Well, the case should be filed away, because after all they cannot prove anything against him. But this is only another warning that one could get into terrible trouble with the Rat."

Muysken knew, too, that Ciske had been working in the bar.

"We must wring his mother's fat neck one of these days," he said. "Or we should simply take the boy away from her. But where would we put him? If we put him with a peasant family, things might go wrong unless the farmer happens by chance to be a superman. I suppose we can only leave the boy to his fate and hope that his opposition to the rest of mankind will disappear in time."

In order not to disturb the canaries, we continued our conversation in Muysken's living room. He said suddenly, "How would you feel if we left that Mr. Alarm of the family welfare high and dry and made you Ciske's guardian?"

I looked at Muysken in amazement and at first did not know what to say.

In the kindest possible manner, my host continued, "I have already spoken about it to Mr. Van Loon. There is practically no obstacle to overcome now. . . ."

"But can I myself add a little word?" I asked, slightly put out.

"Of course," said Muysken, "but I would agree if I were in your place." Suddenly he burst forth, "Damn it all, Bruis, you make me angry. You come running here, in order to talk to me about the Rat, and when I give you a really good piece of advice, you make a face as if you were about to be operated on. We need somebody to put the fear of God into this slut of a mother and you should consider it an honor to help this young boy through his adolescence. He runs no danger at school, only at home. Get yourself the necessary authority there by becoming the boy's guardian! When you feel like it, you can then at least bang on the table with your fist. We will do it this way. You will receive a summons to appear before the magistrate in the juvenile court and we will leave the decision to him."

So this was where all my cleverness had got me. . . . But at that moment I remembered Maatsuyker and decided not to protest any more.

"How do you like this?" said Maatsuyker one day with a certain satisfaction, looking at all of us in turn. "I have received a summons from the juvenile court to go and speak to them about Freimuth.

Now we can at last settle the whole matter." His eyes rested on me. When nobody replied, he continued, "There must be an end once and for all to the trouble we have with this boy. I shall insist on the strongest measures being taken."

"How would it be if you had him put publicly in the pillory?" asked Meerstra ironically. "On the other hand, branding followed by incarceration in a damp and verminous cellar sometimes helps in such not so serious cases."

"I know very well that you all consider me to be an old-fashioned crank," said Maatsuyker, "but all of you with your humanitarian whimsies would like to transform the school into a home for juvenile delinquents. This I wish to prevent."

That was too much even for Jorissen, who said, "Do you mean to imply that we have more offenders in our forms than you have in yours?"

I kept out of all this, and tried to appear unconcerned, but eventually I asked, "When are you to appear before the judge of the juvenile court?"

"Tomorrow at three o'clock."

"I've got an invitation for the same time," I said and produced from my pocket the paper which I had found in my letter box that morning.

Immediately Maatsuyker's good humor evaporated. Then Tedema, who can never keep her mouth shut, interfered. "So much the better; you can go together. That will be much more amusing."

And Jorissen, the fool, added with great seriousness, "Yes, that's true. In such cases one sometimes has to wait for hours before one's turn comes around."

Jorissen was not far wrong. In the courtroom there were a few cases to be heard before our turn came. But luckily we were not put into a boring waiting room, but could take our places in the court. I sat next to Maatsuyker in silence. He still had a sour expression on his face.

What silly preconceived ideas one has about other people's professions! I had always thought that a judge in a juvenile court must be a friendly elderly gentleman, with kindness written all over him. A father figure in a gown with white bands at the neck. Van Loon bore no resemblance to my imagined picture. He was thin and angular and looked a little like a staff officer. His nose seemed to testify that he was not averse to a drop of good liquor. A goatee emphasized the sternness of his expression; a white forelock gave him a more homey air. He sat easily and informally in his chair, playing lazily with a gold pencil. From time to time he shut his eyes for a while. The man in the witness box, who was just assuring the court with great earnestness that his daughter came home every evening at nine o'clock, stopped talking—out of politeness, presumably, in order not to disturb the judge. Immediately a nasal voice broke in, "You may continue your story. I am not asleep and can hear very well that you are lying."

Behind us somebody giggled discreetly. I turned around and saw Muysken.

"He is at his best today," he whispered. "Good afternoon, gentlemen."

Maatsuyker nodded sullenly. He seemed to be not too fond of Muysken after their last encounter.

In the meantime the father in the witness box had finished his protestations of innocence, and Van Loon said laconically, "Well, if I have understood you correctly, your daughter carries on with everybody. We shall put a stop to this as quickly as we can. Good morning!"

Greatly put out by the injustice which he had had to suffer, the man left the court. Maatsuyker shook his head in disapproval.

The type of man who then went into the witness box seemed to belong to a past age. He was wearing an old-fashioned black suit and a very high stiff collar. In his large hands he nervously twisted a bowler hat. The shoes showing from under the narrow trousers were like canoes.

Muysken kept up a running commentary in a whisper for our benefit.

Apparently this strange character had a rascal of a son—compared with whom the Rat was a little angel. But the old man was quite worthless also. We must listen carefully and we would have plenty of entertainment. . . .

First of all the old man was rebuked because he had not appeared in answer to an earlier summons.

"I was ill, your lordship," he pleaded.

"Which means drunk," translated the judge. "Well, we have had your son on probation for three months now, but this has not done him any good so next week he will go on trial. You must not be surprised if he gets six months in a reform school. I have had enough of him."

The curious man seemed to shrink. Then he lifted his birdlike head and protested, "The boy has wild blood in his veins, your lordship. I can't change that."

"If you were to drink less gin and run after women less, perhaps you might," said Mr. Van Loon. "You should stay at home in the evenings and see that the boy is not out on the streets at all hours. You yourself must try to live like a decent man for a while." The judge had changed to a kindlier tone of voice as if he wanted to stress the importance of his words. "This is my last warning," he continued. "I may decide this time to try a milder sentence—but next time the boy goes to reform school."

The father raised both his arms in a theatrical gesture and exclaimed, "I would much rather be buried alive, your lordship!"

The judge nodded and said drily, "Then you will be in the cemetery and your boy receiving corrective training. Not a bad solution! Good day!"

Maatsuyker was shocked. He had imagined a juvenile court to be completely different from this—I, also, to be quite frank. But Muysken grunted with pleasure. "Isn't he wonderful? When you try to play the fool with Van Loon you always get caught."

"But he was the boy's father," objected Maatsuyker.

"That is just the trouble. We suspect that he encourages his son to steal, not that the little rogue needs much encouragement in that direction. Within half an hour that character will be boasting in a bar that he has again given the judge a piece of his mind. . . ."

"Mr. Maatsuyker, please. Will you be so kind as to come up?" Van Loon then asked politely.

Maatsuyker stood in the box like a stupid boy, like a child who has been asked a question he can't answer. Van Loon was looking through his papers and my headmaster was not at all sure how he should behave. He put his hat clumsily on the ledge, and it immediately fell on the floor.

"Now then, Mr. Maatsuyker, you have written me a letter in which you complain about Ciske Freimuth. The Rat, as we call our little friend here, is gnawing at your stomach, is he?"

"I am seriously worried about the boy."

"Yes, yes, he is a troublesome rascal. I know that." The words came quietly from the judge's dais. "But we have to be patient with him."

"Patience I have, but . . ."

"But . . . you would like to be relieved of responsibility for the Rat by our sending him to a 'stricter' school."

"In the interest of the boy . . ."

Van Loon stared at Maatsuyker for a moment and then began slowly, "A 'stricter' school—should this be a reform school? There we send children who have definite criminal leanings, for whom we don't see any other solution. It is a very harsh punishment for a boy. What has the Rat done to merit such strong measures? In a temper he has slightly wounded another boy and he has also broken a windowpane with a stone—I am only dealing with the time since he has been in your school. If we are to punish this with corrective training, I fear that we shall have to send almost 50 per cent of all young boys there. But what trouble did you personally have with the boy?"

Maatsuyker was visibly taken aback. He could not collect himself sufficiently to make his carefully prepared speech. "I'm not worried about myself in this case," he said awkwardly.

"Of course not. I would only like to ask you one more thing. Do you know the child so well that you can say with a clear conscience that corrective training is the only hope for him?"

That stumped him completely! Van Loon's question went straight to the heart of the matter. Had Maatsuyker any real idea what Ciske was like? Why was he so concerned about him?

"I am the headmaster of the school. I do not myself teach the boy, of course, and I have much less contact with him than his form master, but after all I have a certain responsibility and it seems to me . . . how shall I express it? . . ."

"It seems to you slightly embarrassing to have a specimen like the Rat among your other pupils. Is that what you wanted to say?"

I was amazed that someone who did not know Maatsuyker well could express so exactly what was worrying him. This gave me a certain satisfaction—I was not the only one to be severely critical of Maatsuyker.

"Your opinion of the Rat is unfavorable, then," added Mr. Van

Loon. "I should now like to hear the views of his form master."

I found myself in an ugly dilemma. It would not make too good an impression before all these officials if I were publicly disloyal to Maatsuyker. But I didn't at all want to let the Rat down. He was more important to me than the whole teaching community.

"And what have you got to say about your pupil?" the judge asked me. Was I mistaken or was there a flicker of amusement in his steel-gray eyes?

"He doesn't really fit in," I admitted. "But anyone who knows his home conditions can easily understand why. I must admit honestly that sometimes I have felt at the end of my rope with him. His hostile obstinacy has often nearly driven me to desperation, but lately things have changed considerably. He now gets on quite well with the other children, and he has even found a real friend. I am quite satisfied with his progress so far. Of course, I cannot say with any certainty that he won't misbehave again today or tomorrow. That does not depend on me; at four o'clock school is over and from then on the class has no direct influence on him."

"You mean to say that Ciske is a troublesome fellow with whom one might still have a lot of difficulty, but that in the final analysis he is not a hopeless case?"

"The Rat's mother is a fount of corruption." Expressing myself for once in such exaggerated terms I felt that behind me Maatsuyker must be shaking his head with disapproval.

"This should be called a parents' court," laughed Van Loon. "We very often have to protect the children from their natural guardians. Upbringing for them presents no problems. When somebody wants to keep rabbits, he acquires a textbook about them, because rabbits cost money. But children—they just come. Why should one worry too much about their upbringing? Naturally there are people who by reading books turn themselves into pedagogues. The Rat's guardian, for instance. He means well, but he hasn't the faintest idea about his ward. Freimuth does not tally in the least with what he has read in his books. A short while ago this guardian suggested to me that he would like to try parapsychology on the Rat. Do you know, Mr. Bruis, what that is?"

"No," I admitted honestly.

"Excellent! Would you take the risk of becoming the Rat's guardian?"

I was not entirely unprepared for this suggestion. But, once it had been made, I could smell again the stench of cooking cabbage and of cheap face powder. I could see before me the monstrous sideboard with the cut-glass decanters. What could I achieve against such surroundings?

The judge was suddenly irritated. "Why don't you say yes at once? You are young enough to make spontaneous decisions. Who should be the boy's guardian if not you?" Van Loon calmed down again. "Damn it all, he is such a bright boy, Mr. Bruis. Every time he comes here I get some private amusement from this proud little boy. In some respects we could all take a lesson from him. I have a soft spot for children who resist everything they do not like. This boy must be led, but he must not feel the reins. You have proved in your class that you can do it. Make use of your talents outside school and help Ciske on his way."

"But the mother . . ." I said lamely.

"Must the boy suffer because he has such a miserable mother?" the judge shouted at me. "He needs sensible care more than all the others. And if it should be necessary to take steps against his mother, I will be on your side, I can assure you."

"Very well then," I finally agreed. "But I feel quite incapable of dealing with Ciske's mother."

Van Loon was friendly again. "You may come with the Rat to see me at any time. And now I wish you all good luck, Mr. Guardian."

I left the courtroom with Maatsuyker. No sooner were we in the corridor than he said, "I cannot pretend to be wholeheartedly in agreement with the developments. What a to-do about this Freimuth boy! All he needs is to be thrashed, just thrashed; then he will be tamed."

"Well, if the matter is so simple, I cannot understand why you wanted to have him sent for corrective training," I mocked, and Maatsuyker did not pursue the matter.

"To have made you his guardian is, I feel, to make a doubtful combination of competences. How does it combine with the role of a teacher, who must be impartial?"

"You should have told that to the judge," I said angrily. One really could not have a sensible conversation with Maatsuyker. He always rode his hobbyhorse, with the blinkers on his eyes. I don't believe that he is really a bad man, but he is certainly a bad schoolmaster. I saw him one day on a Sunday outing with his family—a school excursion in the true meaning of the word! I can well imagine his saying to his wife, "Rika, if your toothbrush is in the wrong glass again tomorrow, I will have to chastise you!"

ONE day Betty came up to me while she was tidying the classroom after school and asked rather shyly, "Sir, can Dorus come with us on the excursion?" She then blushed to the roots of her hair.

"I don't see how he can," I answered doubtfully. "You know very well that Dorus . . ."

She interrupted me to say, "Oh, sir, we could manage it quite easily. Ciske and I and Sip can push him, and you can lift him into the boat. Verkerk says that Dorus can look after our shoes and socks while we swim. And we can take turns sitting with him. Oh, sir, please let him come!"

I noticed that the conspiracy between "Ciske and I and Sip" must have gone pretty far. They had obviously thought it all out most carefully. "Have you asked Dorus if he would like to come?" I inquired.

"Oh, yes, sir," Betty said quickly, "he would like to come, but he doesn't know if you will agree—you, his mother, and the doctor, that is. But if you allow him to come, the others will surely agree too."

What boundless confidence in the judgment of a teacher! Even medical knowledge must submit to it!

"Which of you first had this idea?"

"I and Ciske," boasted Betty. "Please, sir, do allow it!"

"I'll think about it," I answered.

I realized that it would be wonderful for Dorus if he could come with us to Limuiden and Wijk aan Zee. He had never seen the sea, and it would be no fun for the lad to be left behind. I saw no technical difficulties in taking Dorus with us, but he had not saved up for it as the others had, and it was doubtful whether his mother could easily find the money. But I thought that the money could probably be raised, and anyway I could not allow the plan to be frustrated just for lack of money.

I turned it all over in my mind on my way home. Suddenly I found myself in front of a telephone booth and I went in and dialed the number of Dorus's doctor.

"I have nothing against it," he said in a flat voice, after I had told him why I had phoned.

"Mightn't he get overexcited?" I asked cautiously.

"That one cannot tell in advance. Good day, Mr. Bruis."

So I was covered from that side, even if the doctor's reaction was not entirely satisfactory. I then decided to speak to Mrs. Keulemann the same day.

She received me blushing with embarrassment. Please would I be very kind and not look at the disorder in the house! But there was no trace of any disorder—a spotless home, where everything revolved around poor Dorus. He was lying on a couch in his neat and tidy room. He too blushed deeply when he looked up to see his teacher in front of him.

"I have to talk to your mother about you," I said, "and I don't want you to be present."

Dorus laughed nervously and looked at his mother. Involuntarily I thought of the "best room" in the Rat's home, while I took a seat on the well-polished chair at the gleaming table. How quiet and simple everything was here; even the cat lay curled up neatly on the chair facing me.

"I expect you have heard already that the children wish to take Dorus with them on the excursion?" I asked. "To be honest, I think the idea is not a bad one, and the doctor has no objection. What do you think about it?"

Mrs. Keulemann stared silently in front of her for a few moments. Her voice trembled when she answered at last. "It would be a wonderful experience for Dorus. But won't he be a terrible nuisance to you and the other children?"

I reassured her. A smile appeared on her careworn face. "You tell him yourself, Mr. Bruis. He will be very happy about it." And Dorus certainly was happy about it!

When I sat down beside him and told him that he could come with us, he seized the hand which I had put on his shoulder and, overcome with joy, kissed it. I was a bit shaken. His mother stood by us, her eyes brimming over with tears, and Dorus kept shouting, "I am going to Wijk aan Zee! I am going to Wijk aan Zee!"

I wanted to dance him around the room. I blessed Betty, the Rat, and Sip, and Johnny and all the others who had planned it all. I was proud of my class, which had been so much more thoughtful, more enterprising, and wiser than its teacher.

"Now don't get so excited," I scolded Dorus to hide my feelings. "If everyone were to start behaving like you, people would think that I was taking a crowd of monkeys for an outing."

The cat, who was not used to so much noise in that quiet home, rubbed herself against my knee, arching her back.

"Can the cat come too?" asked Dorus, laughing. "She would be so pleased."

I also met Dorus's father, when he came home from work. He was a silent, thoughtful man. "I have been very anxious to meet you," he said when we shook hands.

"Again, thank you so much," said Mrs. Keulemann, when I finally took my leave after a second cup of tea.

The next day during a geography lesson we talked about the sluices and piers of Limuiden. It was best to do it beforehand, as during an excursion children have no wish to be taught anything. One had to envisage boys and girls swimming, getting their shoes and socks full of sand, and drinking lemonade through straws. I knew from experience that there was nothing I could teach them during an outing. I might talk my head off about dams, lighthouses, and fishing ports, but they would still only pay attention to their candy, to their wet bathing suits, and to the ice-cream vender. I could even sympathize with them. Children react to ordinary lessons just as they react to measles or cold feet: they belong to life, even if they don't know what purpose they serve. But to have their pleasure spoiled by a lesson, they find most inappropriate. Even during that preliminary lesson they didn't give me all their attention.

Only Drikus listened attentively and from time to time nodded approvingly. He was the only one who might during the excursion make a few notes for the essay that would have to be written afterward. That is the way of schoolmasters—after every outing an essay must be written. It follows as surely as the hangover after a night out. One cannot blame children for taking up their pens for such a purpose without much enthusiasm.

The Rat was full of charm that day. For the first time I saw him with a real smile on his face—that was before class, when I whispered to him, "What do you say about your friend Dorus coming on the excursion with us?"

"Wonderful!" he exclaimed, and blushed when I praised him, Betty, and Sip for their good idea.

Betty could be very industrious when she had something practical to do! It was she who made the plans for Dorus. She arranged to call for him with the Rat, who with Sip would push him to the boat. On board, Dorus would stay in his wheel chair, and Johnny was chosen to be the first to keep him company. They had already had their first argument about who was going to push him to the beach and who to the pier. The only thing unanimously agreed on was that I should carry him over the dunes.

Dorus let them plan and quarrel, and just smiled. He was going to come on the excursion like all the other children. Poor little fellow.

With each new school excursion I used to feel that these were quite new children whom I met at the appointed place. They always looked so different, so festive and spruce. Even the poorest, who usually appeared in class in one shoe and one slipper, that day would be decently dressed. Or at least their hair was combed more carefully or they were better washed. Never have I seen a child wear clogs for an excursion; they all wear noticeably shiny shoes, even when these are borrowed from a brother or a neighbor's child. They wear clean shirts and bright ties. Their fingernails are not in mourning.

One always had to laugh at the little girls: they would look at each other's dresses with typical womanly envy. If one of them had a pair of shoes with slightly higher heels than the others, or a coat with a little cape, she would be certain to draw a shower of adverse criticism.

Thus the beautifully turned-out class awaited my arrival. Excited and full of energy the boys and girls rushed toward me and surrounded me, chattering happily. I brought with me that morning (heaven knows why) a walking stick. Perhaps only because I too wished to do something out of the ordinary.

What a day! What a wonderful day!

Cornel Verstaveren, Johnny Verkerk, and Frances Klaver organized a race. That Frances! In class one hardly ever noticed her, but there she was, running faster than any of them. She, who was usually so shy, clutched my arm. The boys were beside themselves with sheer high spirits, and leapt about like goats. The weather was fine, but Drikus had to wear an overcoat because his mother had told him to. A few fathers had come to the pier. When they saw me, they took off their hats, while those mothers who had come along too, smiled with embarrassment.

Only Betty Van Gemert had no eyes for me. She kept looking at the bridge and screwing up her face in annoyance. I understood at once—Sip, Ciske, and Dorus hadn't come yet! Betty was getting worried. She ran up and down and scolded everybody and no one.

"Where are they? It is already ten to and they should be here with the wheel chair by now."

Johnny tried to comfort her. "You silly goose, why do you fuss so much? The boat doesn't go until a quarter past."

By then it was nearly nine o'clock. We were all there except the three boys. I sent Piet Steeman to the corner to see if he could see them. That didn't help much, but at least one appeared to be doing something.

We had to start in fifteen minutes and I was in a nice fix. At five past nine, Piet came running back. "They're coming! The wheel chair broke down!"

In a great hurry, the latecomers approached. Mother Keulemann was with them. From a distance Sip waved the wheel they had taken off, as proof of their story. Betty ran toward them and came back almost at once. "Oh, sir, the wheel came loose on the way."

At last they reached us, Sip and Ciske dragging the chair on the side where the wheel had come off.

"My arms are almost dead," said Sip. "Look at the marks I've got on my hands!"

Sip was not asking for sympathy. He was just full of male pride.

The Rat stood to one side, breathing heavily. In the meantime the fathers present inspected the damaged wheel chair. Betty looked annoyed. Had she been with them, this would never have happened! Poor Dorus. He was quite pale, with beads of perspiration on his forehead. He must have slept badly the night before, and then this had to happen to him just that morning! And the fear of not getting to the boat in time because of the damaged wheel chair.

Bart Oostra, our assistant teacher, was a mechanical genius. He assessed the damage critically. "It can easily be repaired," he said shortly. "Once we are on the boat, I can quickly do it."

It was time to go on board.

"Come on, boys, get into line," I ordered. Oostra carried Dorus onto the boat first and we all followed.

"Once more, many many thanks," said Mrs. Keulemann, who had come up to the gangplank. I smiled and nodded at her.

The Rat ran up to Dorus, who was sitting in the stern. His legs in their braces rested on a bench. Sip for the moment found it more fun to be with the boys, but Betty had decided not to leave Dorus on his own. To be on the safe side, I sat myself with the trio and then had an exhaustive report from the Rat.

Yes, it was the Rat who told me the story, although he addressed himself mostly to Betty.

"We had a terrible fright," he said, "particularly as a blasted policeman appeared and demanded that we go to a bicycle shop to have the wheel repaired. As if we had time for that! But Sip and I made it somehow, although at the end it was heavy as lead."

Dorus squinted at me sideways as if he wanted to say, "Well, what do you think of this fellow, the Rat?"

The boat got under way. When the fathers, mothers, and their children were tired of waving at one another, Wanda Bregman, who had the best voice in the class and knew it, began to sing a well-known sea chantey. A very dramatic song for a class of school children who were on an excursion in a very small boat. It seemed to me that I was seeing the Rat for the first time as he really was—free from all his stubborn hostility.

In the many months that Ciske had been in my class by then, I had only seen the crust, the hard shell which had grown around his real self. I had known that there was another Ciske there, but I had thought that it would be hidden much deeper than it was.

The boys started to play "touch." Ciske did not play, although the others wanted to include him. What had changed him so? The pleasure of having his friend Dorus on board together with all the others despite all the difficulties? The fun of going for an outing on a fine day, as a child among other children? Who could tell? The fact was, though, that my shy little Rat was suddenly revealed as the clown of the whole party. He wrestled with Betty, encouraged by Dorus. Drikus and Gerard Jonker joined in and tried to pinch some of the Rat's candy. Suddenly Ciske started walking on his hands, and did it so well that he might have been trained in a circus—I could hardly believe my eyes.

Johnny Verkerk tried to copy him, but he couldn't manage it. The Rat went on walking around on his hands, making faces at us all the time. The captain was watching us from the bridge and seemed highly amused. Ciske, encouraged by his success, gave an encore. He took one hand off the deck and, holding himself up with the other, carefully kept his balance. Then, with one leap, he was back on his feet.

The captain was the first to applaud. Then all of us joined in. The Rat bowed gracefully in all directions and then went back to his place beside Dorus, who received him with a very proud look on his face.

"One doesn't know what to think," Bart Oostra said to me. "At school he is as stiff as a stick and here he produces a floor show for which he could easily charge admission."

Ciske began to polish the bench with his trouser seat and, as as he was now in the mood, he stuck out his tongue as far as he could and made it touch the tip of his nose. This looked so funny that the whole class giggled with delight. Betty was in tears with laughter.

"You dirty thing," she scolded him jokingly, "have you no hanky with you?"

Johnny almost succeeded in spoiling the happy mood. In order to draw attention to himself, he tried to do some tightrope walking on the narrow balustrade. But I took him by the scruff of the neck and dragged him off. It would not have done if I had come back one boy short!

I couldn't keep my eyes off the Rat! He was again performing for Dorus and the others. Could this be the same silent suspicious creature with the dark eyes, who six months earlier had come into our class?

Inwardly I gave thanks to my class. I would like to have pressed each child separately to my heart. It was they—those little bandits running about in front of me—who had made the Rat into a vivacious lovable little human being.

The gaiety of my class was catching. I felt certain that the day was going to be a wonderful success. Such a school excursion is not by any means always pure pleasure for the person in charge. It is often a devilishly difficult job to keep order and yet not spoil the happy atmosphere. And when in the evening one asked oneself what was the purpose of having such a day out, one would be left with the impression that the orangeade and the sweets had made a much deeper impression on the children than all the fresh air and the wonders of nature. But that day things seemed quite different.

Even Oostra, who had taken up teaching only because his father wanted him to, was like a carefree boy again. He could whistle wonderfully through his fingers. The boys and girls listened open-mouthed to his soulful trills and cadenzas.

"And now you must do something, teacher," said Betty. But I had no act. I could not walk on my hands, nor play the flute on my fingers. All I could do was to imitate, surprisingly accurately, the mooing of a cow. By good fortune we had just passed a ferry laden with cattle, so I mooed loudly across the water at them. When a real cow mooed back at me everyone hooted with laughter and promptly they all started mooing.

The boat tied up, and we set off on our way to Wijk aan Zee. High and clear the children were singing the song about the blue flower which can only be found by a vagabond. People who heard them stopped to listen and smiled at them. Dorus headed the procession in his wheel chair, with the Rat and Betty pushing him.

I left the class to themselves and walked with Oostra at the rear. As no arguments and no screams disturbed the peace, as no boy tripped up any of the girls, I knew that things augured well.

Oostra noticed it too. "It's amazing!" he said. "At first I had no wish to come with such a herd of sheep. Last year I went on an excursion organized by Maatsuyker. I have still not quite recovered from it to this day. It was a real fatigue party! All the sights on the way, mixed up with lectures about Diesel express trains, Utrecht Cathedral with every single historical date, and much similar rubbish. The children were miserable. They would have much preferred to play football or to amuse themselves in any other way. Mr. Maatsuyker behaved just as if he were in school. The only thing that displeased him was that he could not put anyone who didn't pay attention into the corner."

Oostra told his story with a perfectly straight face. He was a nice fellow, but quite out of place in a school. He was aware of this himself too. He would have been much happier in a factory among workmen—more in his place. There was perpetual friction between him and the headmaster. All of us used to laugh at the insolent way in which Oostra spoke to the boss. When Maatsuyker once asked him why he was not wearing a vest for class, Oostra answered laconically, "I *am* wearing my vest, sir. You see, my mother has used it to mend the seat of my trousers." As he spoke he turned his back on Maatsuyker and showed him the patch in the seat of his trousers.

The class was by then a good way ahead of us, and we had to walk quickly to catch up with them.

The boys were showing off like mad. Their conversation turned on the sea and swimming.

"Sir, Johnny says that he can count up to twelve under water. Is that possible?"

"Johnny cannot count up to twelve on dry land!" shouted Sip.

"That's why he can do it all the better under water," threw in the Rat.

"Well, how do you like the sea?" I asked Dorus.

"Very nice," he answered politely and that was all.

He seemed disappointed. I don't know what he had expected to find, perhaps waves as high as a house and hundreds of ocean-going liners. But the good old North Sea stretched out before us calm and peaceful, with little white waves breaking lovingly on the sandy beach.

The boys and girls rushed over the white sand. Such was the magic attraction of the sea that even Betty and Ciske abandoned Dorus in his wheel chair and ran toward it with the others. Oostra set off briskly after them so that in their enthusiasm they would not go straight into the water in their shoes and socks.

I stayed with Dorus. "Are you pleased with your day?" I asked him.

"Oh, yes, sir! It is as much fun as a wedding. I am not a bit tired, but I'm very hungry, sir!"

I lifted him onto the warm sand and whistled for the class to come back. I didn't want them to paddle in the sea as they would only get blisters from it. But it had been agreed that they would bring their bathing suits and have a real swim; that was to be the highlight of the day.

"Get your clothes off!" I ordered. "Who is going to be ready first?"

I myself began to undress to set a good example. The girls moved away a few steps, obviously because they felt it would not do to undress in the midst of so many boys. They started giggling when they saw me in my underpants. As we did not have enough money to hire bathhouses, we had to manage like this.

Drikus wished to stay with Dorus. He had an overcoat with him, but no bathing suit.

"Have a swim in your pants," advised Cornel Verstaveren. "They will dry out in a jiffy."

But Drikus only shook his head. He had coughed in the night and had promised his mother not to go into the water.

I didn't say anything, as one of us had to stay anyway to keep Dorus company.

"Look, Sip has fleabites," cried Johnny Verkerk.

"You are mad," replied Sip, not being able to think of anything better.

The five of us played about on the beach. The sea muttered peacefully.

It gave me enormous pleasure to see the Rat struggling happily against the waves. Afterwards we ate our sandwiches on the beach. It was a very ordinary picnic, but the children loved it. They fell on their bread and butter like starving wolves and Dorus declared, "I could eat ten times as much!" How he loved to exaggerate!

After our picnic we played "cops and robbers." Sip was the leader of the "cops." The captain of the "robbers" was, as everybody had expected, Ciske. But there was someone from whom he had to take orders, someone who had a lot to say even though he could not himself catch anybody, who could only give commands—Dorus. All the threads of the game were in his hands. He only had to lift his little finger and the "robbers" stopped dead. Dorus's eyes shone. What he had until then only read about in books had become reality now.

"There they are," he cried suddenly and pointed to a sand dune over which the Rat and his followers appeared now. With wild leaps and ear-splitting yells, they stormed down the slope and became engaged in a violent struggle with the "cops." Cornel gave Drikus such a hefty shove that he landed in a bramble bush. "Oh, dear, his overcoat!" I suddenly remembered with alarm, but the overcoat lay safely on Dorus's chair. The girls confined themselves to underlining the wild battle acoustically. Only Betty fought like a Valkyrie until at last she was rather ungallantly thrown to the ground by Gerard Jonker.

As the outcome of the battle remained undecided, the two leaders resolved to settle the matter by single combat. Sip therefore climbed on Johnny's back and Ciske had Piet as his "horse."

At last one could see the Rat in his true element. He was smaller than Sip and had plenty to do, taking skillful evasive action. The "horses" stamped their feet excitedly.

"Kill him," screamed the "robbers."

"Kill him!" echoed the "cops."

"Go on, Ciske, let him have it!" shouted Dorus.

Suddenly Ciske stood up on Piet's shoulders. His "horse" stumbled and the shouting suddenly stopped. Then something amazing happened. Ciske could only keep his balance for a few seconds, so Piet exploited this and ran toward the enemy. With one leap the Rat was onto Sip and his "horse," both of whom, of course, were completely taken aback and fell to the ground. Locked together all three rolled down the slope. Only Piet remained standing at the top, his arms thrown up in triumph.

"All right! Now let's go over to the beach house and get some lemonade," I suggested.

"Hurrah!" shouted my children and started to sing a marching song.

And the Rat? The Rat was singing with them! . . .

When we were going home on the boat, Sip sat with his arm

around Dorus, and even Johnny was still. We were all on deck enjoying the windless evening.

"This is how they should always be seen," smiled Oostra.

I sat down among the children and they asked me which of them was the most sunburned. I answered that I believed Dorus was. He had a lovely fresh color and was very happy about my remark. It was probably the first time that he could compare his color with that of the other children. Then it came quite naturally that I could say something about the North Sea Canal and the Y-shaped breakwaters which our great-grandfathers had built so that Amsterdam could be connected with the sea.

"When I grow up, I am going to sea," declared the Rat suddenly —and he meant it!

To be honest, I couldn't imagine the Rat as an upholsterer or a commercial traveler. I could much more easily see him as a stoker on a ship, sweating, covered with grease, with a red scarf around his neck. On land in a leather apron or in a carpenter's coat? Hardly! Perhaps as a tramp in a harbor café? But one shouldn't let one's imagination run away with one—in the end Ciske would probably become an honest grocer. Things always turn out differently from the way one thinks.

"I will be a shopkeeper, like my father," said Johnny Verkerk with conviction. I was quite sure he would.

"And I will be a housewife," added Betty. Of that I had no doubt!

"I will work in an office," declared Drikus. It amazed me that the pupils in my class with the most distinctive characters had already chosen the trades which corresponded to their personalities. They seemed to have grown past the age in which all children want to be bus conductors or railroad engineers.

"And you, Sip?" I asked.

"I will be a man of independent means. Then one does not get callused hands, as my father always says."

"You are quite right," the captain agreed. "Work has never yet made life sweeter for anybody."

Through a veil of mist one could now see the city far off on the horizon. A feeling of regret filled me because I had to return the children, after their day in the fresh air, to an ant heap of houses. They would have to go back again to the narrow tenements, into the small overcrowded rooms, and share the polluted air with their brothers and sisters. Tomorrow school awaited them again. There would again be forty-eight of them in class and they would have to learn simple fractions. Or write an essay. Should I make them write an essay? Ah, why not?

It had been a beautiful day. But what was this one day? For Dorus a great deal. He had experienced more than during a whole year of his sad life. And for the Rat? Perhaps everything. For Ciske had discovered his true nature. And isn't that a great deal?

Dorus was once again sitting in his wheel chair, as we sailed up the last bit of the canal. He did not seem excessively tired, and looked well with his narrow face so nicely tanned.

"I can already see my mother!" he exclaimed.

They all rushed toward the rail, to wave to their parents, who were standing on the shore in a tight little group. Nothing remained of the peaceful magic which had surrounded us a moment before. The children were again back to normal, each trying hard to make more noise than all the others.

Only the Rat did not look toward shore. Whom should he expect to see there? He watched with great concentration the machinery in the engine room. Only when the boat had tied up did he saunter toward Dorus.

Ciske's face had again become clouded with his usual reserve. But when I nodded at him, he smiled back.

Suddenly I saw the smile freeze on his face and his narrow lips fall open in amazement. Motionless he stared at the shore for a second, then, with one bound, shot forward, pushed Wanda roughly aside, and hung over the boat rail. The others looked at him speechless, and Wanda even forgot to scold him.

"Daddy!" cried Ciske. "Daddy!"

Nothing else existed for him in the whole world. No class, no Dorus, no teacher. Nothing but the slim man waving down below.

"Daddy!" Ciske ran toward the gangplank and angrily stamped his foot because it was not yet down. Had the man in charge not kept him back, he would certainly have tried to jump over the rail.

"Just be patient, my boy," shouted the sailor from down below.

I made the children line up, and Oostra took Dorus in his arms. I left the Rat where he was. I didn't want to disturb him in his boundless joy. Crash! Ciske was the first to rush down the gangplank and throw himself into his father's arms. I just had time to see his father lift him into the air, and then I was too much taken up with the other children to pay much attention to the two of them.

All the children shook me by the hand, the better brought up saying, "Thank you very much, teacher."

Sip formulated his thanks with special grace. "It will be an unforgettable day for me, sir," he said. He had probably heard the phrase at some time from one of the ladies who came to his mother's tea parties.

Dorus chattered away merrily to his parents as he sat in his wheel chair.

Then Freimuth came toward me with outstretched hand and greeted me cheerfully. "Yes, I'm back again. I heard that your class had gone on an excursion, so I came here to call for the little monkey."

Ciske stood proudly beside his father. He had been called for like the other children. What a day!

What a day indeed!

"Come and see me one day next week," I said to Ciske's father. "We must have a chat together again."

The hand that Ciske held out to me was as damp as a blackboard sponge.

THE class duly wrote their essays. Among them were some which consisted only of phrases like "and then we went into the water," "and then we had sandwiches," "and then we played." Most of the children found it very hard to put their impressions on paper; they set up a subconscious resistance within themselves because they considered this sort of writing to be pure nonsense.

As I knew perfectly well what had happened on the excursion, they could see no point in telling me all about it!

Betty concocted an impressive piece of prose: a page full of mistakes, inkspots and crossings-out, with the wrongly written words in brackets and the supposedly correct ones right afterward. And yet I was convinced that Betty had told her mother about everything in the most glowing terms. But when she had had to put pen to paper, the situation became hopeless.

Under her essay I wrote in red ink, "Horrible! Far too many mistakes!" And of course she received a bad mark into the bargain. This was the more galling for Betty because she herself thought that her essay was rather good.

The Rat started his essay like this. "When the boat came back, I suddenly saw my father standing there. What a surprise! I rushed toward him, and he shook teacher's hand. Later we went off. I told him about the lovely day and about Dorus's wheel chair. Then he bought me an ice cream."

Only after this introduction came a sensible enumeration of all our other experiences. The most unexpected thing about the essay was the immense part allocated to me in it: "Teacher said"; "Teacher thought"; "and then Teacher pulled such a funny face." The most characteristic thing about it was that he began at the end.

Very characteristic also was the effort of our friend Dorus. It was in a heavy textbook style, but suddenly interrupted by very boyish remarks.

The level of Dorus's essay was much higher than that of the rest of them, so he was allowed to read it aloud.

"It is like a real book," said Sip impulsively.

The class looked at its best pupil with pride.

I showed Dorus's essay also to my colleague Meerstra. "It really is a shame about that boy," he said. "Had God given him healthy limbs, he would certainly become a good teacher. Poor parents with a very gifted child! Those are just the right qualifications. It was a very good thing that you took him with you to the seashore. No one in the world can take that experience away from him."

A few weeks later the long vacation began. About time, too, as far as I was concerned. I was tired and nervous. One cannot just shake off what one goes through with a class as one shakes dust from one's clothes. During the vacation I was going to go on my honeymoon—Susie and I were finally getting married.

In order to justify my guardianship of Ciske *de facto*, his father was trying to get his divorce through. That these preparations coincided with my preparations for getting married, could be considered a tasteless whim of fate. I stood with one foot in the seventh heaven of love, with the other in the depths of depravity. In the morning, for instance, Susie and I might have a lively discussion as to whether we should buy a bedroom suite in beech or mahogany, and in the afternoon I might have to listen to statements from Mrs. Freimuth such as, "If I can get out of it, I certainly will! The dirty bastard! To run off with a strange bitch and leave his own wife with tuppence!"

Susie sometimes used to reproach me because I worried more about a strange divorce case than about our marriage; but that, of course, was largely exaggeration, as I was very happy to be able to get married at last. By the time one is thirty, one is tired of furnished rooms.

On the other hand, it was true that I did think about Ciske a great deal. I now had fairly heavy responsibilities toward him and I had to consider his interests. When the divorce went through, a new and better life would open for the child. But I wasn't quite happy about the divorce; his father seemed to me to be taking the whole thing somewhat lightly. I suspected that that free and easy sailor was simply allergic to all kinds of difficulty.

Smiling and carefree he appeared one day in my classroom. "I have met a woman . . . and now I believe I could have Ciske with me. A month ago you yourself suggested something like this, but at that time I could not even think of it as I had no job and lived like a sick cat—on bad pickings. Now I've got a steady income even if it is only a small one. The woman is a very decent person. She works in a hand laundry as a presser and everything about her is spick and span. Yesterday I took Ciske to meet her and I believe that the two of them will get on fine. What do you think about it? . . ."

To judge by his tone, the matter was as good as settled anyway. Everything was quite straightforward, wasn't it? One met a woman whom one liked, took one of the children to live with her, and everything was fine!

Naturally I found his plan not at all bad, but I refrained from congratulating him too soon. "First of all you must get a proper divorce from your wife," I said, to put a brake on his optimism.

"Ah yes, the divorce," he sighed. "That's a disgusting lawyer's mess, a foul mixup. What's more, Ciske's mother will certainly try to get as much out of it as she can, the bitch!"

Freimuth was willing to take care of the Rat, as he was the apple of his father's eye, but he didn't want to be responsible for the other children.

He spoke gaily about the future. When Ciske went to live with Jane—that was the woman's name—there would also be a home there for his father. The boy would then have been taken away from that slut and would not need to sleep in the coal cellar any more. During his last trip he had been able to save some money, which would buy a number of things, and the remainder could be bought on the installment plan.

"How long have you known the good lady?" I asked him.

It seemed that he had known her for quite a long while. For several years she had been washing his shirts. Recently he again took a bundle around to her and remarked casually that it was really a hell of a job to wash other people's dirty stuff! Just to make conversation, but then somehow they began to speak about marriage. He would only have to lift his little finger and she would consent; but, to be frank, he was rather fed up with the marriage game. As a sailor, a man did not have to buy half a cow when he wanted a pound of beef, did he? And he had told her quite openly how he felt. But when he had called to collect Ciske at the dock and when the boy had told him so happily about the sea, about Dorus and other wonderful things, he had felt disgusted that he had had to take the boy home to the pigsty that was his mother's place.

He had begun to think at night about whether it was quite so impossible to join forces with Jane. So he had gone the following day to Jane's store and showed her two tickets to the movies. After the performance they had drunk a glass of beer in a café and then he had said to her, "Look here, Jane, we are no chickens, we two. If I were to say that I cannot live without you, that would be a damned lie, because that's not how things are with me, and I am sure that that's not how they are with you." Then he had told her about Ciske, and about his dreadful mistake, his marriage. And then he had asked her whether they could perhaps go out together regularly. They could see then how things worked out. "I don't mind," she had said, and they had then had a glass of gin to celebrate.

He had not said a word to Ciske about the whole matter, as nothing had been definitely settled. He brought Jane and the boy together one day, as if by chance. To have said anything to the Rat beforehand would have been dangerous, as he might well have been hostile and intractable. But everything went very well. Nothing much had been said, but one could feel that the two of them would get on well together.

I could see many difficulties, though.

The general attitude to life and its problems has become much more liberal in recent years, but could one just take a child away from its mother and put him to live with his father's mistress? I expressed my doubts about it.

But Freimuth answered simply, "Well then, I must get a divorce at any price; then I'll be rid of the hag once and for all."

"And suppose she won't play along?"

He looked at me in astonishment. "Won't play along? . . . But why, when she has cooked her own goose now! That would be something! She should thank her lucky stars that she's getting rid of me."

"But she'll try to make an enormous profit out of the whole business," I reminded him.

Freimuth once again laughed off the problem. "Well, we'll see. If she won't hear of it, then everything will have to remain as before. I'll go off to sea, Jane will for the time being stay at the laundry, and Ciske will have to put up with his dear mother for a while longer."

Thus our first conversation about the divorce ended.

The next day Freimuth again turned up to see me at school. "I am making things hot for her," he said. "But I am afraid that nothing will come of it. My God, what a viper that woman is! I have thought for a long time that she must have gall instead of blood in her veins, but I didn't think that she could be quite so venomous! . . . I suggested to her very calmly that as it has for a long time been stupid to call our relationship marriage, would it not be sensible to put an end to this folly and get a divorce. Didn't she agree that that would be right and proper? But pff! Madame made a face like a rattlesnake with a stomach ache! She didn't even fly into a rage, which was the most amazing thing. Quite sweetly she said, 'So you want a divorce! Now, when you are earning something, so that you can spend the money with someone else. I would rather drop dead!'

"I couldn't help remarking that there could be worse solutions, but I then suggested we should both try to be realistic. I would free her from the worry of Ciske, which would at least be something, didn't she think? But then she started shouting so loudly that I was almost deafened. She went for me like a madwoman. I couldn't hear half of what she was saying. I thought, Just let yourself go, and when you are tired, I'll give you something to think about!

"When at last she had to stop for breath, I said in a catty way, 'Well, if you have no wish to divorce me, I shall assert my conjugal rights, and shall come back and live here.'

"She looked at me as if I were a visitor from another planet. 'You want to move in here? To stay here?'

"'Of course! It will be fun for you. I could, if I wanted, take over the central-heating job at the shipping line's offices. It is light work with a lot of time off. You could make a fine life for yourself. You wouldn't have to go to the café, and instead you could play games with the children in the evening. And once they are in bed, you could put your feet up and darn socks. I wouldn't disturb you, because I would be sitting in my armchair, reading the newspaper. You could send your sister home, because you would have plenty of time to run the house. You'll see; it will be very pleasant.'

"I said all this in a sweet voice, but every word went home. Give up the café? Not sit any more like a female Buddha behind the counter drinking sweet liqueurs with the customers? And have me at home the whole day instead?

"'You don't mean it!' she whispered.

"'I am quite serious!' I said coolly. 'But you must stop being so moody, Mary. You should know me by now. If I should happen to be in the wrong mood myself I might lose control of my hands.

I might regret it afterwards, but that wouldn't make the plates or the mirror whole again.'

"I was ready for the outburst of rage which followed. 'Monster' and 'brute' were probably the kindest expressions which she threw at my head.

"'Well, Mary, should our new marriage begin like this?' I asked her very calmly. 'I find you have become somewhat rough in your manners. Where shall I sleep tonight—here in the living room or in your bedroom?'

"I thought she would have a heart attack at any moment, but I took off my jacket and sat down casually in an armchair. 'Put the kettle on and make some tea!' I commanded.

"Her face was like a red balloon; she disappeared into the kitchen to drink a glass of water. When she returned, she was relatively calm. 'Get out of here,' she said menacingly. . . ."

Freimuth finished his story. I had listened to him in silence.

"I really believe that everything is a question of money with her," he said, staring straight in front of him.

"Tell me frankly, Freimuth," I asked bluntly, "is the boy your only concern?"

"No, not entirely," he admitted. "I myself would also like to start life over again."

Maatsuyker was not enchanted with those activities of mine which had nothing to do with my school duties. For once he was quite right; my room sometimes resembled the office of a lawyer who specializes in divorce cases.

In the afternoon Mrs. Freimuth appeared to speak to me as Ciske's guardian. When the Rat saw his mother in the hall, he went pale and he passed her without a word of greeting. He hated her more than anything else in the world.

Mrs. Freimuth started without any introduction. Her worries were about money, and nothing else.

At that moment, I had no time for her, because I had a date at five with Susie. We had to take some measurements in our new apartment. In my head everything was going around and around: prices of carpets, vacuum cleaners, stoves! And now Ciske's mother . . .

"You must be sensible," I told her sharply. "Freimuth cannot pay you ten guilders a week. I'll try to get him to agree to five."

"Then I shall not agree to a divorce."

"And suppose he moves back into your apartment?"

"He should just try it! I'll make his life a paradise on earth."

One thing I did understand about women was that, when they had this dangerous glint in their eyes, one shouldn't start arguing with them. What was more important was that it was already half-past four!

"You must know best what to do," I told her. "But you must please leave Ciske out of it; otherwise I will go to the juvenile magistrate the very same day."

It was probably stupid of me to have said this, because she hissed at me, "Ciske, Ciske, Ciske! That wretched boy! His father too is very full of him now. But I can see through the whole game. He wants to take my son to that washerwoman! And even Ciske is too good for that!"

By a particularly ill stroke of luck, while Mrs. Freimuth still had her hand on the doorknob, Freimuth appeared in the doorway. The two glared at each other without moving, before the old hatreds flared up. The woman then lost her temper completely and started hurling insults at her husband. A few children were running along the corridor and Meerstra came up, peering anxiously over the top of his spectacles. I was sure that Maatsuyker would appear on the horizon in another moment.

My God, what a situation!

Meerstra, with whom I left the school buildings, laughed at me. He found it funny that I was so angry about the mess in which I had got myself.

AND then my class found out that I was getting married. One cannot hope to keep a thing like that a secret, but still I kept asking myself how the children had found out about it.

When I came into the room, an enormous bunch of gladioli was lying on my desk. "Congratulations on your marriage from us all," I read on the attached card. Who the "us" were I could read in the faces of my pupils, and I immediately got to work shaking forty-eight children by the hand, which of course produced a lot of movement and noise.

Meerstra stuck his head in the door and wanted to know what was going on.

"Mr. Bruis is getting married," said Johnny, and Meerstra pretended to be very surprised. He rushed toward me and shook both my hands.

"And he has never told me a thing," he lied.

"Nor us," laughed Betty.

And then they began to sing so that the windows rattled, "For he's a jolly good fellow!"

Attracted by the noise, Maatsuyker now put in an appearance. "What's the matter?" he asked Meerstra.

"Bruis is getting married."

I must admit that Maatsuyker behaved better than I would have expected. Our last quarrel was quite recent, and I wouldn't have been a bit surprised if he had said, "Oh, yes, I know. But must you therefore make so much noise?" But he only laughed, shook me warmly by the hand, and said, "And now back to work, everyone."

In the afternoon I let the children draw what they liked. Most of them chose wedding scenes—the teacher in morning suit and top hat, at his side a fully veiled bride—or fantastic wedding cakes. The Rat, who could draw better than any of them, drew a peaceful picture of the future: a man and a woman holding hands over a cradle. The precocious Johnny Verkerk laughed not quite innocently at the drawing. I asked Ciske if I might give his picture to Susie as a present. He was very proud.

After all this, I said, "Get the arithmetic books out of the closet, Sip. We must do something sensible too today."

"Ohhh!" muttered the class in disgust. Up till then it had been such a lovely day.

"Don't you like arithmetic?" I asked with feigned surprise.

"Oh, yes, certainly, but not today," replied Johnny, and even Drikus shook his head.

"Well, what then? . . .

The Rat shouted, "*Robinson Crusoe!*"

Without waiting for my approval, they moved up together, three in one row, and more where possible.

Those are the pleasantest hours in any class. There is nothing more touching than the attentive children's faces when one reads to them. How completely they are absorbed in listening! How much I have always loved my boys and girls during such short hours. I would like, in one enormous gesture, to press them all to my heart. How much I wish at such times that they will preserve some slight memories of school in their future lives. A memory of the time when they did not know the grimmer side of life and were trying to become decent and orderly people.

Suddenly the spell was broken. "Sir, look. . . ." Betty was pointing to the window, where I saw Susie's radiant face. I was a bit embarrassed. What could Susan want here?

"Miss Tedema asked me in," explained Susie when she came into the classroom. "Oh, what wonderful flowers these are!"

They all smiled. And then Susan, also, had to shake forty-eight small hands.

The bell rang and the class broke up. The children looked a little uncertainly at Susie, and Susie looked a little uncertainly at me when, with the skill that comes from practice, I put Dorus up on my shoulder to take him to his wheel chair.

"So that was Dorus," she said when I came back. "You must always be nice to him, or you will have to answer to me."

When I moved to kiss her, I saw that her eyes were moist.

Miss Tedema came in smiling. "Have you got a moment to spare?"

In the headmaster's office Maatsuyker and the others were

assembled. Maatsuyker made a short speech and wished us luck in our new life on behalf of himself and my colleagues. "A marriage can be compared with a school," he said. "We get a portion of responsibility allocated to us and we must see how we come to terms with the joys and the disappointments."

The last days before the long vacation.

I had no child in my class who would have to repeat the course. I had succeeded in dragging even Betty along with the rest. Exercise books, textbooks, and all school equipment were put away tidily. On the last day of term, the geraniums would be divided among the children, so that they could look after them at home. The Rat was to take the fish home with him.

I had no idea that the children were preparing another surprise for me and that the bouquet of gladioli was not to be their only wedding present.

Suddenly Sip's hand shot up. He said that he wished to "be excused," and I gave him permission. When I looked up again he was back in the room—with a large package under his arm.

"Go on," Johnny urged him and Sip said, "This is also for your wedding, sir. We all hope that you will like it." I must have looked rather taken aback, for Sip then pushed the package into my hands. "Take it; please, sir."

"Have you all gone mad?" I asked jokingly. "I daren't unpack this."

Their faces shone with pleasure. I unwrapped the sheets of paper, revealing a bright red fruit dish. It was so enormous that I was quite amazed by it.

Forty-eight pairs of eyes were watching me anxiously.

"How wonderful," I exclaimed. "How extremely kind! Is this really from you?"

"Yes," said Johnny, "we saved up for it."

"It is a wonderful thing. I am quite overcome. When I look at the dish in ten or twenty-five years' time, I'll think of you all and remember that you were the nicest class I ever had. Then I'll see your faces before me again, and hope that you have not forgotten me entirely."

When the lesson was over, I took Ciske to one side. "Listen," I said quietly, "we won't be seeing each other for a month. Your father will be at sea all the time. I am counting on you to be a good well-behaved boy. You know what I mean, eh? And you must not answer your mother back and make her angry."

For a moment his steel-gray eyes rested on mine. Then he nodded. I was not particularly easy in my mind. Was I wrong or was there some of the old reserve in his look? But I hadn't much time to think about this, as, to my amazement, I saw Muysken's head appear in the doorway. He gave me his podgy hand and then held out a cage with a canary in it.

"Every wedding must be marked by a present," he said. "In the first few weeks you won't need any chirping, because your wife will do it all; but, later on, it won't do you any harm to have a prize-winning canary in the house!"

I had always considered enormous fruit dishes and canaries to be the symbols of petty-bourgeois life; they had seemed to me as objectionable as stone dwarfs in the garden and tea cozies. And yet I was as pleased as punch with the presents from my class and from Muysken. I was really pleased, but I was not quite sure how Susie would react to the livestock and chattels I would be bringing home.

"Ah, there is our young friend," called Muysken and took the Rat playfully by the scruff of the neck. "Yes, and there's the boy who got that terrible stab with a knife! Did you suffer a long time from the effects of it?"

Both boys, the Rat and Johnny, laughed with embarrassment. They had both completely forgotten the whole painful episode. We had all come a long way since then.

WHEN the long vacation rolls around, the children are happy. When it is over, they are also happy. This used to strike me forcibly every year. When you asked them, "Are you pleased to be back at school?" they would exclaim in chorus, "Oh, yes!" and "No-oo." They feel somehow obliged to find school horrible and vacation wonderful. But how can one explain that most of them, on the first day of school, run, smiling and happy, to their teacher, as soon as they see him coming around the corner? Why is it always just the first school day that is so particularly nice and happy? And why is one personally so displeased? When everything is back to normal again, with the children sitting at their desks, the geraniums again on the window sill, and the fish in their aquarium, back in place, there is no class and no teacher who are longing for the Christmas break.

When I looked at my class on that first morning of the new term, I could not discover much evidence of blooming health. Indeed the schools had been closed for a few weeks, but who cared whether the children really enjoyed their vacation or not? Sip Eisma was one of the very few who looked better than they did a month before. He had been staying with his uncle in Ernewouden, on the most lovely part of the coast in Friesland. Full of pride he showed his arms and legs. None of the others was as brown as he. Even Cornel Verstaveren, whose parents had a summer bungalow, seemed pale beside him.

And the Rat?

I didn't like the look of the Rat. It seemed to me that he was even grayer than before. He seemed somehow distrait. During the reading class he could not even find the place.

What could be the matter? Were things going wrong at home?

No, the vacation had done the child no good. When his eyes began to roam aimlessly around the class and I could at last catch his eye, he smiled shyly at me. For a whole five minutes after that the Rat concentrated gallantly, but then his thoughts again escaped somewhere else.

At four o'clock I kept the Rat in as he had to correct a few sums. "Why were you so inattentive today?" I asked him. "Is there anything the matter with you?"

"No, sir."

"How did you enjoy your vacation?"

"Very much, sir."

"So you had a nice time?"

"Yes, sir."

He answered all my questions mechanically. It was quite obvious that he was putting on an act. Children do it frequently without being conscious of it. Even if Ciske had wanted to tell the truth, he would not have been able to. Grownups and children often speak a different language. A child who does not tell the truth is not necessarily always lying!

Only when I asked the Rat whether he was pleased to be back at school did he say with real conviction, "Oh, yes, sir!"

That was genuine enough. School was Ciske's refuge, the place where he felt safe. The Rat, I was sure, had not had any pleasure during the vacation.

The class was set to write an essay about their vacation, and I read in the Rat's book, "And then I was asked to run a few errands for our neighbor. She gave me five cents, and I bought myself some candy. That was lovely!"

Apart from this, there was nothing "lovely" to be found in Ciske's essay. Only at the end he wrote again, "And then we went back to school, which is lovely!"

That afternoon I went again to visit Mrs. Freimuth. In the "best room" there was a smell of cigars. In the ash tray lay a heap of ashes. This did not necessarily mean anything, but in this case I had a definite feeling that when I appeared a man had been hastily shoved into the kitchen. The lady had obviously had a visitor.

She pretended to be extremely pleased to see me and she even congratulated me belatedly on my marriage. Nothing further had happened about the divorce. Her lawyer had advised her to insist on getting forty guilders a month at any rate.

"Then indeed nothing will come of it," I said. "It is rather silly, really, because not only do you lose twenty guilders, but you must also look after Ciske." I had to suppress a desire to comment on the cigar ashes and hint at the possibility of a new life for Mrs. Freimuth, but I was too shy to be so outspoken. "How did Ciske behave during his vacation?" I asked instead.

She shrugged her shoulders. "How should he behave?" she answered harshly. "He has been around the place pestering his mother. One should thank God when children go back to school."

The boy had not been at home much, she continued. Mostly just for his meals and at night. He had sat a lot with Dorus at his house and had, whenever possible, slipped off in the evenings to see his father's woman.

"What, don't you know? His father has got himself a mistress. Too funny for words—a common washerwoman. And after that he wants to tell me what to do! He should be pleased that I don't divorce him for adultery. Then he would have to pay up! Pay through the nose until the day of his death!"

One thing Ciske's mother made quite clear: Ciske would never be able to see that sluttish woman with her blessing—"Auntie Jane," as Ciske called her. (He called her that, of course, only to irritate his mother.) But she knew perfectly well that he was visiting her behind her back. She couldn't keep an eye on such a boy all the time, especially as she was so busy herself. Once she had followed him when he had said he was going to Dorus. But where did he go? Straight to the washerwoman! Well, she had shown him then where he got off. And at night she had been locking him in.

Now I could see quite clearly why the Rat had been so pleased to see the end of the vacation.

SOMETHING was in the air. I could not explain why I felt it, but I did. I was worried that the Rat fell silent whenever I mentioned home to him.

Maatsuyker asked me during the break one day, "How are things going with the Rat now?"

"Excellent! He is a changed boy, quite different from the child who came here some months ago"—I did not need to exaggerate.

"True enough," admitted Maatsuyker, "we have not had any trouble with him for quite some time. But let's wait and see if things remain that way. I don't trust the boy an inch."

Earlier I would have been very angry at this lack of confidence. Now I felt that the doubts expressed by my headmaster were not quite so unjustified. Just because I was so pleased with the Rat, I could not suppress a certain fear of the future. Why did the child stare so grimly into space when the moment before he had been so gay? Why was he suddenly, in the middle of an arithmetic problem, so far away in his thoughts? Why did he start when I called his name? What was going on in his mind?

For Dorus, Ciske would still walk through fire and for Betty and Sip he would run until his feet bled if necessary. I also knew that he was fond of animals. He was even fond of the fish in the tank and was very unhappy whenever one of them died a peaceful death.

If the Rat had only been my pupil and nothing more, I could have been reassured in every respect. But fate had decreed that I be concerned with his welfare outside school. How could I, though, be responsible for a child who spent a great part of his day outside my field of vision?

It became quite obvious to me that the Rat was hiding something from me. Something new and unknown had crept into our relationship. This did not mean that we didn't understand each other any more—quite the contrary. Only recently I had chased Ciske around the desks after class and shoved his head into a wastepaper basket. He had stuck out his tongue at me in reply. A boy does not do that when he does not like you. When he does it, as a joke and not to be naughty, it proves a certain inner bond. If Johnny had done it, he would have been sharply rebuked. The fact that I was prepared to take it from Ciske proved that our relationship was now capable of withstanding a knock or two.

Ciske was never resentful when sometimes he had to be punished, but he could not bear to be humiliated. In that case he was quickly offended and ready to seek revenge.

Piet Steeman, who sat just behind him, could best testify to this. One day during class I saw Ciske turn suddenly and give Piet a well-aimed blow in the eye. I took him by the collar and put him in the corner. Piet sat in his place with the face of a martyr.

"Piet shouldn't tease him," said Sip, springing to his defense. "Piet said that the Rat has to eat from the garbage pail at his mother's."

Ciske was very good at binding books, and did it very willingly. With Piet and Johnny I asked him once to stay on a little after school break. Piet wanted to go home after a little while because he had been asked to a birthday party, and Johnny went too because he wanted to meet his father's train. I stayed on alone with the Rat and we had a little chat.

"And when is your father coming back?" I asked.

Without looking at me, Ciske answered, "He went yesterday to Aalborg and Stettin, to the Baltic."

"Oh, dear." I was most surprised. "And how long was he here then?"

"Five days."

"Did your mother object to your going to see him?"

"I didn't ask her; I just left her," said Ciske and again he did not look at me.

"And have you since then been to see . . . ?" I wondered how I should refer to "Aunt Jane."

No reaction at all from the Rat!

Something was wrong. I had a definite impression of this. Was it normal for Freimuth not to have come to see me when he was in town for five days? Or was I imagining things?

I felt at times that the Rat was now playing an active part

in the Freimuth marriage tragedy. Ciske's temperament did not allow him to be a silent witness of the horrible quarrel between his parents. He would intervene—and leave nothing undone to help his father. When it came to the point, he would again be the old fighting Rat! And I racked my brains to think how to cope with the dangerous traits in the boy, the cold cruelty which could suddenly swamp all his good qualities.

It seemed to me as if invisible demons were hovering around the child but I could not let myself become a prey to my imagination. Was Maatsuyker by any chance right when he spoke about the "critical clash of personalities"?

Good God, how difficult it all was!

BETTY, our talkative little "class mother," gave us a report one day about her visit to Ciske's "auntie."

"How nice she is, teacher! She and I laughed ourselves silly over Ciske, when he made the cat do some tricks! And the Rat could almost go on the stage as a ventriloquist. Not really, teacher, but he can speak without moving his lips and he pretends that it is the cat saying funny things. It was altogether a lovely afternoon. Just as if it were somebody's birthday. We had tea and cakes. And later on, we went to a milk bar and had cookies. Really, she is so nice!" said Betty dreamily.

"It must really have been very nice," I said, very pleased.

The next day I learned from another source that the friendship between Ciske and his father's friend had not been broken off. Mrs. Freimuth paid me a call.

"I just wanted to make sure that you didn't hear about it from the other side," she said to justify her visit. "Well, yesterday I again followed my dear little son—without his knowing, of course.

I wanted to know what he has been up to and, as his mother, I am after all entitled to know, don't you think? He has been coming home late recently. I don't really care about this, of course, but once or twice lately I have found hard candy and chocolate in his pockets after he has gone to bed. I'm not a fool! The woman is of course trying to entice Ciske away from me with sweets. But she should be more careful, I must warn you, Mr. Bruis!"

"Well, tell me what happened."

"Just as I expected, Ciske went straight to that wretched female. I followed behind him, I assure you. I grabbed him by the collar on the stairs. I am quite good-natured, but not a fool, and they must not all imagine that they can fool me so easily. And now I want to show you what kind of a little beast your pupil is."

Mrs. Freimuth lifted her skirt and showed me a puffy leg. Through the thin silk stocking I could see the varicose veins. Not a pretty sight! What was I supposed to look at? Then I noticed on the shinbone a deep blue mark.

"This is how he treats me," she said, almost in triumph. "And look here now. . . ." On the hand, too, she had a few bloodspot places. "He bit me! He drew blood! I just wanted you to see it so that you would realize what kind of a boy he is! And yet you continue to rush to his aid when his mother sometimes acts badly toward him!"

"And what happened next?" I asked, without paying any attention to her poisonous asides.

"Oh, it was wonderful," she sneered. "The washerwoman appeared on the stairs, and Ciske clung to the banister. He was not to be moved, much as I shook and pulled him. And then you should hear the blasted woman! She started acting the grand lady! How a woman like that has so much nerve, I can't imagine! 'Cis, go with your mother now!' she said. And she held her head very high, the countess of the ironing board!"

Mrs. Freimuth paused for breath but I didn't interrupt, and let her go on.

"I then gave her a piece of my mind and she took it lying down too. She just said to the boy that he should now go with me. After which he let go of the banister. I gave him a slap on the face so that he reeled under it. And suddenly the great lady found her voice again! Not loud and noisy, for she's much too ladylike for that. But she planted herself before me and said that I had no right to beat the boy in her house. And then she showed me the door—like in a movie, Mr. Bruis. People started gathering in the street to hear what it was all about. So I only shouted in her face that I forbid the boy once and for all to visit his father's mistress."

"And what in fact have you against Ciske's calling on that lady from time to time?" I asked.

Mrs. Freimuth was quite disarmed. "You're a fine schoolmaster, you are! And you want to set an example for the children? This is a fine thing! Should I look on without saying anything while you too try to turn the boy against me?"

I let her carry on like that for the while, and then I quietly, but unmistakably, showed her the door.

THE following Wednesday I called on the juvenile court judge, Van Loon. He was wearing a light gray summer suit and looked much younger than when I had first met him. I reported to him about why I was worried about the Rat.

"The child has become the apple of discord between his parents. The mother would gladly get rid of Ciske, but she does not wish to give pleasure to the other woman. She's not concerned about Ciske; it's the principle that matters to her!"

Van Loon smoked for a moment in silence, then he nodded. "Yes, it is an unfortunate case. Moreover, the mother hates the Rat because she cannot dominate him. What a stupid tyranny! She wants to lord it over him and to torment him, nothing else. And the Rat, of course, is the best means of irritating her husband. But for the moment we cannot do anything about it. One can act against evil, but not against stupidity. That is like tilting against windmills."

"In the meantime Ciske's life will be ruined, and we are supposed to just look on helplessly?"

Van Loon nodded. "For the time being at least. First something must happen so that we can take action, my dear sir. The law punishes a person who steals a pencil, but there is no legislation against those who daily drive others to the brink of despair."

With this dubious consolation, I found myself again in the street. And as I nonetheless wanted to try to do something, I decided to call on "Aunt Jane."

I introduced myself as Ciske's guardian and his teacher.

"Oh, yes," she said, embarrassed, and let me into her apartment.

"Aunt" Jane was no beauty. She had a broad face with eyes set too wide apart. But those eyes were kindly and her face was a pleasant one with a peaceful expression.

She looked at me questioningly and somewhat fearfully. I decided not to beat around the bush. "You had a quarrel on the staircase with Ciske's mother, I hear. I would like to speak to you about it."

"Yes, that was wrong."

"Most important, it was wrong from Ciske's point of view. We must do something to prevent the boy from being drawn too deeply into the whole affair, don't you agree?"

Aunt Jane nodded and sighed heavily. Life had never given her anything free, and she had had to struggle hard to earn her daily bread, without having the support of love and happiness. The sailor had suddenly invaded this gray reality like a messenger from a sunny country. She had clung to the dashing man and to his child. And now she had no peace at all.

"We must think about the child," I said. "It would be better if Ciske didn't come to see you for the time being. It will be hard on him, but his mother insists on it."

Aunt Jane's kindly eyes slowly filled with tears.

"You are fond of Ciske, aren't you?" I asked. "You must make this sacrifice for him. Things are hard enough for him at home as it is."

She dried her tears. "Can't I see him again?" she asked softly.

How fond she must be of the boy! I thought what peace and happiness he could have with her! I was overcome by a helpless anger against fate which could come between people like a stone wall.

That dreadful mother! For the sake of twenty guilders a month she was prepared to ruin the best years of her child's life. Twenty guilders—and Aunt Jane could enjoy the happiness for which she yearned, Ciske could have a home, and the sailor could start a decent life.

"Perhaps things will sort themselves out soon," I said to comfort her. "I will in any case do everything in my power to help you. But please don't make my task more difficult."

Aunt Jane was very unhappy, but there was nothing I could do to help her.

"When is Mr. Freimuth expected home?" I asked her before I left.

"Next month."

When I got home that evening and the whole house smelled of tea and Susan was waiting for me with her lovable smile, I felt almost ashamed of my happiness. I could not imagine that this peace could ever be disturbed.

Wasn't it natural for people to make life pleasant and beautiful for each other? Why should there be all these broken, bewildered, miserable people who have no inkling of what we call happiness?

"You are very quiet, darling," said Susan, stroking my hair. "Is anything the matter?"

"I would like to have the Rat come to live with us." I laughed as unconcernedly as possible. "Then he would feel really secure! It really is a shame that one does not always apply such obvious remedies."

YOU must use your head," I said to Ciske the next day. "Your Aunt Jane is a very nice person and I like her. And, if everything were straightforward, I would be all in favor of your going to see her. But you know in this case that your mother does not wish it. Do try to understand that you may spoil everything if you visit her in secret. Perhaps things will get easier for you soon. . . ."

The Rat's face was quite blank. I was quite prepared to see him shrug his shoulders with indifference, but instead he looked at me frankly with his gray eyes and said, "I'm not afraid of her."

"And your mother is not afraid of you!" I warned him.

Perhaps that was foolish on my part, because Ciske's look became aggressive and he said, "And yet she *is* afraid! I have heard her telling one of our neighbors that sometimes she can't sleep for fear."

I couldn't do anything except warn the Rat in all seriousness. At such moments I would willingly have exchanged the Rat's toughness for Drikus's well-behaved obedience. Instead I had to treat the boy like a grownup. With his determination and his wise eyes he forced me to it.

In class, work was progressing satisfactorily enough. This was confirmed by the schools inspector, Mr. Kakebeek, after he had listened to a few lessons.

We were just having geography when he came in. Dorus was telling what he knew about the tides, when suddenly the child began to talk about the influence of the moon on the waters of the earth. I couldn't believe my ears. I had never spoken in class about this so presumably Dorus had collected the knowledge from his own reading. I could have hugged him! Kakebeek looked amazed.

With assumed innocence I pocketed the praise which the inspector bestowed on Dorus, the class, and therefore myself. Of course, our visitor noticed very soon that Dorus Keulemann was a particularly bright child. "Good wine in a fragile glass," he said. "May I have a look at his exercise books?"

"This Dorus should become a teacher some day," he mused—as if that were the pinnacle of all human achievement!

Gerard Jonker, for example, was also bright. He learned what had to be learned and he remembered it all. But Dorus's interest extended far beyond the subject under immediate discussion; he absorbed everything worth knowing, whatever he could read about. He would think about it all very hard and master it completely.

It was a pity that I didn't any longer stay at school with him during the midday break. I suggested to Susan that we invite the boy home and she agreed readily.

"The Rat should come as well some day," she said. "I only know about him from hearsay, and I'd like to know him better."

So we invited Dorus and the Rat together and, so that the trio should be kept intact, also Betty. Unfortunately the chatterer talked so much about it in class to impress the other children that the rest of them became jealous. For the two boys, our invitation was a pleasant secret; for Betty, however, it was an opportunity to boast in front of her girl friends.

"When will it be our turn to come?" Wanda and Tilly Verhoef immediately wanted to know.

"Betty is always allowed everything!"

"What is Betty allowed, pray?" I took care to defend myself. "To tend the flowers and to keep the classroom tidy! Would you like to have to do the the dusting?"

They had no answer to that, of course. But inwardly I had to admit that they were right. A class, and especially the female element in it, has a definite instinct as to whether or not the teacher has "favorites." So the girls knew that Betty occupied a special place in my heart. On the whole, they didn't seem to mind, though, because Betty was so stupid. But to be invited to my house was really going too far!

Even the boys were a bit jealous, although they were better able to hide their feelings. Only Johnny Verkerk could not conceal his envy and whispered, "The Rat is teacher's favorite!"

He immediately realized that he had gone too far, and blushed deeply. I called him to come up to me and looked at him for a long while in silence. Embarrassed and a bit afraid, he stared at his feet.

"What do you mean by that remark?" I asked him at last.

How would Johnny answer that one? The class waited tensely to see how the matter would end. Johnny had spoken too hastily and now he was caught.

"Well?" I said sternly. "Say something! You usually talk such a lot."

But Johnny could not find his tongue.

"Tell me!" I ordered.

Dejected, Johnny whispered at last, "Because Ciske was allowed to visit you, sir . . ."

"Listen to that now!" I interrupted. "So that's it. Because I wanted to see Dorus in my house and two children had to bring him and take him back, you say such stupid things. Aren't you ashamed of yourself?"

Johnny had given me a welcome opportunity to justify my invitation. Only Sip looked at me askance. He too belonged to Dorus's transportation group. Why hadn't I invited him too? But Sip, luckily, was not one to bear a grudge. To console him, however, I made him run an errand for me right away.

The visit of Betty, Ciske, and Dorus was, incidentally, very pleasant. Susan and I almost forgot to put the bright red fruit dish on the sideboard where it was most noticeable. That would have been a terrible omission!

"Our fruit bowl," exclaimed Betty immediately after greeting my wife. "How lovely it looks there!"

Betty behaved like a friend of the house of long standing. She subjected everything to close scrutiny and even cast an interested glance into the kitchen. She might almost have added, "You have arranged it all very nicely here."

At the beginning the boys were shy and terribly polite. The Rat perched himself on the very edge of a chair and did not say a word. Dorus gazed, as if spellbound, at my books, but Betty did not share his enchantment.

"My brother also reads a lot," she crowed sweetly, "but he takes a different book each week from the library around the corner from where we live."

In her tone one could detect a note of contempt for unpractical people who bought books instead of borrowing them from a library!

"What do our visitors feel about a glass of lemonade?" asked Susan.

"Can I help you?" Betty reacted immediately and got up in order to go with Susan into the kitchen.

Dorus sat with a French illustrated book on the couch and tried to translate the captions under the pictures. The Rat gave himself the task of arranging a pile of magazines in chronological order.

"It's nice here," Dorus said with a sigh.

"Really nice," agreed the Rat.

When we all had glasses of lemonade in front of us, Betty said abruptly, "Do you remember, Ciske, we were given such nice things too at your Aunt Jane's?"

"Mind your own business," groaned the Rat.

"Well, I can't say you are being very polite," laughed Susan. "One doesn't speak like that to a lady."

"A lady!" said the Rat angrily. "She's just a very stupid little girl."

The "lady" who was "a stupid little girl" laughed, without being hurt. She had not meant it like that. But when Dorus, too, began to scold her, she hung her head contritely for a moment.

"Betty is always worrying about things which don't concern her," said Dorus and exchanged significant glances with Ciske.

So he was in on the secret! Would he influence Ciske in the right direction and prevent him from making a fool of himself? A child learns most from another child, also with regard to matters of behavior.

When Betty had disappeared into the kitchen once again to wash the glasses, I decided to put out a few feelers. "Typical of Betty," I said, "to start talking about Aunt Jane without any reason. You don't speak to anybody about it, do you?"

"When my father comes back next, I'll go for a walk with him and Dorus," declared Ciske, probably only to prove to me how much Dorus belonged to them.

"Yes," beamed Dorus with pleasure, "and when he moves to his father's place I can call on him as often as I like. Aunt Jane has already agreed to it."

The two of them thus agreed on everything. A child finds everything very simple and does not understand why stupid grownups make everything immeasurably complicated.

AT THAT time Dorus had one French lesson with me a week. So far he was my only pupil. I hoped very much to get a few paying ones as well, because life is very expensive for a young couple, especially when they have to think about getting together a layette. Yes, the prophecy which Ciske made during art class some time before seemed about to come true—a little earlier than was financially justifiable! And yet Susan and I were very excited that we, too, were going to have a child of our own!

The weekly French lesson brought me a bit closer to Dorus, and now I had no great difficulty learning more about the Rat.

"They are having a lot of fights at Ciske's house," Dorus told me willingly. "But Ciske will soon be leaving his mother."

"Do you know that for certain?"

"Yes, it is already fixed. As soon as his father is back again. We look in the paper every day to see where his boat is now. The day before yesterday it was already in Danzig. It might be back in Amsterdam within two weeks."

"All right, and now conjugate the verb '*écrire*'!" I reverted to the French lesson. "*J'écris, tu écris, il écrit, elle écrit* . . ."

But Dorus was not paying attention. "How horrible Ciske's mother is," he started again. "He is never allowed to go out of the house after tea. He has no fun at all!"

"He has you," I said, smiling.

"But I don't belong to his family. I am only his friend."

"Well, friend, then conjugate '*lire*' for a change!"

Dorus rattled through the conjugation so well that it was a pleasure to hear him. The irregular French verbs didn't cause him any headaches.

"Yesterday evening Ciske had a fight with his Uncle Henry," said Dorus abruptly.

I immediately remembered the cigar ash, and I believed I knew whom Dorus was referring to.

"That Uncle Henry sits in Ciske's home every afternoon. And Ciske has to keep an eye on him, as his father asked him to. But he doesn't quite know how to do it, because the man only talks to his mother. And yesterday he sent him out of the room. But how can Ciske keep an eye on him when he is not in the room? So he just stayed where he was. And Uncle Henry was furious and kicked him, and he got a shaking from his mother besides."

"Now Dorus, you must translate 'he must go away'!"

"*Il faut qu'il parte,*" laughed Dorus. "Were you thinking of Uncle Henry?"

We continued to work seriously for another fifteen minutes, but I was unable to stop visualizing the Rat, Uncle Henry, and Mrs. Freimuth. What a den of iniquity! How could I get the boy out of there?

As his guardian I had the right to appear at Mrs. Freimuth's without warning; and, as I had to get to the root of the matter about Uncle Henry, I set off. To my disappointment, I didn't find the gentleman there and the apartment didn't smell of cigar smoke. But Mrs. Freimuth's manner seemed to indicate that she was expecting an intimate tête-à-tête. She did not ask me to sit down. No, I was certainly not welcome there, but I very much wanted to meet Uncle Henry face to face.

Without being asked, I took a seat on the settee. Ciske's mother remained standing and looked at me in an unfriendly way. After the usual skirmishing about the Rat, the "washerwoman," and the "ne'er-do-well of a father," I tried to lay a trap for her. "During the last argument, you had a man to help you," I said.

She stared at me in cold fury. "So he has been telling tales again, has he? I'd like to give him such a kick that he would fly into a corner."

"I didn't hear it from Ciske, but from another boy at school."

Mrs. Freimuth laughed scornfully.

"Would that be the same man who fled to the kitchen the last time I came here?"

There was fear in her eyes now. This the wretched boy could not have told me!

"Well, don't let's talk about it," I said magnanimously, "but you will notice that I have eyes everywhere. I do not set myself up as a judge of morals, but I represent the interests of your son. As far as I am concerned, you are welcome to marry the man! I even advise you to do so. What do you think about that, eh?"

"I? Marry?" she burst out. "Not a chance! No, Mr. Bruis, I know men too well. At first they promise you all the stars from the sky and later they reveal themselves as dirty egotists. No, I don't want to get married again and the other party does not want to either."

"In any case I wish this man to have nothing to do with the boy," I said with authority. "He has no business having anything at all to do with the boy."

I had come to the end of what I wanted to say and could not extend the visit any further. I reached for my hat and was about to take my leave when "Uncle Henry" came in. At that moment I was better pleased about it than was his lady friend.

"Oh, excuse me," he said, very surprised, "I did not know . . ."

Mrs. Freimuth blew her nose and from behind the handkerchief explained who I was.

These two would have made a lovely couple! Uncle Henry looked like a moderately prosperous building contractor. His hair was plastered down on his red skull, he looked dull and bestial, he was wearing a heavy gold chain over his fat belly, and his suit must have cost twice as much as mine. He smelled of cigars and gin.

"As you are here," he said to me, "you had better know that Ciske is a shameless boy."

"How do you mean?"

"No good will ever come of him. One cannot do anything with him. Things cannot go on like this, I tell you!"

By then I had heard enough. "May I ask why you should be so concerned about him? Who are you to worry about Ciske's upbringing?"

"That's my business," he said rudely. "I don't have to explain to anybody about it."

"I am warning you," I added threateningly. "You and Mrs. Freimuth! If you push things too far, I'll apply to the juvenile court to order the boy to leave this house."

"Threats don't hurt anybody," laughed Ciske's mother. But then suddenly she shouted, "You and these family-welfare people! You all make me vomit. . . . All this interfering is slowly making me sick. I am mistress in my own house, I and no one else but me! Now get out!"

In the street I met Ciske. Under his pullover he was clutching a book. He looked at me uncertainly. Should he stop or run along? Always when I saw him at home or in the vicinity of his house, he looked frightened.

"What book have you got there?" I asked him.

"*Pieter Marits!* Dorus lent it to me."

"You must look after it carefully. It is Dorus's most beautiful book."

The Rat looked at me as if he wanted to say, "Yes, that's how Dorus is. He lends me his favorite book." And he pressed the book to him even more lovingly under his green sweater. "I'll wash my hands before I start to read it," he promised. "And I won't lend it to anybody else."

I stood for some moments looking after him, when he entered the house from which his mother had just thrown me.

THE following morning the Rat was not at school. None of the children could explain why, not even Betty or Dorus. Again and again my eyes wandered to the empty place next to Sip. Something must be wrong. What could have happened?

I was not surprised when, toward midday, Maatsuyker put his head around the door and asked me to go to his office, where Ciske's mother was waiting for me.

"My room stinks to high heaven of her cheap perfume," said the headmaster. "She does not want to tell me what is the matter."

"Do me a kindness and come with me," I asked Maatsuyker. "Try to forget for a moment that you don't like the Rat. I have the impression that Mrs. Freimuth wishes to remove the boy from our school, and this would be a terrible blow for him."

"Listen to that now," replied Maatsuyker. "Mr. Teacher Bruis needs my help for once! I admit that I am not overfond of the boy, and I would be pleased if we could get rid of him without an accident of any sort; but if this awful woman with her forbidding smells comes too near the child, she will hear from me. He is still a pupil in our school. That is what matters. I'll come with you."

Was Maatsuyker perhaps human after all?

We entered the room together to find Mrs. Freimuth waiting for me. The first thing the headmaster did was to open the window wide. "It smells like hell in here," he said distinctly. "And what business brings you here?"

Fixing her eyes angrily on me, Mrs. Freimuth rattled out the sentence which "Uncle Henry" must have taught her to say. "I have only come to inform you that my son Ciske is leaving this school, because his teacher is turning him against his mother."

"Dear madam, you are talking nonsense," said Maatsuyker. "And you know damn well that you are!" When she started to interrupt him, he stormed at her like a sergeant major. "Be quiet! Here I do the talking. You can answer later when I allow you to speak!"

I had never seen my boss act like this.

"For a year we have slaved away with the boy. If it were not for Mr. Bruis, he would have gone to the devil a long time ago. And now you come along and say, 'I'm taking the boy away from school!' This is the limit!"

"As a mother I must insist on my rights," screeched Mrs. Freimuth.

Maatsuyker glared at her in open hostility. "'As a mother,' you said, didn't you? Aren't you the mother who allowed her son to work in a bar, and who locked him up in a coal cellar?"

I took great care not to get mixed up in the argument as Maatsuyker seemed to be in great form. With his stomach protruding and his hands stuck deep in his trousers pockets he faced Ciske's mother.

"Moreover, I wish to draw your attention to the fact that you are married," he went on, "and that therefore the father also has the right to decide whether the child should be taken away from school or not." My heart gave a leap. What a good idea of Maatsuyker's!

"The father!" exclaimed Mrs. Freimuth in a fury. "The father! He doesn't give a damn for his children. He doesn't even want to support them."

"He wants to, but you prevent him from doing it," I put in. "You should not make these exaggerated claims."

"It's all quite clear," continued the headmaster. "When we get a written request from Ciske's father, the child can be taken away from this school, but not before. And if he does not come to school this afternoon, you will have the police at your house, do you understand?"

Mrs. Freimuth behaved like an offended queen. She cast a poisonous glance at me. "This is just in your line, isn't it?" she shouted. "Two men against a defenseless woman! You bastards!"

"Please get out of here," ordered Maatsuyker. "You can open your mouth as wide as you like at home but not here."

"I believe that you have been handling the lady with kid gloves, Bruis," said Maatsuyker after she had gone. "She is the one who must be treated rough. . . ."

In the afternoon the Rat was back in school. He looked pale and tired.

"So here you are again," I greeted him. "Are you pleased?"

He nodded vigorously. I noticed that his eyes were sad. What must the poor child have suffered when his mother forbade him to go to school! Kept away from Dorus, from Betty and Sip! Ciske must have been dragged straight down from seventh heaven when he got home yesterday, overjoyed about *Pieter Marits,* proud of the trust shown by Dorus in lending him his most wonderful book.

"Tell me what happened," I said gently. God, how sorry I was for my little Rat!

"Well, yesterday Mother told me I could not go to school any more. When I wanted to run here in the morning, she locked me up in the attic. I hammered on the door so hard that she came back and dragged me into the coal cellar. And then today at mid-day she said suddenly, 'Go to school now!' "

That was Ciske's unadorned report. The boy told his story without emphasis. His fingers drummed nervously on the desk. Something had again been broken in the Rat.

The other children obviously felt that something out of the

ordinary was going on. This was not their normal Ciske! It was a quiet, sad little boy who could only understand with difficulty that he was again sitting in his old place.

I purposely didn't call on him. He must first find his feet again. He was staring at his reading book, but his thoughts were goodness knows where. From time to time I gave him a wink, but the Rat behaved like a sick person for whom normal life had become strange.

The last lesson of the day should have been singing, but I didn't feel up to it. "Drawing instead," I ordered, and there were several shouts of "Wonderful!"

The Rat remained apathetic. He tried to draw a horse, but it turned into a dog. I was glad when the bell rang and the class could be dismissed. I would like to have given Ciske a word of encouragement on his way home, but thought better of it. What was the use of words? The child surely felt anyway that I was on his side.

"Go on reading your *Pieter Marits,*" was all I said to him. He nodded, and Dorus smiled at him from his chair.

THAT evening I was more uneasy than ever before. I had not liked the Rat's manner that day at all. What should I do? In despair I paced up and down my room. Susan looked at me quizzically but did not ask me any questions. Ciske, now you are between the four walls which are called your home! Ciske, boy, don't hang your head! Hold out! Ciske, Ciske, Ciske! The thoughts were running around and around in my head. I had to keep wiping the perspiration from my forehead.

At half-past nine, Muysken of the juvenile police knocked at my front door. I let him in. He told me that Ciske had killed his mother. Ciske! My Rat!

I felt the ground slipping away from under my feet. I was so shaken that I could only stare at Muysken without saying a word.

He nodded gravely. Yes, Mrs. Freimuth had ordered Ciske to bed early and tried to take his book away from him, the book he had borrowed from Dorus. She had torn it out of his hand, thrown it on the floor, and, in a senseless rage, trampled it under her feet. The Rat had become mad with rage. He had grabbed a knife which was lying on the table and had thrown it blindly in his mother's direction. It had penetrated Mrs. Freimuth's jugular vein; she had died within a few minutes.

"And the child?"

Ciske had fled instinctively to his Aunt Jane. She had taken him to the police.

DORUS knew what Ciske had done. He became very ill and ran a high temperature.

"What on earth is happening, Mr. Bruis?" his mother lamented. "Dorus has been rambling for hours. It must be something to do with Ciske, but what . . . ?"

As quietly as possible I told her what had happened. She looked at me, pale as a ghost. "It is a sin," she stammered, "it is a sin. . . ."

I sat by Dorus's bed and held his hot hands. His pulse was very fast.

"It's not fair, it's not fair!" moaned the sick child. "His mother was bad, a horrible woman. It isn't fair to put Ciske in prison. You are all so unfair, so horrible. . . ."

Dorus freed his hands and began to beat his fists against the wall. I put my arm under his back and lifted him into a half-sitting position.

"Now stop this for a moment, Dorus, that's a good boy."

His unhappy eyes rested upon me.

"In a few days you will be able to see Ciske. You are his best friend, aren't you? When he asks about you, I cannot tell him that there's something wrong with you. Just try to be brave now, and think what you want me to say to Ciske for you."

Dorus listened greedily to my words. The tension inside him eased, and he began to cry plaintively. I let him cry.

"The class thinks that Ciske has done a terrible thing," I went on. "But we are all calm and we have made up our minds to be brave. You must be brave too! We don't believe that Ciske is a bad boy. And when he comes back to us, he will find nothing but good friends."

Perhaps it was my voice that had a soporific effect, as Dorus had closed his eyes. I laid him back on his pillow and tucked him in. Then I tiptoed out of his room.

NEXT day I ate some sandwiches in the empty classroom, having decided not to go home for lunch. Susan would understand.

I cleared out the Rat's drawer. The untidy exercise book, full of fantastic drawings, the penholder, the pencils, the eraser, a piece of tape, a key. I put the things in the closet, feeling just as if the Rat had died.

Although I was well aware of the child's guilt, I could not suppress a feeling of defiance which welled up inside me. I cursed and swore for all I was worth; it must have sounded pretty silly in the deserted room! Damn it all! Now the Rat was delivered into the hands of strange people! Abandoned by God and man! And that was what I had worked for for over a year!

Was it the child who was really guilty? Were not the guilty people the adults who had brought him to this? It would be Van Loon's task to establish that clearly before God and the world. For me there was only the sad, lost little Rat, who now had nothing left to which he could cling. He had become like a part of myself.

Making a sudden decision, I put on my hat, ran into a tobacco store, and telephoned the psychiatric department of the juvenile prison. A matter-of-fact voice gave me the information that, on Mr. Van Loon's instructions, I would be able to speak to the boy in three days' time. He was relatively calm—perhaps too calm, considering what he had done. That was all.

When I returned, my colleagues were standing around in groups in the corridor. They stopped talking when I appeared.

"I *am* sorry for you, Bruis," said Tedema warmly. "Truly sorry!"

Jorissen squared his shoulders. "Why sorry for Bruis?" he asked. "Bruis has no reason to reproach himself. He has taken enough trouble with the boy."

"If I were you, I would go home now," advised Tedema. "You look like a ghost."

Maatsuyker shook his head. He said gravely, "I leave it entirely to you, but I would advise you to go back to your class. All this moping at home is no good. And it will be better for the children if everything is as normal as possible."

He was right of course. "I am not worrying about myself," I said sharply, "only about the Rat."

"How is Dorus?" asked Meerstra.

"He is completely overcome, of course. Ciske is his best friend."

"And how is Ciske himself?"

"He is apparently very calm," I said and went to my classroom.

"Sir," Johnny Verkerk called out, "will the thing about Ciske be in the newspapers?" He sounded almost envious.

The afternoon dragged slowly on. Reading, writing, then science. It was torture. What was going on in the children's heads?

For the last lesson, I brought the stuffed squirrel from another room and put it on my desk. When to the question, "Tell me now, where this animal lives," Betty answered, "Under the ground," the spell was suddenly broken for the children and they burst out laughing.

"She is mixing it up with a mole," commented Sip.

The class began to forget. The lesson became almost normal. Someone from outside would not have noticed that we had lost one of our number because he had murdered his mother. How lucky children are that they can forget so quickly!

That evening Freimuth called on me at home. It was not the same Freimuth I had met before. "This is terrible," he sobbed.

"Well, my good fellow, the child has given you your freedom. Now you can marry Jane!"

It was vile of me to say that and I regretted it immediately.

"Are you trying to say that I . . . ?"

"No, of course I don't mean to imply that you put the boy up to murdering his mother! But I consider it particularly objectionable to use children as tools to further one's own ends. You made Ciske spy for you, and even without that he had a difficult enough time at home. That's what I hold against you, Freimuth."

"I want Ciske back," he burst out. "I'll get a job ashore and have him with me!"

Now! Now! When it was too late!

"I'll move to Rotterdam or somewhere like that, and start a new life in a new place."

Freimuth was a broken man. His sailor's cap hung limply from his hands.

"Jane wants to get married when Ciske is free again, but not before," he added. "She does not want us to build our happiness on the tragedy of this child. Tell Ciske when you visit him that his father is waiting for him, and that he loves him dearly. . . ."

"By the way," I asked, suddenly remembering, "what are you going to do about the other children?"

"I haven't had time to think about them yet but obviously I can't look after them myself. I'm only a sailor. I'll have to send them to an orphanage, where at least they will be well looked after."

I rose and shook Freimuth by the hand.

"Thank you very much," he muttered hoarsely and disappeared.

WHEN I entered the quiet building of the psychiatric department at the remand school (the detention home where Ciske was being held until his trial), I was overcome by a feeling of uneasiness. From the street the noise of everyday activities penetrated into the prison, the sounds of life itself. Had the Rat irrevocably forfeited this life? Would he never be able to return to the company of happy children?

The head of the department showed me a door, and looking through the small window in it I saw Ciske sitting on a wooden bench. He was swinging his legs, exactly like a boy who is momentarily bored during vacation. Here he was, the Rat, my pupil. I had given my whole heart to the boy and yet I had been unable to prevent fate from striking him down.

Ciske jumped when I went into the cell. So, he was not as unconcerned as he had appeared. At once he hung his head and began to bite his knuckles nervously. He wouldn't look at me.

I couldn't feel anything but a deep, painful sympathy for the cowering child, for this sad little bundle of humanity which—without understanding it completely—had taken upon his conscience a mortal sin.

I felt, not for the first time, how relative guilt can be. A fraction further to the right or to the left and the knife would not have killed the woman, only wounded her. In Ciske's defense, mitigating circumstances would certainly have been found. But because Ciske happened to hit precisely the fatal place, he would be stigmatized for the rest of his life.

I put my hand on his head and stroked his hair. I could find no words. The boy was trembling like a captive, frightened bird. All of a sudden he began to cry, although he tried to keep back his tears. But when I pressed his head lovingly against me, he broke down completely—Ciske was now no more than an unhappy child.

If only I could have taken him home with me! But I had to

leave him here, in this bare cheerless building, in which the Rat was a serious, perhaps even an interesting, case. What could I do to lighten for the child the burden of his tragic fate?

"Dorus sends his love," I said finally. "He wants me to tell you that he does not mind at all about the book. He will always remain your friend, he has assured me. Isn't that wonderful?"

The Rat continued to sob.

"Betty and Sip also send their love," I lied.

The boy pressed his wet face against my hand. Wordlessly he begged for my protection, which I was unable to extend to him any more.

Through the little window in the door, the head of the department made a sign that my time was up.

"Listen, my dear boy," I said to the Rat, "we won't discuss now what you have done. It was a terrible misfortune. But you must remember that I won't abandon you because of this—all right? Nor will the others, Ciske!" After a moment I said quietly, "And now I must go, Ciske."

He clung desperately to my arm with both hands. I could feel his loneliness, his utter misery. Gently I freed my arms, and Ciske lifted his pale face to me. The Rat's eyes imploring me to help him were the last thing I saw as I left.

THE newspapers devoted whole pages to Ciske's case. Public interest was still as lively as on the day it happened. The whole country felt obliged to discuss the extent and the type of punishment to fit the circumstances.

I personally saw the case like this. Here we have a child who in a moment of passion has thrown a knife at his mother and has quite accidentally given her a mortal wound. I consider as fair only a form of punishment which will insure that the boy does not do something like this again.

The orthodox legal experts were inclined to establish a precedent with the case. An unusual deed must be followed by an unusual penalty. This case, they said, could not be heard by the juvenile court, which they considered to be the sentimental creation of modern psychologists, but must come before a jury at an ordinary trial! Another group supported the idea of compulsory special education. A third advocated the infliction of a penalty, but one that would not prejudice the child's future.

I followed the arguments in the press with close attention. I hoped that Ciske's trial would at least be postponed long enough for it to take place in a quieter atmosphere! How difficult it must be for a judge to pass a just sentence when everybody feels entitled to play the judge!

Poor Rat . . .

"I have never yet had a case before me in which I have had to apply to a child's wrongdoing considerations other than purely educational," Mr. Van Loon admitted to me; he had told me that he was to be Ciske's judge.

The question which Mr. Van Loon was asking himself was this: matricide . . . how are we to punish Ciske for it? He was thinking about retribution from the very beginning.

The question which I was asking myself was: a tragedy . . . how can we save Ciske?

Poor Rat!

I was amazed when the chief psychiatrist of the remand school, Mr. Arnoldi, asked me to visit Ciske for a second time, as he had made it quite clear to me on the first occasion that the contact between Ciske and his former companions was to be kept to a minimum.

"I would rather like to see how the boy reacts to people from his previous environment," Mr. Arnoldi said.

So I was to be invited for experimental reasons!

"Despite careful observation I cannot say anything definite about the boy," said Mr. Arnoldi when he met me at the remand school. "Other children are more relaxed after a week here and end up behaving quite normally. But this Freimuth is so shut in on himself. Not that he has given me any grounds for complaint!

He behaves well and is diligent in his lessons. He is very conscientious. But it is impossible for me to establish whether or not he regrets his action."

In a way I felt glad that someone else now had to concern himself with the Rat. "Yes, I also had the greatest difficulty at first in getting a word out of him, but in time I overcame this."

"He does not seek any contact with the other boys. When they play, he sits alone in a corner of the yard. I discovered by chance that he loves flowers and plants, so I let him work in the garden, and he is quite useful there. But recently he hit a boy, who had trampled on his rose bed, really hard. He is certainly aggressive, this boy!"

"Such an incident seems quite normal to me and I would say that we couldn't make a greater mistake than to explain such ordinary reactions as characteristic of a matricide."

"I'll bring him in," said the psychiatrist, bringing our talk to an end.

I tried to think how I could manage to be left alone with the Rat; if I was to get him to talk to me, we could not have witnesses.

Mr. Arnoldi had apparently not told Ciske who was waiting to see him, because the Rat seemed very surprised when he saw me and hesitated in the doorway.

"Well, come on, go to him," Mr. Arnoldi encouraged him. "Your former teacher will not eat you!"

But Ciske did not move; he just looked at me with great big eyes. Did I seem unreal to him? An apparition from a time long past?

At last he came slowly up to me as if he were sleepwalking. Only when I winked at him and put out my hand did his mask-like face relax and a shy smile appear on his lips.

"Well, Ciske, here I am again," I said.

"Good morning . . . oh, good morning, sir," he answered softly.

"How are you, my boy?" I tried to get the conversation going, but Ciske shrugged his shoulders and did not answer.

I observed him closely; his face had an unhealthy color, almost gray like the tweed suit he was wearing. It was clearly going to be difficult for both of us to re-establish our former intimacy.

The Rat was the first to break the spell. "How long must I stay here, Mr. Bruis?" he asked abruptly. "I have now been here forty-six days." Forty-six days! So he was counting them. When one is as young as he was, forty-six days is an enormously long time.

"I am to give you greetings from a great many children," I evaded the question. "In the first place from Betty and Dorus, of course. But also from Sip and Cornel; in fact, from the whole class."

"What are you doing now at school?" Ciske wanted to know.

"Fractions! And how far have you got?"

"Also to fractions. But it's very easy."

"Are you allowed to trim and to bind books here?" I asked. "He is very good at that, Mr. Arnoldi. It's a pleasure to watch him do it."

The chief psychiatrist looked thoughtful. "One must have a very sharp knife to trim pages," he said at last, "and I don't know . . ."

I was very worried. That careless remark of mine could have done a lot of harm. I knew that look on Ciske's face. Now one would not be able to do anything with him.

Mr. Arnoldi realized that his allusion to the knife had been a blunder, and he therefore added in a conciliatory tone, "Well, if you do it so well, we can try it one day."

"I can't do it at all," said the Rat gruffly.

We had clearly reached a dead end in our conversation. "Ciske must now go back to his class," the psychiatrist said.

But a sudden spirit of rebellion awoke in me. I didn't want to let the child go away like this. I *had* to speak to him! But how could I get rid of the psychiatrist? I tried the direct method. "I'm sure you won't mind, Mr. Arnoldi, if I speak to the boy alone for five minutes?"

Arnoldi hesitated. He obviously felt that my visit had no purpose unless he could be present and observe the proceedings. "Well, all right, if you insist," he muttered at last. "But only five minutes."

"Now then, you little rascal," I started when Arnoldi had gone, "tell me, now that we're alone together—you're not very happy here, are you?"

Ciske gulped. Tears welled up in his eyes. For a boy who was not given to tears, that meant something.

"You see, my boy, you must accept things as they are," I tried to console him. "I also would have preferred to have you back in class, but you must understand that Mr. Van Loon can't agree to this."

I drew him close to me but he looked away at a corner. I turned his face to me and looked into his eyes. "Do you know that Mr. Maatsuyker has asked me to remember him to you? You would never have expected that, would you? Yes, Ciske, none of us thinks that you are bad, and you must try not to let us down. You must try very hard. You must not immediately hit a boy just because he has walked on your rose bed. Of course, there is nothing wrong if you want to box with somebody from time to time, but you must learn to keep your fists to yourself otherwise. You deserve to be punished. I am sure you must see that for yourself. But it won't go on forever, so chin up, Ciske!"

Ciske had not averted his eyes. His lips trembled while he listened attentively to me.

For me the Rat was not a "case" about which articles are written and discussions held. With a little more love in his life, everything would be different for him. Although we had not come around to talking about Aunt Jane, Dorus, and Betty, I knew for certain that in his loneliness he was longing for them, for the bit of love that each of them had given him, each in his own way. But could I, in the course of the miserable five minutes which were allowed to us, reawaken in him his belief in this love? Ciske's eyes were wet, and a helpless and nervous little smile played about his lips. For the first time since I had known him, I found his face lovely. His eyes, full of tears, were fastened on me as if some consolation were still to come from me.

"You promise me then that you will try hard to control yourself?" I asked him. It was the only thing that I could think of to say. He looked at me anxiously. I would have to go soon and he would have to stay here alone. Why is it always so difficult to give a child like Ciske a sense of security?

Our five minutes were up and Arnoldi returned.

The Rat's predicament had put years on me. I no longer attached so much importance to the small things with which I had to cope. What more could happen to me? One of my pupils had killed his mother. That puts the normal misdemeanors of a class in quite a different perspective.

I really could not be very angry when Johnny Verkerk carved a rude word on the door of the wooden closet where we kept the maps. Johnny was just a precocious boy—there will always be boys like him and one always has to count on having some of them in one's class. Or Piet Steeman! When, the previous week, he returned the book he had borrowed from the school library, there were grease marks all over the pages and a cheese rind stuck into it as a bookmark. Once I would have been terribly angry about such carelessness, but this time I limited myself to showing the book to the whole class, which looked at it with disgust. Of course, I took care to appear very indignant, but in fact I didn't much care. I knew that Piet Steeman after writing his lines would remain the same careless boy as before. He was hard-working, but had very dirty habits. All the daily transgressions of the children had become quite unimportant to me; only the essentials still mattered. At that moment these were Ciske and Susan, my wife.

We had spruced up an empty room in our home and there stood an empty cradle. There was a neat pile of snow-white diapers in the closet. But even the joy of my coming fatherhood was overshadowed by the tragedy of the Rat.

The shadow of the Rat hung over me. In class everything went on as usual. Sip sat alone on the bench which only a short while ago he had shared with the Rat. The children had long ago become accustomed to the empty place, but I hadn't. It even seemed to me that this wasn't my old class any more. Sometimes I felt a longing for new faces, perhaps even for a new school where I could start everything anew. Had the boy met with a fatal traffic accident or died of pneumonia, I would probably have got reconciled to the loss, but the thought that he was now in a remand home awaiting trial, while we were calmly solving our arithmetic problems, was dreadful!

To test the children's reactions, I said to them after my second visit to Ciske, "Do you know who sends you his regards? The Rat!"

Most of them acknowledged this in silence. Wanda Bergmann continued to cast on her wool, Frances Klaver calmly tied her hair ribbon, and Cornel Verstaveren, who had been naughty and was standing in the corner, did not even turn around.

"Is he behind bars?" asked Johnny Verkerk shrilly. He was undoubtedly the sensation-monger of the class.

"You're crazy," said Sip without much conviction.

The others sat quite still and no one asked how Ciske was. After class Dorus remained behind for his French lesson, and Betty Van Gemert was busy tidying up.

"Oh, sir, please tell us something about Ciske! Is he miserable?" they both asked.

Oh, yes, the Rat had two friends left. We sat down together on a bench and I told them that Ciske had become a gardener, that he was still learning fractions, and that various people in the home were being very kind to him.

Dorus looked at me searchingly. His fine face seemed to me old and wise.

"Is it nonsense what Johnny Verkerk said? I mean about the bars?" he asked.

"Of course it was nonsense," I reassured him. "Such a remand home is like a strict boarding school. It is not very nice there, but the children are not ill-treated. They are just not allowed to go out."

"So it *is* a prison," stated Dorus gloomily.

"How mean!" said Betty with true womanly sympathy.

I LEARNED in the meantime that Van Loon was not inclined to be vindictive toward the Rat. But I was still not sure whether he intended to help the Rat rather than just punish him. But, anyway, I understood his attitude better than that of, for instance, Jorissen, my colleague. When, during break one day, we were discussing the Ciske case yet again, he said harshly, "Let this venomous snake remain in captivity for a time. At least we are then rid of him for a while!"

I declared that, in my opinion, a few months in a reform school constituted a proper deprivation of freedom for a child and that suitable supervision in the future should keep Ciske on the right path.

But Jorissen laughed cynically. "You speak as if the boy had stolen twopence and not killed his own mother. A few months in a reform school and the case is settled, eh? That would be too simple!"

Tedema looked at him steadily with her pale tired eyes. "A child who has willfully and with premeditation stolen twopence," she said calmly, "can be in the long run much more dangerous than a hothead who once threw a knife at somebody."

"And I maintain that if evil is not nipped in the bud, it will go on growing," Jorissen replied angrily.

Meerstra reflectively chewed on the butt of his cigar. "I would like for five minutes to borrow the robes of the judge of the juvenile court," he said slowly, "and sentence the boy to be taken into a decent family, to people who have some love to spare for such a little fellow and who would not continuously talk of 'guilt and expiation'. I hate all this useless, juristic mumbo-jumbo. Why complicate matters so? It is all a lot of dangerous twaddle; to repay evil with evil. Under certain circumstances one can do this with an adult, with a thoroughly depraved character, but not with a child. If you pronounce a vindictive sentence on the boy, you lightly commit spiritual infanticide, in the name of the law, too. . . . Do you understand?"

Meerstra was not the sort of person to express his views rashly and without reason. He had certainly given the matter a lot of thought. How strange that his opinion was exactly the same as Aunt Jane's! I had called on her a day or two before and had a cup of tea with her. While I was sitting opposite her, not knowing how to get the conversation going, my eyes had fallen on her hands; they rested, tired and work-worn, on her lap. These chapped and callused hands spoke of a hard life, but they had stroked Ciske's hair. They were kind honest hands.

"Mr. Freimuth is now pressing me very strongly to marry him," she said at last. "He thinks that he will then more easily get permission for Ciske to live with him, once he has served his sentence. Perhaps he is right. But I don't know yet what I'll do. . . ."

"Would you perhaps like to come with me to see the judge?" I suggested.

Her eyes shone. "Oh, yes, if it's possible, I would like to," she said with gratitude. "You may think that is presumptuous of a silly woman! But when I read the newspapers, I ask myself what all these smart alecks know about the boy. *I* know him. He often used to come and have a good cry here. If he could come to live here and we all could keep an eye on him, there wouldn't be a better-behaved boy. Don't they want to make a decent man out of him? If they drive Ciske too hard, he will just become obstinate. But I suppose a judge is there to punish people. I am heartbroken about the whole thing, quite heartbroken!"

"Wouldn't you spoil the Rat too much?"

"Did you ever hear of such a suggestion? I come from a family of many children. No one can tell me how to handle the little rascals. No boy ever came to any harm from a well-deserved smack! If he is the right sort of boy, he has forgotten it within the hour. Would you like another cup of tea, Mr. Bruis?"

That second cup, which I accepted, was responsible for my seeing Ciske's father again. He walked unannounced into the room and looked surprised to see me sitting on the couch.

Freimuth had aged. He had become thinner and his hair was graying at the temples. "I wanted to call on you this week anyway," he greeted me. "I am going to sea again on Saturday."

He sat himself at the table and began to drum on it with his thick fingers. We did not have much to say to one another.

"Perhaps it would be right if we became man and wife before the law," said Aunt Jane at last.

Freimuth started. "I thought you did not want to get married as long as Ciske was inside."

"I am going with Mr. Bruis to see the judge. As long as we are not properly married, there is no possibility of Ciske coming to us here. But when I can declare that I will care for the boy like a mother, they are bound to see that I am fond of him, aren't they?"

Freimuth stared into space for a moment or two. "This is wonderful," he said finally with a wry smile. "You want to marry me in order to get Ciske. Well, I hope you won't have anything against my putting in an appearance from time to time?"

"That depends entirely on you," answered Aunt Jane.

Was Freimuth's manly pride seriously hurt? He said without enthusiasm, "All right, I agree to everything. Prepare the necessary papers. When I come back from the Baltic, we will get married. It's the boy that matters. Let's leave it at that."

"Who started talking about marriage, you or I?" asked Aunt Jane bitterly.

"Everything's fine!" said Freimuth wearily.

AND then eventually came the day of the Rat's trial. A great multitude of people had gathered in the courtroom, mostly people concerned professionally with delinquent children. But their lively conversations, which betrayed so little personal sympathy, sickened me.

Muysken and one of his colleagues from the criminal police came quietly up to me where I was sitting with Maatsuyker. We had been called as witnesses.

"What a lot of interest there seems to be in this case!" laughed Muysken with a touch of irony. "It seems as though the Rat will become famous. Usually things are much quieter here. One witness, a hearing of the case for the prosecution and then for the defense; then suddenly the sentence. If they don't agree at once, the interested parties are sent out of the room, and the judge, prosecuting counsel, and counsel for the defense put their heads together. This is how things used to be always, at least as long as old Van Everdingen was the state prosecutor. Now they've got a new man, a former official from the provinces. I am curious to see whether the new broom will sweep well. Van Loon does not seem to think much of him, because he usually does things behind his back. Today too he has called a whole series of witnesses. It's very boring!"

"Yes, but they must investigate the case thoroughly, mustn't they?" Maatsuyker asked uncertainly, seeking information.

"It's all nonsense," growled Muysken. "They have the evidence and a heap of reports. No, this Mr. Sweering only wants to make himself important. You should see the indictment he has composed. 'Seeing that the accused has been guilty of the death of his mother, Joanna Maria Theodora Freimuth, née Geesthoven, through a powerful sharp intentional blow with a knife, that is, with the intention to kill . . .' etcetera, etcetera. Can it mean anything except to the person who wants to make himself seem important?" Muysken wiped the perspiration from his forehead.

All of a sudden a hush fell over the room; Ciske was being led in. An enormous policeman escorted him to his place. The man was wearing a helmet and a sword and the little boy beside him seemed even smaller than he really was. I was of course immediately up in arms. What a performance! Why should the Rat be led in by an armed policeman? I presumed it was part of the prescribed ceremonial for a court session—some relic of the nineteenth century.

Even Maatsuyker, who was by no means as sensitive to such things as I was, started muttering under his breath, "My goodness, is all this necessary? And he is wearing a revolver, too. They must fear that the boy has a bomb hidden under his shirt."

As soon as Ciske was placed in the dock, I walked up to him. I didn't care whether this was allowed or not. Ciske must know that he had friends in the courtroom.

"Well, my boy," I greeted him. "I just wanted quickly to say hello to you."

Ciske had been staring at the floor, but now he lifted his narrow little face to me in surprise. He looked tired. He was pale and his eyelids were swollen. He had probably not slept at all during the previous night, from sheer nervousness. How sorely punished is such a child, apart from the official sentence!

"Good morning, sir," he whispered to me in his hoarse little voice.

The heavily armed policeman did not rebuke me; at close quarters he looked decidely benevolent. "Is that your teacher?" he asked the Rat kindly.

The child nodded shyly and I ruffled his unruly hair. I didn't quite know what to say to him next. "Have courage," I finally brought myself to say.

"Will you be here?" he asked in a frightened voice.

Poor Rat! Where is your courage and your proud independence? Where is all that I liked in you? Now you are nothing more than a pitiful little heap of humanity facing the powerful apparatus of justice.

"I will sit close behind you," I promised. "Don't be frightened."

A young woman in a gown came up to us, counsel for the defense. "I am Mrs. de Hoop," she introduced herself. "Are you Mr. Bruis, his teacher?" and suddenly she said to the Rat, "You have brushed your hair very neatly today. You are looking very nice."

Ciske smiled with some embarrassment. He immediately stopped looking so edgy. Mrs. de Hoop looked at him kindly and chatted to him, as if she wanted to divert his attention from all the people present. Her sympathetic attitude encouraged me a lot.

"Ah, here is Mr. Van Loon! Get up, my boy," she said and bowed slightly toward the judge who, followed by the prosecutor and the clerk of the court, now entered the courtroom. Mr. Van Loon looked fleetingly around and immediately opened proceedings.

The prosecutor read out his frightful accusation.

"All right, and now come up to me, my boy," said Van Loon without a pause. "You know of course why you are here. We need not go into that at length. It is a terrible story! You find it terrible too, don't you?"

Ciske looked at his feet and nodded slightly. This tiny sign of contrition was apparently too modest for the prosecutor. His stiff posture and his sharp face didn't allow one to hope for much leniency. He undoubtedly was not the sort of person with whom one could establish pleasant contact.

"Sit down now, my boy, I shall speak to you later," said Mr. Van Loon. "First witness, please!"

A police official read a dry report of all the depositions which he had collected in connection with Ciske's action. He did not forget to mention that the child must have been very angry because of the damaging of the *Pieter Marits* book, nor that the sharp knife which he threw at his mother was lying within his reach. He stated that there could be no possibility of the Rat's action being premeditated. Muysken, who was called next, went into a lot of detail and the judge gave him every opportunity to do so.

"You have known Ciske for a long time," he interrupted at last. "Tell me what impression he makes on you!"

"He is not really a bad boy," said Muysken. "With a little guidance he would be a splendid little fellow. His mother drove him to the unfortunate act."

"It is easy to blame the mother now," interrupted the prosecutor, "when she cannot defend herself any more."

But Muysken did not allow himself to be put out. He said slowly, "I have no desire to find fault with the deceased. I am accusing Mrs. Freimuth as she was when she was alive. She hated her own son and made life miserable for him as often as she could. She set him to work, against the law, in a café of doubtful reputation. Shortly before the event, she even tried to take him away from his school, a school where he was happy. You see—I am only establishing facts."

The judge interjected, "On this point Mr. Muysken is certainly correct. Conditions in the boy's home left much to be desired."

"I ask: why was the boy not withdrawn from the custody of his mother?" interrupted the prosecutor.

"Because at the time there were not sufficient grounds for it," snapped Van Loon.

Maatsuyker coughed nervously when he was called into the witness box. I was curious to know whether he would let himself be bullied. Which Maatsuyker would testify—the confident man who had at one time put Mrs. Freimuth in her place, or the pedantic schoolmaster?

He proved himself to be a model headmaster springing to the defense of his pupil. But this only came to light during the course of the cross-examination. The prosecutor first put a few questions to him.

"You often had trouble with this boy, am I right?" My heart missed a beat. If only he would now refrain from dragging up trifles and from speaking about the incident of the pocketknife!

But Maatsuyker said in a voice like honey, "Ah, complaints, complaints . . . with children there is always this sort of trouble.

It is always so at that age! The boy had first of all to get used to a real school. But as soon as he understood what it was all about he was a good boy. We had got him on the right road when the tragedy occurred."

Mr. Van Loon looked at Maatsuyker for a moment in amazement. He had once heard him speak very differently from the same place.

"Aren't you convinced," the prosecutor urged, "that the seeds of the offense lay dormant in the boy for a long time?"

"How can you make that assumption? What child would deliberately kill his mother? The worst boy would not do it, let alone this little fellow. We are faced with a dreadful tragedy. It might have happened to any child with a short temper! We cannot forget what the boy must have felt when his mother spoiled the beautiful book that belonged to his friend."

"Did you ever meet the mother?" asked the judge.

Maatsuyker nodded.

"What impression did she make on you?"

"To answer the question truthfully would be somewhat painful, after the woman has met her death in such an unfortunate manner."

But Van Loon insisted. "You can speak quite freely about her."

Maatsuyker took a deep breath, and then he continued. "Well, if you insist . . . I did not have a very high opinion of her. I have come to know a great many mothers, but Mrs. Freimuth was quite unique. She was stupid, selfish, brutal, mean, and, to cap it all, she was a . . ."

"I must protest against the name of the victim being dragged in the mud like this!" interrupted the prosecutor, but the judge said immediately, "The witness is giving, at my expressed request, his personal views on Ciske's mother. I consider this indispensable for the conduct of the case."

While the grownups argued, the Rat was playing apparently unconcerned with an empty matchbox. Suddenly he plucked the sleeve of the policeman. The man leaned toward the child and Ciske whispered something in his ear.

The square-shouldered man laughed and nodded. Together they left the room. The excitement had obviously got the better of the boy. . . .

The trial continued. The chief psychiatrist, Arnoldi, gave a good report on Ciske. I was beginning to hope that the prosecutor would not be able to make much headway against such a mountain of favorable evidence. Yet the prosecutor had still to be reckoned with—although he was the only person who was antagonistic to the Rat.

I was the last witness to be called. I was feeling extraordinarily calm and was determined not to be intimidated by the prosecutor. This was all I could do for the small boy in the dock. I felt much encouraged by the realization that I knew him better than any of the people who had given evidence so far.

"Mr. Bruis," the judge began, "we all know that the boy's surroundings and his relationship with his mother were of decisive importance. Can you add anything to this as his teacher and guardian?"

So I held forth, presenting Ciske as I saw him: as a strong willful personality, with a very pronounced sense of right and wrong. "That is what brings the boy over and over again into conflict. With a humane and understanding upbringing, the obstinate traits might have been developed into virtues. With a tyrannical, vulgar, and selfish mother, however, the daily friction increased until it reached catastrophic dimensions."

"So, his mother is again to be blamed for everything?" the prosecutor interrupted.

"Yes, certainly, his mother," I replied sharply. "Without taking that woman into account we cannot judge either the child or his crime. And it makes no difference that she is now dead. Anybody who wishes to get at the truth would agree with me."

"Do you mean to say that, without the influence of his mother, the boy would have been a little angel?"

"Hardly an angel but certainly a vivacious, useful boy. Hotheaded and obstinate, perhaps, and liable to indulge in foolish pranks, but definitely not a delinquent."

"So it was his mother's fault that, two years ago, he was caught stealing from a store?"

"Yes, because she let the child wander around in the street without supervision. She did not succeed in creating a home for him in which he could feel secure."

"According to you, then, there are no blemishes on this pure child's soul?"

"No, there were some, but we were well on the way to removing them."

"Have you the impression that the boy regrets his action?" the judge now intervened again.

"Most certainly! When he ran to Aunt Jane to confess the deed, he was nothing more than a frightened little wretch who felt completely helpless."

"He was frightened, certainly, but did he feel any remorse, do you think?"

"I don't believe that one can distinguish fear from remorse in a child."

Van Loon was emotionally quite ready to agree with me on many points, but he was, after all, a judge and he had to be impartial. "We cannot, with the best will in the world, leave out of consideration the fact that Ciske killed his mother. I admit this is a tragic case, but we cannot just for that reason not punish him at all."

"But he has been for some months in the remand school," I ventured to remark. "Isn't that already an impressive punishment for a small child?"

The judge was silent, just tapping his pencil on the table.

Suddenly I remembered my call on Aunt Jane. "I should like to add," I said, "that the woman who brought the boy to the police is shortly to marry his father. She is a sensible kindly woman, who is ready to have the child come to live with her. The boy would have for the first time a home life with some warmth and affection. And I myself would keep an eye on him to the best of my ability."

"Well, we shall see," interrupted the judge.

I don't know whether it was the formal atmosphere of the room, the somber blackness of the official robes, but I suddenly had the feeling that I was not speaking to living people. It seemed to me that I was like a man who wanted to deliver a letter personally and saw it disappearing into a pile of several hundred.

"The court is adjourned for an hour," said the judge suddenly.

"You will see, the prosecutor will demand the severest penalty," said Maatsuyker while we were eating our sandwiches in the refreshment room. "He is very crafty. He hoped to get some support from me. But he'll have to wait a long time for that!"

"Yes, yes," I mumbled distractedly and looked away from him.

"You once heard me speak very differently, didn't you?" said Maatsuyker frankly. "Well, I am not the sort of man who will not admit it when I have been unjust. One goes on learning all one's life and one cannot easily get to know children. I did really believe in the beginning that a type like Ciske Freimuth should be handled with great firmness. And even later I was convinced for a long time that you were handling him too much with kid gloves. But when I saw the boy looking so small and helpless beside that great big policeman, I suddenly had the feeling that I ought to make amends to him."

When we returned to the courtroom, Ciske was again in his place. Maatsuyker walked up to him and said kindly, "Well, skipper, and how's the boat?"

Ciske laughed a little, even if he could not understand why the stern headmaster had suddenly become so friendly. He looked at me questioningly. The police escort produced a sports paper from his pocket and began to read it.

The Rat profited from this favorable opportunity to whisper to me, "I have had a letter from Dorus." He was radiantly happy to be able to produce a crumpled piece of paper from his jacket and give it to me to read.

"Dear Ciske," I read,

"My mother has given me the money to buy a new copy of *Pieter Marits*. When you come back, you can borrow it from me. I am reading a lot now because I am very bored while you are away. Betty comes to see me sometimes, but I cannot play with her very well. Do you know, dear Ciske, that I have been given a new wheel chair, one that I can propel myself and which has a real bicycle bell? You will be amazed when you see it. Our cat has fallen out of the window and now she is lame, walking on three paws. I am sorry for her, but it serves her right for trying to catch birds!

"Mr. Bruis is very pleased with my progress in French and says that I may be able to go to the secondary school. That would be wonderful! I have no other news, except that the doctor has to take off Cornel Verstaveren's thumbnail, because he got an enormous splinter under it. It hurt him a lot and now he cannot do any writing at school. Much love, dear Ciske, also from my mother.

Dorus"

What a fine boy that Dorus is, I thought. He writes such a tactful letter to his friend who is in trouble. Not a word about what happened. For him the Rat had remained the same, and Ciske had certainly felt this, as otherwise he would not have been so pleased with the letter.

A smile appeared on the judge's face when he saw Maatsuyker and myself standing by the Rat. "Come here again, my boy," he said kindly, after he had taken his place on the bench.

I saw Ciske go pale. For a moment he had managed to forget his surroundings, but now he was brought back to reality with a jolt.

"Now tell us quite frankly whether you are sorry for what you have done."

"Yes, your honor."

"Do you understand that it was a dreadful thing that happened?"

"Yes, your honor."

"Do you think that you deserve to be punished for what you have done?"

"Yes, your honor."

"Right then, sit down again. The prosecutor may now speak."

In the meantime I had been worrying about this stubborn prosecutor who by all appearances knew only the doctrine of an eye for an eye. Was this Mr. Sweering at home a warm-hearted father who would help his eldest son with his algebra and sit his youngest daughter on her potty? But with the best will in the world I could not visualize him with his children on his knee, singing to them! When he rose from his place I had only the feeling that he would move in now for the kill!

With great feeling he began to draw a picture of the pitiful woman whose cruel fate it was to die by the hand of her own son. He called her self-denying and dutiful to the last. Only someone who had never known Mrs. Freimuth, with her brightly colored lips, the mole under the short veil, the hands overladen with rings, who had never had evidence of her boundless egotism, who had never heard how she shouted at Ciske or how she used to lock him in the coal cellar—only such a person would have found the prosecutor's words moving.

"This boy has always been worthless," he continued. "The murder was only the logical expression of the bad instincts which have always lain dormant in him. Had he not once already attacked a schoolmate with a knife in the class in which he apparently felt so happy?"

I felt with burning shame that this man was trying to discredit my class. Dorus, Sip, Betty, and all the children who had made Ciske into a human being. Unconsciously I made a violent gesture, but immediately I felt Maatsuyker's restraining hand on my arm. "Sit still, Bruis! Let him tell his story!"

The prosecutor cast a reproving glance at us. "It is most improper," he continued, "to try to shift the responsibility for the crime onto the boy's mother. I believe that, on the contrary, this child would have developed his bad tendencies in any surroundings. I am most seriously concerned that among his advocates there are also his teachers, the educators of our youth. Should we not fear for our schools when just the very people who should hold in check the evil instincts of their charges, try to develop them instead?"

Maatsuyker understandably took these accusations much to heart. "You see, now it is we who are really the guilty ones," he growled.

"The obduracy of this boy can only be cured by strong measures. While the emphasis is usually on rehabilitation when one has to sentence a minor, in this particular case I see the need to apply punishment for its own sake. Only after the boy has served his sentence should one attempt to re-educate him. I ask, therefore, that the accused be awarded the maximum sentence permitted for his age: six months at reform school, without any remission and without taking into account the time spent in remand school."

"If he had the right to ask for capital punishment, he would certainly ask for it," said Maatsuyker quietly.

Ciske himself had not paid any attention to the prosecutor's speech. He sat there like somebody who daren't switch off the radio, although he is bored, because others are listening to a lecture on the cultivation of cotton in the Sudan. When the judge addressed himself to him, he almost jumped.

"Did you hear what the prosecutor said, Ciske?"

"No, your honor."

"He wants to send you to a reform school for six months." Ciske stared open-mouthed. Van Loon observed him closely. "That is a severe punishment, my boy," he said softly. "Sit down again now."

The counsel for the defense, Mrs. de Hoop, who spoke next, confined herself rigidly to a statement of the facts. She did not make any harsh comments about Ciske's mother, but briefly expressed her regret that the woman had not been deprived much earlier of the opportunity of harming Ciske.

"The picture that my opponent has drawn of Ciske," she said, "reminds one of the negative of a photograph. The outlines are accurate but the dark parts are light and what is light appears dark. It might be better if we made a positive print from this negative. This boy is not a born criminal, but he could be made into one if he were given too severe a sentence. It would be the first time in the history of the Amsterdam juvenile court that it sent a child to a prison school. For habitual offenders that institution might be appropriate, but where there is the slightest hope that a juvenile delinquent can be restored to the community as a useful member of it, I consider committal to prison school quite unsuitable. The boy who sits here in front of us has been sufficiently punished already by the three months' detention in the remand school. I should consider it understandable if the prosecution were to ask that he be sent for a time to a rehabilitation center. This would give him an opportunity to prove that he deserves to take his place among us again."

Ciske in the meantime had been following with his eyes a fly which was buzzing around the courtroom. Then he began to watch intently how the judge drank a glass of water.

Even the squeaking shoes of the court usher provided an object for his attention.

"Come up here once again," said the judge when Mrs. de Hoop had finished speaking.

"Now tell me once more quite frankly, Ciske—did you hate your mother?"

"Yes," answered the Rat without hesitation.

"When you threw the knife at her, did you want to kill her?"

"No, sir, certainly not. . . ."

"But you wanted to do something to hurt her, didn't you?"

"I don't know. . . . She had spoiled Dorus's lovely book!"

"And you considered that this was a good enough reason for throwing a knife at somebody?"

Ciske was a bit taken aback by these questions, but he recovered almost immediately. Suddenly the words tumbled out of him. "It was not only because of the book, sir. She had been bullying me for a long time. Because of her, I had to stay away from school; and when I did not want to, she locked me in the coal cellar. She used to look on without doing anything when Uncle Henry beat me. And I have never done anything to Uncle Henry. And then the book. It was Dorus's property and *such* a lovely book. Even teacher told me that I must not make the smallest mark on it. And then she tore it up and threw it on the floor. That's why I threw the knife at her. I didn't mean to kill her, sir."

The courtroom was completely quiet while Ciske was talking. The boy had never spoken so coherently and frankly at any of the previous questionings. "The knife just happened to be lying there," he added as an afterthought.

"And now you are sorry for what you have done?" asked the judge.

"Yes, very, very sorry, sir. I was so terribly frightened when I saw all the blood."

"Yes, my boy, I am quite prepared to believe that you did not kill your mother intentionally, but do you realize now what may happen when you do something in a blind rage? This time you have killed your mother, next time you will use a knife on somebody else who does something you don't like. No, Ciske, one cannot behave like this. You have now spent three months in the remand school, and I will take account of that, but you must go for three months to a reform school so that you will understand that one cannot act as you did when you are in a temper. After these three months we will see what we can do for you."

"Can I go to my father and Aunt Jane after the three months?" asked the Rat between his sobs.

"Would you like so much to live with them?"

Ciske nodded passionately.

"Well, we shall see," said Mr. Van Loon. "I cannot promise anything definitely now."

So he could not promise anything? The child was now crying freely. He put his head on the hard barrier and his thin body was racked with sobs. The Rat, the proud tough Rat, stood there in the public eye and cried! I walked up to the crying child and put my arm around his shoulders. "Don't cry, Ciske," I comforted him. "Better days will come soon."

Did I believe what I was saying?

Walking between Mr. Arnoldi and the enormous policeman, the Rat left the courtroom.

A TWO-DAY holiday enabled me to accompany Muysken and Ciske on their journey to the reform school at Nijmegen. I didn't like leaving my wife alone because she was expecting the birth of our first child any day, but it was she who wanted me to be with Ciske.

"Go with him," she said. "It's the last thing you can do for the Rat for the time being. I'll be quite all right by myself."

Muysken did not object at all to my going with him and Ciske. "We don't have a reserved compartment," he said, "so how can I forbid you to sit next to us?"

"Aunt Jane would like to see him off at the station," I whispered to Muysken. "Would you allow her to? She has promised not to make a scene."

"All right, all right," agreed the police official. "We must only hope that the boy will behave calmly too."

He beckoned to Aunt Jane, who had kept herself shyly in the background. "Hullo, Ciske," she said.

The Rat swung around and stared at her in surprise. His eyes then wandered uncertainly from Muysken to me and back again. Smiling with embarrassment, Aunt Jane stretched out her hand to him, but Ciske flung his arms around her neck. He clung to her, a very small, very helpless little boy. Aunt Jane was almost overcome with emotion. What should she do? Hadn't she promised not to make a scene? And now look how the boy behaved! Could one be expected to remain calm under these circumstances?

"Aunt Jane, Aunt Jane," sobbed Ciske and pressed his small head against her ample bosom.

"Now, now, now," the woman soothed him. "Don't fret now, dear boy. We shall see one another again very soon." Her voice trembled a little, but she kept her composure.

"I'll get the tickets now," growled Muysken, who was visibly moved. "Don't squeeze your aunt to death," he added, trying to keep his voice normal.

"Will you promise to be a very brave boy?" asked Aunt Jane in a firm voice.

The Rat nodded.

"I'll write to you every week if I can. Good-bye, dear Ciske."

Slowly Jane loosened Ciske's grip around her neck. Quickly, and without looking around, she crossed the waiting room. Clutching the package of candy, which she had bought him, Ciske stood looking after her until she disappeared from his view among the crowd of travelers.

In the train each of us followed his own thoughts. The Rat, who sat next to me, pressed himself into the corner. Muysken sat opposite us. One of our fellow passengers tried to start a conversation about the fine weather, but as we showed little inclination to join in, he returned, rather hurt, to his newspaper.

From Utrecht on we were alone in the compartment. Each minute our hearts became heavier. For me, too, it was a hard punishment, as it is not exactly proof of a teacher's talents when he has to take one of his pupils to such an institution.

"How old are the other boys there?" asked Ciske at last.

I couldn't answer his question; he would have to wait and see.

"The others thought that one must be sixteen to be sent to a reform school."

"What others are you referring to?" asked Muysken irritably.

"The boys in the remand school, sir. They said it was a shame that I was being sent there. One has a brother who once escaped from a reform school because they had beaten him up there. Do they beat people up there?"

"No, that's nonsense," said Muysken. "If you behave yourself properly, nobody will hurt you."

"I will not let myself be beaten," said the Rat with determination.

It suddenly struck me that I had never beaten Ciske. Not because I was in principle opposed to a sound slap—Johnny Verkerk and a few others had occasionally felt my hand—but because the Rat was not the type of child one could beat. Perhaps it seems silly, but there was something in his eyes which demanded respect, and one could not easily lift one's hand against him. Wasn't there always a fight in his home whenever anybody smacked him? At that moment I felt that in the reform school they might perhaps have too free a hand with the boys. All Ciske's good intentions and all his promises to Aunt Jane might be completely forgotten.

"In a few years' time you will think quite differently about the whole thing," Muysken said to divert Ciske's thoughts. "Then perhaps you can serve on a training ship, and swim, row a boat, climb the mast, perhaps even win sea battles! I can just see you as an admiral. De Ruyther started like this, you know; he too was anything but a good boy when he was young. And yet there are now many streets named after him in Dutch cities. Who knows, perhaps there will one day be an Admiral Freimuth Street too."

The Rat started laughing; Muysken had struck the right note.

"Can people visit me there?" Ciske asked suddenly.

"Of course, my dearest child," replied Muysken with heavy irony. "There will be a children's tea every day with lemonade and strawberries. In the morning they will bring you ice cream in bed or a cup of coffee and ask whether you have slept well. And every Sunday there will be a lovely excursion into the country."

This acted on Ciske like a shower of cold water. His spirits sank noticeably, especially since we had just stopped at Arnhem. "Now we are nearly there," he observed in a small voice. "Soon we will pass the Rhine and then comes the Waal." His voice trembled as we crossed the railway bridge over the river. He bit his lips.

The Waal! This was the symbol for the approaching, terrifying Unknown!

From the station at Nijmegen I telephoned the reform school and asked if, as teacher and guardian, I could accompany my ward there.

"Certainly, why not?" a sympathetic voice replied.

THIS is where you must get off," said the streetcar conductor. When I looked at him in astonishment, because we hadn't said a word to him about our destination, he said with a smile, "We usually know on this line."

He didn't mean any harm, but the Rat squirmed with embarrassment and would not look at the man.

"The building there on the left." The conductor pointed it out. I had expected a somber mass of dirty-yellow brick, with barred windows and heavy iron gates, but the reform school looked almost friendly. The house had clean walls, partly overgrown with vines, and a broad drive led up to it. Many a school in Amsterdam makes a much more unpleasant impression than did this prison for juvenile offenders. But when we had rung the bell and were waiting to be admitted, I suddenly realized very sharply that the next few steps which Ciske took would deprive him of his freedom.

A woman in a gray uniform received us in silence. She led us into a waiting room, where we sat in silence on upright chairs, having lost all desire to speak. Ciske was shaking with nervousness. What would remain of the old Rat after his discharge, I kept asking myself. Would they not kill precisely that passionate temperament that made him so lively and so lovable? Would they not destroy his small but distinct personality?

It seemed only a few days since the Rat had walked on his hands on board the excursion ship.

The woman who had opened the door for us returned. "Please come in now."

The Rat got up with a jerk. Muysken also rose to his feet. Should I join them? Why not? After all, I had received permission to accompany Ciske here.

The governor of the prison school put down his cherrywood pipe as we entered his room. "My name is Reinders," he said by way of introduction. "Please sit down."

Ciske remained standing between our chairs.

I was pleased that Reinders was a plump man in his fifties and not a dry surly prison official.

"I don't usually get pupils from Amsterdam," he said with mild irony. "And when one appears, he is accompanied by two policemen. Well, please sign here that you have delivered the boy safely."

"Oh, so you're his teacher and his guardian?" he said to me when Muysken explained. "It is not often that a boy's teacher comes here with him!"

Next he took Ciske's personal particulars. "Well, my young friend," he said to him, "put your belongings on this table. We shall keep them safely for you. Empty your pockets now!"

The Rat complied. First appeared the package of candy Aunt Jane had given him.

"These will go into the common pool of candy," said the director. "Well, hurry up, boy."

The Rat next produced a pocketknife, a handkerchief, a piece of string, and a cork from the unfathomable depths of his trousers pockets. These were all his possessions.

"And now you must have a bath," ordered Mr. Reinders.

"But . . . but I had a bath only yesterday," stammered Ciske awkwardly.

"Two baths have never yet harmed anybody. And you must remember one thing: when I or one of the other officials or teachers speaks to you, you must get up and stand at attention. Do you understand?"

Ciske had heard, but had he understood? He nodded, but remained in a nonregulation posture.

Reinders pressed a bell and an official appeared who was to take charge of the Rat: a large man with a bushy moustache and a dull face. In silence he beckoned to Ciske. The boy looked apprehensively at me. Must he go now? Was the strange man taking him with him now? Couldn't he even say good-bye to us?

"You can now say good-bye to these gentlemen," Reinders prompted him. Ciske then followed the unknown giant obediently.

As I was there, I thought I would like to know something more about the institution. "I am here for the first time," I began.

"It does not matter," replied the director and relit his pipe. "You are a little too old to be taken in here."

Against my will, I had to laugh. Not so much at the joke which Mr. Reinders had made, but from pleasure that a director of a reform school should appear so informal at a first meeting.

"Joking apart! You would, I'm sure, like to know how things are here," continued Reinders. "Well, we are not exactly a finishing school, as you of course understand. But when the boys have been here for a few weeks, they get quite to like it. The first month is hard, one might say very hard. It would be unfair to deny it. All new boys get a separate room for their first four weeks."

"A cell, you mean to say?" I was frightened now.

"Ye-es, but those are the regulations. Regulations dating from the year 1905 . . ."

". . . which were probably out of date even in 1905," I said bitterly. I was furious. To shut a child up in a cell for a month? Good God, can't grown-up people think of anything better than this? To stand in a corner for half an hour is a blow for a child. But to be locked up in a cell for a month! "Don't you ever make an exception?" I asked as calmly as I could. "I mean, when a child is as young as Ciske Freimuth?"

"I cannot break the regulations," said the director. "But, my dear sir, what do you want?" he continued bitterly. "We are a penal institution. We have anyway now shifted the emphasis toward re-education. Do you realize that I have the right to punish an unwilling pupil by confining him to his cell for forty-two days? That I can give him nothing but bread and water every other day? But when I tell you that we have a day for outings and a football team, that should prove to you that we are not child torturers."

Mr. Reinders had become quite red with excitement. He looked as offended as any schoolmaster who feels his professional honor is being attacked.

"Yes, yes, I am sure that you do your best," I said, as I had no wish to upset him. "Nevertheless, I consider it scandalous that a child of Ciske's age should be locked up in a cell!"

There was a loud knock at the door, and the official who had shortly before disappeared with Ciske reported that the new boy was ready.

"You might just catch the four o'clock train," said Reinders pointedly.

We got up and left the room. In the corridor I saw the Rat—in prison clothes. He was wearing a pair of gray trousers and a shirt which buttoned up to the neck. Under the wide trousers legs I could see heavy workman's boots. I hardly recognized him, the uniform seemed to have obliterated his personality. This was no more my brave merry Rat.

Like a hunted animal he leapt toward me and pressed his head against my breast. The despair of the trembling boy affected me deeply. I freed myself gently from his arms and took his narrow hand in mine—it was like a bird's claw, warm and damp. He looked at me, but I could not see any tears in his eyes. I could see only fear—nothing but fear.

The large man who was to look after Ciske, took him by the shoulders. Ciske bowed his head, and with small halting steps, he followed the man down the long corridor.

Only then did I fully realize that Ciske, my pupil who should be sitting next to Sip in class, who should be learning geography and fractions with us, had now been sent to a reform school.

WHEN in the evening I got back to Amsterdam and climbed the stairs to my apartment, making as little noise as possible in order not to wake Susan, I heard the muffled crying of a child. I did not at once understand that during my absence I had become a father. Only when I saw the nurse and the light coming from the bedroom did I take it all in.

At a loss, I stood clumsily at the foot of Susie's bed. She smiled at me, tired but happy. "Don't you at least want to see your son?" she asked.

For a long time I stood over the cradle and looked speechlessly at the bright red, wrinkled, old face of this new crying human being, whose father I was.

"How do you like him?" asked Susan.

I sat on the edge of the bed and kissed both her hands in silent gratitude. "How was it?" I asked anxiously.

"All right. Everything was quite normal. He weighs just over seven pounds."

The nurse then pushed me firmly out of the bedroom into the living room, where Muysken's canary was happily trilling a song. I could at last relax a little.

Was I happy? At the very moment that I had the feeling that I had lost a son in the Rat, my own son had come into the world. In my heart, the two children fought for supremacy. The result was that I could not think clearly about either of them. I was very tense but realized that I was tremendously hungry.

Nobody seemed to give a thought to me. In my loneliness I reached for the bottle of Bols. I could guess that my solitary drinking would upset the nurse.

"Of course, men always take the easy way out," she said indignantly. "Their way of assisting at a delivery is to get themselves drunk."

Why must women always be so unpleasant toward a young

father? Even Tedema, who two days after the event appeared with a basket of fruit and a little bonnet, treated me with condescension. She declared that I looked a little green around the gills and much too pale to be a father. And yet Tedema was on the whole a person one could respect.

Our nurse was for me a white ogre. She must have chosen her profession solely to have an opportunity to demonstrate her scorn toward the partner of the marriage who was not lying in bed. If Susan had any pain when feeding the baby or a slight temperature, the nurse would look at me at once reproachfully, as if she wanted to say, "It's all your fault, you hateful man!" She even handled the dirty diapers of John William, as we had decided to call our son, only with the tips of her fingers, as if they were mine and not the baby's.

But worst of all were the meals we had to have together. The lady hated well-seasoned food, so I had to be content with the thin soup she made, and with French beans. And in default of better nourishment, I fed myself on my suppressed anger.

It was about the third day, when as we were again sitting facing one another at the table, that she suddenly began to cry. Crying women have always completely defeated me.

"What is the matter?" I asked dully.

No answer.

"What is the matter? Can't you tell me?"

"Why are you always so hateful to me?" she said at last with some difficulty.

Now it was my turn to search for an answer. I looked at her in astonishment, and suddenly I felt real pity for her, with her sad eyes and the ageing face. It could not, after all, be much fun to spend one's life washing diapers dirtied by other people's children.

"Would you like a glass of water?" I asked clumsily.

She got up angrily and left the room.

"What have I done wrong now?" I sought Susan's advice.

"More or less everything," she laughed. "Try to be a bit nicer to her! A few weeks ago her engagement was broken off and one should really be very sorry for her."

With my mother-in-law too there was trouble. She insisted that John William should wear socks. I could not understand why.

"Every sensible person knows that a baby should have warm feet and a cool head."

"And because my head was kept cool when I was an infant, I declare that it is nonsense for a baby to wear socks," I retorted. . . .

"You should have dealt with the matter in quite a different way," said my clever Susan later.

"How?" I asked irritably. "Tomorrow she will come here with the idea that the baby should wear rubber boots."

"You should have put the socks on John William's feet, and then, as soon as Mother had gone, we could have taken them off again."

This is known, I believe, as feminine diplomacy.

Susan, who had insisted that I accompany the Rat to Nijmegen, had not once asked about the boy. Did no one exist for her now but her own child? And how did I feel about things? I must honestly admit that at that moment I worried much more about the fact that John William had that day eaten half an ounce less than the day before than I thought about Ciske locked in his cell. But I had promised myself not to be a selfish father. On the contrary; through the love for my own child, my affection for other children should grow.

Did this mean that I was not as pleased as I should have been with my son? The fate of the Rat rose like a wall of mist before my other thoughts.

Betty and Sip appeared one day with an enormous bunch of lilacs. The nurse took the flowers from them at the door, as if it were something quite normal, but luckily I noticed them going away and called them back. The thoughtfulness of my class was after all more important than the formal kindness of neighbors. Such a bunch of lilacs represented forty-eight times threepence, for which the children must have asked at home. I therefore received the two delegates of the class in the living room.

Betty sat herself in Susan's chair, like a small grown-up woman, completely at home. She was calling on me for the second time, and made sure that Sip, who was wriggling self-consciously on his chair, should take due note of it.

"Look," she said, "there is our fruit bowl."

But the fruit bowl was not to be seen.

"Has it been broken?" she asked, frightened.

"Oh, no," I said as if such a possibility did not exist. "It is just that it is so nice and big that it takes up too much room at the moment when there are so many other things to find a place for. I have therefore put it carefully away in the kitchen, so that nothing should happen to it."

A little later I gave them each a small cake and a glass of lemonade. Sip crammed the pastry into his mouth with his hand; Betty ate hers neatly with a spoon. How charming she looked in her light dress, with her blond locks on which the sunlight played! A pity that the Almighty, probably in absent-minded admiration for the lovely head, had forgotten to put any sense into it!

"May we see the baby?" asked Betty with her irresistible smile.

I could not very well refuse this polite request. And so Betty and Sip were the first visitors outside the family circle to set eyes on the world's wonder, John William Bruis. On tiptoe Betty walked into the bedroom, with Sip close behind her. The latter was very embarrassed when he saw his teacher's wife lying there in bed, and stopped six feet away.

"Good morning, Mrs. Bruis! And my best congratulations," he said.

"Children, you shouldn't spoil us so. Such lovely lilacs!"

Betty went up to Susan and shook her warmly by the hand. "I am allowed to see your baby," she said. "Mr. Bruis has said so."

"Is it a boy or a girl?" Sip wanted to know.

"A boy, of course," I answered proudly.

"Well—" said Sip, "it might just as easily have been a girl, sir!"

I had hardly pulled the net curtain back from the cradle when Betty called out excitedly, "Oh, such a lovely baby!"

"You can't see a thing," stated Sip soberly. He was right; one could see nothing but three hairs of John William's head, he had huddled so deep under his blanket. I uncovered him a little.

"How do you like John William?" I asked Sip.

"I haven't seen him at all so far. Betty is always putting her head in front of me."

"Well, Betty, let Sip have a look!"

"What does a boy understand about babies?"

"Well?" I asked Sip.

"He's all right," he said. But he said it as if he had just had a look at a new pencil box.

Susan laughed. "Would you like to have such a baby brother?" she inquired.

Sip looked at her with gentle scorn and answered, "We have one already. I am the oldest at home and I have two brothers and a sister."

"When you are married, you must let us come and admire your baby," I told Betty and pinched her cheek. "Promise?"

"Yes, Mr. Bruis," answered Betty, without finding the idea in the least embarrassing. She added spontaneously, "When I am married, I want to have at least six children."

"Then your husband will have to earn a lot of money," said Sip soberly.

When Susan got ready to feed the baby, the boy discreetly left the bedroom.

"If you are very quiet, you can stay here," my wife said to Betty.

When Sip was sitting opposite me in a deep armchair in the other room with his legs crossed, and looking at me with his steel-blue eyes, a secret wish arose in me: that John William should be like Sip! So strong, so pleasant-looking, so natural! And when Betty emerged from the bedroom with shining eyes I wished I could have a daughter soon, in addition to my son, a pleasant girl like this Betty Van Gemert, either with or without many brains.

And the nurse had wanted to send these two away from the house! Unbelievable!

Dorus, too, came to visit our son. He brought something special —a board with the word "Welcome" on it. Some stamps which he had soaked off were stuck neatly around the word. When my best pupil shook hands with Susan, something happened which I had almost expected: Susan took Dorus's small face between her white hands and kissed him on both cheeks.

"You are a dear, dear boy," she said softly. She had to bite her lip to hide her emotion. ("If this boy dies, I cannot believe any more in a just God," she assured me afterward.)

Dorus's eyes seemed to implore me to rescue him lest my wife kiss him again! I understood his youthful embarrassment and took him with me into the living room.

"What do you think Ciske is doing now, sir?" asked Dorus suddenly.

I could only shrug my shoulders. "Let's hope he is reasonably happy," I said, feeling somewhat guilty. "Do you think about him a lot?"

"Of course!" Dorus was almost offended. And smiling shyly he confessed, "I say good night to him every night and Betty does the same. We have promised each other to do so. But you must not tell anybody about it."

And Betty too! She had never mentioned the Rat to me, although she usually wore her heart on her sleeve.

I had of course said nothing to Dorus about the Rat being locked in a cell. That would have worried him too much.

"My father says that I must not associate with Ciske any more when I go to the senior school," said Dorus thoughtfully.

Damn it all! So it had started! And yet Mr. Keulemann was not a hard-hearted fellow but a decent workingman who desired nothing better than to be left in peace. And now this decent man had said, "A delinquent, a boy who has killed his mother, is no company for my son. And especially when he is going to a secondary school."

"I'll talk to your father about it when the time comes," I promised Dorus. "Don't worry about it now. We will cross that bridge when we come to it."

But even if I succeeded in making Keulemann change his mind, he and Dorus's mother would never act toward Ciske as naturally as before, and the sensitive Rat would immediately feel it and consider himself branded for life. My God, what would this child have to face when he was free once again!

When Dorus had gone away in his wheel chair, I sat down immediately to write to the Rat. I told him about John William, about the lilacs brought by Betty and Sip. I mentioned that Betty started screaming with excitement about the baby even before she set eyes on him. And so on for page after page. The letter became a really long one. It would reach Nijmegen on Saturday, so Ciske would have something to read and something to think about on the endlessly long Sunday.

I decided, moreover, to go to see Ciske the following Saturday. Maatsuyker would certainly let me leave school one hour earlier for that purpose.

No, I would not abandon the Rat, not even now that I had my own son.

AT THAT time everything seemed to conspire to banish the Rat from my thoughts. Not only on the same day that I lost Ciske did I acquire a son of my own, but something else happened soon afterward that preoccupied me a lot. One morning Maatsuyker brought a strange man to my classroom.

"I am Mr. Riemens, a headmaster from the southern district of the schools association," he said, introducing himself. "I would like, with Mr. Maatsuyker's permission, to listen for an hour to your lesson."

God Almighty, I thought, this too just at this time! About three months before, I had written to a private school which was advertising for a teacher of French. I had never had a reply from them and had forgotten all about it. As I had never taken this application very seriously, I had not mentioned it to Maatsuyker or to my other colleagues. I had just hoped I might be lucky, as four hundred guilders more would after all have been a welcome increase in salary for a teacher who was at that time expecting an addition to his family. And not only the four hundred guilders, but also the events connected with the Rat had prompted me to apply for the job. For a while I just could not stand being faced with the empty place next to Sip. Such emotional states disappear in time, of course; and then, just when I had, so to speak, outgrown the whole thing, I was faced with this Mr. Riemens. He seemed to notice my surprise.

"I know I have descended on you without warning," he said, "but the teacher whom I engaged for a trial period did not appeal to me and now I have to start looking for someone else. As I am in a hurry, I wanted to make your acquaintance on the spot."

In spite of this explanation, I was inclined to believe that an unprepared lesson represented for him a better test than a well-organized one. But that did not worry me as I was not particularly interested in the whole thing. Briefly I explained things to Maatsuyker and put a chair for the visitor at the back of the room.

It is strange how a class can feel instinctively when something out of the usual is afoot. If Mr. Riemens had been one of the school inspectors who often visit classes, the children would have behaved quite normally. But no, they felt at once that this man was somebody of importance! And therefore they behaved particularly well and paid a lot of attention. I felt cold shivers run down my spine upon finding myself in front of such an exemplary class.

Like an experienced bank clerk Sip calculated 15 per cent of 250 guilders, and Wanda shone with her knowledge about the surface of a cube and the perimeter of a rectangle. In order not to create the impression that I had forty-eight little geniuses in my class, I gave Betty an opportunity to say something too. And she immediately began to talk such nonsense that I can't even remember what it was about. I had to restore the balance at once, so I got Dorus to do some calculations in hectoliters and deciliters, which he could do very well.

After fifteen minutes, all the children seemed to have forgotten about our visitor, and I had certainly forgotten him. Then Cornel Verstaveren said loudly and distinctly, "You must be crazy!" when Drikus wanted to persuade us that the frame of a picture is two square centimeters larger than the picture together with the frame!

Mr. Riemens looked up in astonishment, but I could see that, behind the hand which he held in front of his face, he was laughing. My first impression of him was that he was quite a fellow.

Apparently my method of teaching pleased him, because he suggested that I give a lesson in French—I would be the French master—at his school. "I can then get to know you and you can get to know us," he said kindly. "This afternoon, if you can manage it."

I agreed, and promptly at two o'clock I entered a paradise of a school, a building full of light and air. Through windows which were almost as big as the walls, the sun smiled into the classrooms, shining on flame-red geraniums, on tables and chairs which were well spaced, on the well-polished parquet floor, and on the few but well-chosen pictures on the cream-painted walls. It shone, too, on the heads of twenty children whom I was to teach in an ideal classroom.

What riches! How rewarding to be able to spend the years of one's youth in such a school! How amazed my forty-eight children would be if they could see this school!

The French lesson went by without a hitch. The seventh form was well advanced; one could see that they had received good training.

But one could also observe something else—something which is difficult to put into words: the naturalness of good behavior, which can only be achieved perhaps when one's grandfather and great-grandfather have eaten with a knife and fork and not sat at the table in shirt sleeves.

Naturally, even in such a class, there are bound to be dunces and bright children; stubborn, suspicious, honest, and open children—just as in my school. In spite of this, one cannot escape the feeling that even virtues and vices can be displayed on different levels.

And then my hour was over.

"Go back to your homework," said the headmaster. We left the twenty children to their own devices and he took me to his room.

"Well, you have done well," he said to me, obviously pleased. "If it is all right with you, you can begin with us next week. I shall apply to the schools governors to arrange for your resignation from the council school."

I didn't answer at once. I had had during the French lesson a feeling that I was almost betraying my old class. Four hundred guilders more pay—well and good—but what about my forty-eight boys and girls? A strange feeling: I needed only to nod my head and I could turn my back on my past and start work in these wonderful surroundings.

In spite of this I hesitated. "May I have until tomorrow to think it all over?" I asked uncertainly.

Riemens raised his eyebrows. "Don't you think you would like it here with us?" he asked.

"Oh, yes, yes! It is not that but . . . I will tell you quite honestly. I find it mean to abandon my old class. Also, I ask myself whether I don't really belong to the council school, whether I can't do much more for working-class children than for your pupils who have a good life anyway. Naturally I should have thought about this before I applied for the job. You are quite right in thinking that."

I then told Mr. Riemens what I had gone through with the Rat, how depressed I had been when I had applied, and how much I had longed for a change of school at that moment.

Riemens listened to me, a deep frown on his face, with great attention. I was most grateful to him when he nodded understandingly when I reached the end of my story. "Let's have a cigar," he said kindly, "and then we can talk further. Yes, Bruis, I understand you fully and completely. What you have told me is proof that you take your job seriously. I too once had to make a similar choice before I left a village school. I don't want to press you. Think about it in peace and quiet. But I would like to say one thing. Don't think that we are a snobbish school. The children here may be somewhat better clothed, washed, and fed, but they remain simple school children and are treated as such. Their fathers are doctors, chemists, lawyers, civil engineers. Whether the children turn out to be the intellectuals of tomorrow or not depends solely and exclusively on the quality of their brains. You will admit that such children are also worthy of some loving care and attention!"

I WALKED up and down the streets of Amsterdam and thought furiously until my head swam, but when at last I went home I had reached no decision.

The pros and cons of the change that lay within my reach had caused a real battle to rage in my mind. What are you worrying about? I asked myself again and again. Within a year your old class will be leaving school. Dorus, Betty, Sip, Drikus—they won't stay with you forever! The next moment, I was scolding myself:

You are a coward. Admit that what you care about is the money. Four hundred guilders! And a nice small class, longer vacations, and children without snotty noses and dirty faces!

First of all I must talk to Susan about it, I decided in the streetcar. I had deliberately not told her about the trial lesson, as she would have worried too much. I knew that she must carefully count every cent, as our financial position was precarious. Good heavens, a baby is expensive! The layette, the doctor, the nurse, and all the other things which are needed! We didn't even have a baby carriage, and, apart from that, John William did by no means get everything he needed. We had no constant hot water and no decent bathroom. Susan had to carry pails of water around the place. She was certainly not a young mother who had everything.

Why is a teacher's income so miserable? He has to prepare forty-eight or so children for their future lives, and yet he earns no more than a post-office clerk who sells stamps!

When I got home I found a woman there who wanted to sell us a second-hand baby carriage for thirty-five guilders.

"Twenty-five," said Susan. But the woman said that this would be a ridiculous sum for a carriage with solid rubber tires, a wind screen, and other special features.

"You should not have answered my advertisement," she said huffily as she took her leave.

"She's quite right," sighed Susan. "The carriage is not too expensive at thirty-five. But I would have to have borrowed the money for it from Mother, and I already owe her fifty."

I find borrowing from mothers revolting. One then has no right to protest about John William wearing socks in his cradle!

I told Susan about the trial lessons and all the heartbreak connected with it.

"Wonderful!" she exclaimed, sitting up in bed. "This is the answer! Four hundred guilders! The rent! Have you thought about that? Oh, darling, I would like to jump out of bed and dance around the room. I have never really told you how difficult everything is for me. I preferred to have a little cry when you were at school."

Susan pressed her head lovingly against my shoulder. When I stroked her face, I felt that she was crying. I held her close to me.

When she had had her cry, she lifted her face to me, and smiled at me through the last tears.

"I don't think you are at all pleased," she said. "What funny creatures you men are! Can't you be a little happy at the thought of six weeks' vacation in the summer? You have been looking so tired recently. Oh, I am so happy for you!" Susan beamed with pleasure.

That very evening I wrote to Mr. Riemens that I would accept the new job with much pleasure, but when I went to put the letter in the box, I was overcome by new doubts. If I mailed the letter now, it meant an irrevocable parting from my class. Betty would be sad. It wouldn't matter much to Dorus, as he would soon be going to secondary school anyway. Sip? He would get on perfectly well with my successor. Piet, Cornel, and Johnny? They could stand a shock. Perhaps they would all find a change quite amusing in the end.

And the Rat? It wouldn't be so bad for him as he couldn't go back to his old class anyway.

My colleagues? They were not children.

The letter fell with a dull thud into the box.

WITHOUT much enthusiasm I worked away at my old job for the next fourteen days. The schools council had found it appropriate that I remain for another two weeks with my old class, although Bart Oostra, the assistant master, was available immediately and was eminently suited to take my place.

I caught myself postponing the teaching of decimal fractions; my successor could start on them!

Maatsuyker was very sorry that I was leaving. "I am so sorry we must part," he said sadly, "but I won't try to keep you, as the other school will give you better opportunities. I don't consider it right though that experienced teachers should be taken away from the council schools."

Tedema and Verbeest were pleased at this step up for me, and Bart Oostra was quite overcome with excitement. "That is a wonderful school, Bruis," he exclaimed. "A friend of mine worked there when it was being built. The most modern of the new ones—a real palace for children! You should be pleased to get away from this old shack here."

Only one person was opposed on principle to the new step in my career—Jorissen. He accused me of selling myself.

For me it was most important to know what Meerstra would say about the whole thing. He stood silently in the corridor while I was telling the others about it.

"I would like to explain to you in detail about my decision, Meerstra," I began when we were alone, and then I told him about my struggle with myself. "Tell me quite frankly, do you think I am making a mistake?" I asked him at the end of my story.

"You would be stupid if you acted differently," he replied. "In principle I think as little of private schools as you do. All schools should be light and roomy and all classes should be small, but our good old shack will not become more attractive if you stay. And in your new position, after all, you won't be just sitting around twiddling your thumbs either. And you can use a little more money in any case." He patted my shoulder in a fatherly manner. "You have my blessing. . . ."

So far everything was in order. What remained was the rather difficult task of telling my class that I was leaving.

"Now listen, all of you," I said one day before we began our lessons. From the tone of my voice they could tell that I was not going to tell them about some new arithmetic problem or about a participle ending. They sat very still on their benches and this made me uneasy. "Well then, the thing is this"—I searched clumsily for suitable words—"I shall be leaving you soon."

They all looked at me in surprise—Sip, Wanda, Betty, Dorus, and Piet Steeman and his friend Cornel Verstaveren. Most of all I was surprised by Drikus, that good boring boy. I had never been particularly nice to him. Often I had had to keep myself in check not to shake him hard just to put a bit of life into him. Drikus went quite pale and tears appeared in his expressionless eyes. Was he fond of me? Or was he crying out of anxiety for the future? Whichever it was, I decided to be nicer to him in the last few days.

"Why are you leaving, sir?"

"Where are you going, sir?"

"When will you be going, sir?"

"Who will come to us now?"

I brushed the questions aside with my hand and told them that I would be going to another school. "To the school with the glass walls; you must have seen it."

"Oh, yes! The school where all the poor children go," laughed Cornel, and Piet added, "The one where the pupils are so hungry that they are nearly blind?"

By their scorn they took their revenge for having lost their teacher to other children. I didn't rebuke them, and therefore they were encouraged to laugh so loudly that Meerstra put his head around the door out of sheer curiosity.

"What's going on here?"

"I have just told them that I will be leaving, and they are very pleased about it, as you can hear."

They naturally began to protest wildly, and Meerstra, as a joke, took me by the collar and asked them, "What shall we do with him?"

"Kill him," shouted Piet Steeman excitedly.

"Spank him," screamed Sip.

To be honest, I had visualized the leave-taking quite differently, but I was not displeased that it was as it was. What use is sentimentality to anybody?

AND then I got a letter from the Rat! I was in a hurry to get to school when I found it in my letter box, and I had therefore to wait to read it in class.

"Dear Mr. Teacher," wrote Ciske. (How long must he have sucked his pen before he decided to use this respectful form of address?) "Thank you for your long letter. I read it on Sunday at least ten times. I am glad you have a baby now and I find that John William is a lovely name. I can write this letter as my exercise in composition. I hope I don't make too many mistakes in it. The day after tomorrow I will come out of here and will be allowed to join the others. I am not looking forward to this. I can see them marching in the courtyard. How can I keep step with them? They take much too long strides. I don't know any of them yet for up to now I have not been allowed to speak to anyone.

"My teacher here is very pleased with me. Yesterday I calculated the area of at least thirty figures, and in dictation I made ten mistakes, but the words were mostly very difficult, the teacher said so himself. The teacher does not speak as much as you do, but he is all right too.

"I had a letter from Aunt Jane, but she made a lot of mistakes.

"Dorus, Betty, and Sip can write to me too; I would be pleased to hear from them.

"Once a week I must have a shower and once a week, on Sunday, I go to Mass. I quite like Mass. The priest wears a long coat. He has been to see me a few times because he wants to teach me how to pray. But this I find very difficult. I can only say Father, Son, and Holy Ghost and Amen. I have a picture of the Holy Virgin Mary in my room, and she looks rather like Betty in it. She has a round face like Betty.

"The priest is a very fine man.

"Best greetings from Ciske Freimuth."

I folded up the letter. It was high time I turned my attention to my class.

"Please, sir, I have forgotten my letter about being absent."

"Please, sir, can I leave school fifteen minutes earlier because my mother wants to buy me a pair of new shoes?"

Because of the demands made on me by my class, I had no time then to reread the Rat's letter.

One needs time to read between the lines of a child's letter. It is difficult enough for an adult to write about his problems; how much more difficult it is for a child!

Meerstra, to whom I showed the letter during break, was struck by one thing: Ciske was not pleased to be released from his loneliness; he was not feeling very sociable. One has heard that often about people who have been kept in solitary confinement too long. We didn't need to talk about the blow the child had received. When they had stifled the last spark of life in a boy like Ciske, then perhaps he would appear good and attentive. An easy method, that!

Maatsuyker did not see things in quite such a somber light. "The Rat will pull through," he believed. "When he is released from that damned cell, he will revive all right. Such a boy can take quite a lot."

I don't know what came over me but I next showed the letter to Verbeest. "Damned interesting," he exclaimed when he had read it. "You must read your Kierkegaard again. Without knowledge of the psychology of the soul you cannot understand this."

"What do you mean?"

"Why? To study character of course! The fear of being admitted again into the community . . . damned interesting, I tell you."

"The only question is what is damned and what is interesting," I said irritably and left him standing there.

The following Sunday I would go to Nijmegen. Susan had been up for the last few days and the nurse had gone. My mother-in-law was helping with the housework until our new maid was properly trained. She was now a bit more friendly toward me, since I had got a job at a "nice" school.

IN THE corridors of the reform school spring cleaning was in progress. A whole crowd of boys was busy scrubbing the floor. They poured buckets of water over the stones, scrubbed and mopped, and everything was done without a single word uttered. I couldn't see the Rat among them.

The governor received me with relative friendliness. I had been in a bit of a hurry to make my visit, he thought. How was the boy? Oh, quite well. No, there had so far been no complaints about him. He was probably busy chopping wood at the moment.

Reinders walked with me through the bleak scrubbed passages. In the courtyard a few boys were busy tying up brushwood into bundles for kindling. They were working busily away, while their supervisor smoked his pipe in comfort.

One of the boys chopping wood was Ciske. Was it really he? The small boy in ill-fitting prison clothes, so much smaller than all the others?

One could see that he found the work distasteful. To chop the knotty branches with the tiny hatchet! But here at least they were not afraid to entrust him with a sharp tool as they had been in the remand school. Contrary to the scrubbing squad, the wood choppers were engaged in lively conversation. From the distance I could hear all the known Dutch dialects!

"Freimuth," called Mr. Reinders.

Ciske turned around sharply. He lifted his head, clicked his heels together, and held his arms stiffly at his sides. He had let the hatchet fall.

When he recognized me, Ciske made a slight movement as if he wanted to rush to me. But, after an uncertain look at the governor, he remained standing stiffly at attention.

I walked up to him and held out my hand. He took it limply.

"Well, you didn't expect to see me here?" I greeted him. He looked a little confused, almost frightened.

"Go and wash your hands, Freimuth," said Reinders. "This afternoon you need not work. You may go for a walk in the garden with Mr. Bruis."

Reinders said that in a matter-of-fact but not unfriendly tone, and in the same voice he continued to speak to the others. "And you get on with your work! In a few hours I want all this wood to be stacked in the shed! You should be able to manage that."

With my hand on Ciske's shoulder, I walked with him through the garden. We were both a little embarrassed. What had we to say to each other?

Everything was so strange. Ciske himself! His clothes! The boy was now under the stern discipline of the reform school, and he was unable to overcome a certain shyness. He had been here for four weeks. In all this time he had not really laughed; he had not led a normal boy's life. Could one wonder that he had become a little detached from the world?

"Have you heard that I am going to another school?" I asked him at last. I was glad to be able to give him a piece of news which might perhaps interest him.

The Rat stopped walking and his mouth fell open. "You . . . you are leaving the children? But why? Do they know? Who will teach them now?"

"I am going to the school with the glass walls. You know the one I mean—in Arcadia Street."

"Ah, the one with the flowers. . . . But that is a school for rich children." A certain respect showed in Ciske's eyes—almost as if he had wanted to say, "You have done well!"

"Mr. Oostra will now take my class."

"Oh, he is also a good teacher."

The ice was broken, and I told him then that on Monday I would be going to the juvenile court with Aunt Jane. "I will ask the judge whether you can go to your father and Aunt Jane when you come out of here. You know that they are going to be married, don't you? That's a good thing isn't it?"

Ciske looked at me thoughtfully. "Won't I have to go away from them ever?"

"But, my boy, why should you go away from them? When you have undergone your punishment here, no one will ever speak about it any more. The thing must come to an end sometime, mustn't it?"

The Rat clasped my arm all of a sudden and smiled happily. "It will be wonderful if I can go to Aunt Jane!"

I determined to try everything to make his heart's desire come true.

"I won't be allowed to go back to our old class, I suppose?"

"But would you like to?"

"Back to the children? I don't know."

"Wouldn't you prefer to go to a completely new school?"

"I don't know," said Ciske and we were both silent for a long while.

"But that's not so very important, anyhow," said the Rat abruptly. "You are going away, and Dorus is going to a secondary school. I would only have Betty and Sip. And I could see them anyway if I wanted to, couldn't I?"

"But of course!" I said. "It might perhaps be more convenient if you went to a school somewhere near where Aunt Jane lives. I will write on Monday and tell you what we have arranged with Mr. Van Loon."

"If only he says yes," said the Rat feelingly.

"How are things with you here?" I asked hesitantly.

He shrugged his shoulders and looked at me. How should he answer? Everything was hateful.

"Are you pleased to be out of the cell?"

"Oh, yes. Now I sit with a whole lot of boys in a very large class. But the teacher is quite pleased with me. You could ask him! I am always quite quick with the answers."

How docile Ciske had become! Before he did not give a hoot for anybody's opinion. Fear must have broken his confidence in himself. Good God, what problems this boy did set one!

"I sit next to a boy who is already fourteen," Ciske said. "He is even stupider than Betty. And what mistakes he makes! Sometimes thirty or forty spelling mistakes on one page! He can't even speak properly. He has to stay here for another six months."

"What has he done?"

"We are not supposed to know. We must not speak about what we have done. But I do know," Ciske looked carefully around and then whispered. "He broke into a house. Quite professionally, he and a whole lot of other boys. But you must not tell anybody I told you, teacher!"

Ciske had completely forgotten that he himself had been in trouble with the police for shoplifting.

"There is one boy here who has done some smuggling. He's a fine boy. When the others tease me, he is always on my side. He is leaving here in a month. Then he goes quietly over the frontier again, he says."

Ciske was now in fine form. If it were not for his clothes, I could have believed that I had my old friend with me.

"The governor," said the Rat suddenly and was transformed on the spot into a nervous inmate of a reform school. At the end of the path we met Reinders.

"Well, Freimuth, walking around is nicer than chopping wood, isn't it?" he said to Ciske who stood stiffly in front of him. "Well now, listen to me, my friend. I have just spoken to your teacher and to the chaplain. They are quite pleased with you. Report to Mr. Zwart, your teacher. He will give you a red ribbon. Do you know what that means?"

"That I have tried hard," said Ciske hoarsely.

"Well then, you can fix the ribbon to your sleeve. And moreover, you may work in the garden in your free time. You like doing that, don't you?"

"Oh! . . ." Ciske was delighted, and would probably have jumped for joy had he not remembered the correct posture. He looked at me fixedly. "Will you tell Mr. Van Loon everything?" he asked. . . .

"Well, do you find him completely broken?" asked Mr. Reinders after Ciske had walked away.

"Yes," I answered frankly, "but I believe that he can still be saved. He has become so terribly docile, so nervous. In a little while he will become a hypocrite who is showing off his virtue. You should have known the boy before! His lively spirit has been completely suppressed here."

I would not have been surprised if Reinders had become angry at this, but he only laughed and said ironically, "That lively spirit of which you speak killed his mother."

"But is it right to remind him of his sin for several months?"

"You don't know what you're talking about!" Reinders was really angry then. "You are prejudiced and will not see anything good in the reform-school system!"

"I would very much like to but I can't when you lock children up in solitary confinement and let them run around in shaming prison garb," I retorted. "Look for yourself." I pointed to a group of eight boys who were at exercise in the courtyard. "Perhaps you have grown accustomed in the course of years to such a sight, but I find it humiliating! Perhaps seven out of the eight will not suffer any ill effects, but for the eighth this is an evil humiliation. And I pity him because he is the one who has some pride, some feeling of shame and of honor."

"Let me assure you," Reinders continued, "that it is salutary for all here to be curbed for once. The good this will do them will appear perhaps much later. I can see quite clearly that there is a good core to Ciske Freimuth, but he murdered his mother and has therefore earned his punishment. Don't you think, too, that the prosecutor would have a fit if he knew how mildly we are treating him here? It is quite unusual for him to be awarded a red ribbon after so short a time. But I wanted to encourage him."

The eight boys at exercise marched, turned to the rear and to the right and to the left, and reacted like automatons to the sharp words of command.

"Halt!"

They stopped dead.

"About face! Quick march!"

Like eight mechanical dolls they disappeared into their cells. I shook my head, but Reinders resumed his explanation.

"You should not attach so much importance to these external things! Do you know perhaps a different method of providing some fresh air for them? I cannot let them lounge around and give them an opportunity to boast to their comrades of their heroic deeds. Don't forget that I have to deal with thieves, housebreakers, tramps, and similar elements, not to speak of those who have committed sexual offenses. No harm will be done to their little souls by my giving them half an hour of drill!"

I would have liked to contradict him, but he continued. "No, let me do the talking! You should be present when they all gather together for their singing lesson. When you heard their voices you might have tears in your eyes. You see the tall youth, the one with the pail? He is a real delinquent. He has been sentenced twice for breaking and entering. He is a very hardboiled lad, but last week he whimpered like a little dog, because as a punishment I excluded him from the singing lesson. You must sometimes look at the other side of the coin, Mr. Bruis."

I was again quite ready to consider Reinders a splendid fellow. I was quite impressed with how he could warm to his subject.

At the end of the hall Ciske emerged, looking proudly at his red ribbon.

"Now tell us quite frankly, Freimuth. Can you stand it here?" asked Reinders.

Ciske did not really understand what the question meant. He looked pleadingly at me.

"Hadn't you imagined that things here would be much worse?" Reinders made his question plainer.

Against my will, I winked at the boy. He should not hide anything and say that everything is fine here!

"Now that I am no longer sitting in a cell by myself, things are not so bad, sir," Ciske stammered and suddenly tears welled up in his eyes.

That answer told quite enough.

"Well, you may have another little walk with Mr. Bruis," said Reinders. Turning to me he added, "The chaplain would like to speak to you afterwards. He will be waiting for you in my room."

Ciske took me to the dormitories and showed me the bed in which he slept. A carefully made bed, over which there was a picture of the Virgin Mary. I sat on the bed and pulled the Rat to me.

"You have tried to conform here," I praised him, "and it is wonderful that you have already earned the red ribbon. Mr. Reinders is pleased with you, and so am I. Now you must stick it out for a little while longer. Then you will get out of here and can live, let's hope, with Aunt Jane."

Ciske's sad eyes brightened a little.

IN THE governor's room there sat a young priest smoking. The smell of fine tobacco filled the room and made me feel at once well disposed toward the unknown young man.

"My name is De Goey," he introduced himself and flicked a speck of dust from his black coat. "Mr. Reinders told me of your visit and I wanted to meet you."

He had a beautiful voice with a singing quality to it.

"I am interested in that boy," he began without any preliminaries. "He is so young among all these big boys. I don't consider him to be spoiled. For me he is nothing but a child who has been overtaken by sin."

"I am glad that you have formed that opinion of him."

"His offense is nevertheless not a trifling one. The sin which overcame him is a mortal sin, Mr. Bruis. I don't know whether you are a believer, but he has sinned not against one human being or against human beings in general—he has also sinned against God. And God alone can lift the burden from his soul."

"Have you noticed any signs of contrition in him?" I asked after a short silence.

With a pleasant smile on his kindly face, the chaplain answered, "With a child of his age, that is difficult to ascertain. Is regret not a form of fear quite often?"

"Could you establish contact with him easily?" I inquired with interest.

"Well, you know, for the moment he is soft as wax. One has only to talk to him in a way which is suitable for a child, and one is his good friend at once. In spite of this, I shall not abuse his temporary accessibility. It would not be fair to win over his soul in such an easy way. I would so much like to coax this Ciske to a kind of confession."

Not being a Catholic I didn't know what to reply to this. I looked at the priest a little uncertainly. At last I allowed myself a question. "Don't you fear that confession might strengthen the feeling of sin?"

"Then you don't know the meaning of confession," he said with conviction. "Even such a childish confession can bring release to a heavily burdened conscience. Of course, I can only give him absolution when he expresses real regret. But our dear Ciske does not understand the seriousness of his terrible sin. Only in perhaps five or six years' time will the sin begin to press upon his soul, and therefore I would like to divert the burden from him a little. If he can then remember that Mr. de Goey already once absolved him of his guilt, it will be easier for him to bear. I know it very well, Mr. Bruis. The forgiveness which is necessary in order to gain admittance to God's beautiful heaven, that forgiveness I must leave to God. But whatever I can do here on earth to make life a little easier for him, I shall do."

What goodness emanated from this man! He was appointed to give Ciske this support which I, an old skeptic and a doubter, could never give him.

"I hope my wish does not remain unfulfilled," the priest sighed. "Until now I have been unable to move Ciske to a simple prayer. He says, 'God the Father, God the Son and the Holy Ghost,' but only to give me pleasure."

"But the picture of the Holy Virgin?"

"Oh, yes." The chaplain laughed heartily. "I bought it once for myself. It is so much nicer and more natural than the pictures of the saints which one usually sees in the stores. Most of the children rattle away their Ave Marias without noticing what picture faces them; but Ciske, the boy who cannot pray, is surprisingly the one who feels the difference between the cheap reproductions and the lovely little picture. I have wondered about it and it gives me much pleasure."

I looked gratefully at the kindly priest. When I got home that day I would know that I had not abandoned Ciske to his fate. There was somebody there who had some feeling for the Rat.

I TOOK over my new class and started to give lessons to children whose names were Henry, Eric, Connie, and so on. Dr. Van Haanraadt Dros came around and asked me to be lenient with little Jimmy because of his recent pneumonia, and Mrs. Rollinant inquired whether she should be worried about Stanley's increasing nervousness. I listened to children talking about vacation trips to St. Moritz or the Riviera. They talked about their electric trains and their meccano sets with which one could build dredgers over a meter high. Minnie Versteer apparently was often given a whole can of sardines for her breakfast, of which she usually ate half, throwing the rest into the garbage can.

I didn't receive any notes which said that Dirk wouldn't be able to come to school in the afternoon because his shoes wouldn't be ready at the shoemaker's. And Gerard Jonker's father was a mechanic in a factory owned by Wim Norden's father. And Wim Norden was a pupil in my new class.

Sometimes I cursed myself for an opportunist. In the first week I thought it was all a dream and that I would wake up one fine day in my old classroom. I imagined myself telling my forty-eight children, "Last night I dreamed that Cornel Verstaveren had thrown half a can of sardines into the garbage can, just because he was not hungry any more. How do you like that?"

"Such things don't happen," they would all say.

Yes, I had come into quite a different milieu. But were the children whom I now had to teach different from other children?

When Wim Norden was allowed to bring the globe from the attic, he looked just as pleased as Gerard Jonker. And Connie Fabie could, in an unobserved moment, blow her nose just as loudly as Betty Van Gemert. Freddie Hylkeman's fingers were sometimes as dirty as those of Piet Steeman—Freddie was the son of a well-known surgeon, but a real little tramp, who ran about with untidy hair and scratches on his knees.

Connie Mathot was almost as stupid as Betty and just as lovable and clinging. On the second day she was already hooking herself on my arm.

Children are children, and work was going wonderfully well at my new school. Mr. Riemens did everything according to his own methods. He had taken something from all the existing systems of education and had created for his school the notion of "communal individualism." The children had to fulfill a certain program, but they could, when they had finished it, help a classmate with his work or devote themselves to their useful hobbies. The various classes worked, whenever possible, together, for such things as physical training and singing. And club life was very much encouraged.

We had clubs for animal and plant lovers, for photographers, and for football players. We had a theatrical group and a school orchestra. In the seventh form there was even a dance club.

"A school does not exist for work alone," Riemens maintained. "I don't see why the children should have to seek the pleasures of life outside school."

There was a great spirit of friendliness among the teaching staff. They all spoke of "their" school and devoted much time to it outside of the actual lessons. On my first day I was nominated to be producer of the theatrical group and I was told that, because during my military service I had been a sergeant, I was to go for one week to camp under tents with the boys.

"Besides you are the youngest, Bruis," said Van Kalsbeek, an old schoolmaster with a goatee. He was very friendly toward me from the outset and told me off when I addressed him as "sir." Riemens was referred to as "Principal" and Miss Telders as "Sister." She was going to be retired in a year's time and her eyes filled with tears whenever she spoke about it. Her job was to give special tutoring to children who had been ill, so that they could quickly catch up on lessons they had missed. A wonderful arrangement! That school did everything for the children—and for the teachers, too. There were special people to take over singing and art, so that one had some free hours, in which one could correct exercise books.

At half-past ten, a cup of coffee was served for the staff and milk for the children. How pleasant it all was!

And yet the separation from my old class had not been easy! When the bell rang for the last time and I sent my pupils home for the last time, I shook hands with each one of them in turn. I had looked into the eyes of every single one of them, into friendly, open, embarrassed eyes. Only the eyes of Johnny Verkerk were not quite honest. I could read in his look quite clearly: Now you are nothing more to me! A pity—for Johnny was not a stupid boy, but he was shallow and malicious. He won't be a good man in later life, I thought, he's much more likely to be a loud informer, who is always elbowing other people out of his way, who will certainly not know his teacher if he meets him after many years.

Drikus bowed to me; he seemed upset. He had something of the faithful dog about him, a dog who did not want to be parted from his master. Piet and Cornel, the two big rowdies, said warmly, "Good-bye, Mr. Bruis," and began to argue as soon as they were out the door.

I noticed how Betty and Sip were helping their friend Dorus down the well-worn stairs. With a laborious pumping action Dorus set his wheel chair in motion. Betty walked on his right and Sip on his left—the three best-behaved children of them all. Only the Rat was missing.

Had I not just abandoned a crowd of naughty boys and girls to whom I was devoted with all my heart?

"Yes, yes, Bruis, this has been your last day as an educator of the children of the people," said Jorissen pointedly.

Wasn't he right in fact?

But did it help to brood any longer about it all? It was all finished and that was that.

MY VISIT to the juvenile court, in the company of Aunt Jane, proved to be completely superfluous.

"Naturally the boy can go back to his father," said Van Loon, as if there had never been any question about this. "If you, Bruis, as his guardian wish him to stay with his father and his stepmother, it would be very much out of place for me to raise any objection."

A pity that I had not called on him earlier! I might have spared the Rat a lot of worry. However, it was good to know now that everything was in order.

"How is our young friend?" asked Mr. Van Loon.

I don't know why, but this question irritated me. There he sat behind his desk, smoking the inevitable cigarette, looking so neat in his gray suit, his fine hands playing with his valuable ivory paper knife. The man who decided the fate of children!

"Well, there is still hope," I answered gruffly, "that perhaps a glimmer of life will be left in him. But this will be purely accidental. He should really come back squeezed out like a lemon."

"So you consider that my verdict was wrong?"

"Totally wrong, but luckily there is a chaplain at the reform school who cares a little about his spiritual welfare. But that could not really have been foreseen when you sentenced him!"

"How unpleasantly you are expressing yourself. You are probably thinking I am a torturer of children, but that even so I won't succeed in breaking the Rat's spirit."

"In any case your verdict was a dangerous experiment."

The judge looked at me scornfully. "All education is an experiment, Mr. Bruis. And a good educator is nothing more than a bold gambler. The cleverest man cannot calculate with certainty what results will be achieved by his educational methods."

Aunt Jane listened to our verbal duel without saying a word. She had come prepared to play a silent role. She fumbled nervously with her purse. Suddenly Van Loon turned to her. "Now you say something! When Ciske is with you and he is playing, with matches, for instance, although you have told him at least six times not to do it, what do you do?"

Aunt Jane looked perplexed. "When he plays with matches for the sixth time, although I have forbidden it . . . But no, that couldn't happen."

"Why not?"

"Because I would have smacked him already the second time. Children must not play with matches!"

"And do you think that it is right to slap a boy?" asked the judge, amused.

"Of course it is right," said Aunt Jane without hesitation. "I would warn him once, but after that he would have to face the music! But what *are* you gentlemen talking about?"

I WENT with Aunt Jane to bring Ciske home from the reform school. She was terribly nervous. She sat there in the train opposite me in her Sunday best and wept.

I too was in a badly nervous state. I knew only one thing with certainty: Ciske had remained for me a real friend, although I didn't know for certain whether he still felt any ties with me.

"Now pull yourself together, woman," I scolded Aunt Jane when she stood trembling in front of the gate of the reform school, waiting for it to be opened for us. Like an obedient child, she tried to hide her tears.

But when we were in the corridor and saw Ciske, all self-possession left us, and I must honestly admit that I could not master my emotions any longer. At the end of the long hall stood my old Rat, the real boy as I had known him, in shorts and a blazer. It seemed as if a bad dream were over. When Ciske recognized us, he ran up to us and flung his arms around Aunt Jane's neck.

I was almost frightened. I had never seen him like that. There was nothing in him but joy and happiness. Aunt Jane, of course, was unable to utter a single word. With her work-worn hands she just stroked his back lovingly, and pressed her tear-stained face against his cheek. At last she said, "Now, Ciske, my dear boy, you must let me go! What will people think?"

Then it was my turn. Ciske put his arms around my waist and pressed his head against my stomach. He did not seem to give a thought to the strangeness of this greeting! He did not care about anything: he was free; free; free! The three months were over. Everything had come to an end.

"I must say good-bye to the governor," he said with a certain self-importance.

"Well, be careful he doesn't keep you here!" I teased him. "One never knows!"

Ciske then proudly showed me his outstretched arms. "Look how I have grown in these last three months. The sleeves of my jacket are much too short for me."

Aunt Jane, who had regained her composure in the meantime, looked at the jacket and said, "That doesn't matter. We can cut off the sleeves altogether. Some boys are now wearing sleeveless jackets."

Then Chaplain de Goey came up to us and I introduced Aunt Jane to him. "This is Ciske's second mother," I said.

"Thank you," stammered Jane inconsequentially.

"Let's go to the governor's office for a moment," suggested De Goey. "The governor is still busy somewhere else in the building so we can have a chat while we are waiting for him."

"Listen carefully now, my boy," said the chaplain when we had all sat down. "In half an hour's time you will again be in the street outside and will once more be just an ordinary boy. Then your punishment will be finished and you will be able not to think any more about the time you have spent here. But even so, I would like to give you something, a small present as a memento. You didn't expect that, did you? There was somebody here, wasn't there, who always showed you a friendly face, who has been kindness and gentleness itself. Do you know whom I mean?"

"Yes," exclaimed the Rat without hesitation. "You!"

The young chaplain tried hard not to laugh. His eyes shone with merriment. "No, you silly boy. You must not think of me, but always of the Holy Mother of God!" De Goey then produced from under his cassock the picture of the Holy Virgin.

"Oh! . . ." exclaimed the Rat, very surprised. "May I . . . may I take it with me?"

"You may certainly say thank you to the chaplain," said Aunt Jane, but Ciske did not say anything, he just looked in rapture at the picture in his hands.

At that moment Mr. Reinders the governor came into the room. "Well, well, what sort of meeting is this?" he asked.

Aunt Jane sprang up hastily from her chair and made a rather awkward bow.

"All right, please don't disturb yourself," said Reinders. "Now Ciske can sit down in my presence. Boys who have behaved well here have the right to sit in the place of honor. That's the custom here. Sit down, Freimuth."

Ciske fully realized the importance of that moment. So this was the "leave-taking"! He had been longing for this little ceremony for three long months.

"What have you got there?" asked the governor.

"A picture of the Holy Virgin, sir. The chaplain gave it to me."

"Well, I am very pleased to hear it, my boy. Now you will get something from me too. It is not very valuable, at least not to the outside world, but it will be the more valuable for you. What have I got here?"

"My red ribbons," whispered Ciske.

"Correct, your ribbons. You have earned them honestly and they belong to you. You have not won them lightly. In fact, you have gritted your teeth and persevered. Now you must hang these ribbons up somewhere in your home where you can always see them. Best of all, next to the holy picture. Yes, that's the best place for them. If ever you are at a loss to know how you should behave, look at them, and when you begin to think how hard it was to earn them, everything should be all right. Now let's shake hands. You have been a good boy, and you have taken your punishment like a man. I have been very pleased with you, my boy."

This then was the "leave-taking." Warm, brief, and not in the least sentimental.

Ciske then went off with Aunt Jane to collect his things.

"He has become much tougher," said Reinders, "even physically. He is broader in the shoulders and fuller in the face. If I had had to keep him here for six months, it would not have done him any harm. A healthy boy can stand a lot. The training here is short but hard."

"One must wait and see how he adjusts himself to everyday life," I said.

"You will have a harder job restraining him than spurring him on. The little devil has preserved a great deal of his fiery temperament."

"If you have a moment and the opportunity, please write and tell me how he is," said De Goey.

Ciske was ready for the journey. His jacket over his arm, his suitcase in his hand, he was now in a hurry to get away. The last ties which bound him to the reform school were severed. Freedom called him.

"Good-bye, and thank you very much," he said to the governor.

The latter replied, laughing, "There's nothing to thank me for! I was pleased to oblige!"

"Good-bye, Father," said the Rat, rather moved, looking at De Goey with wide-open eyes.

The young priest took the boy's head between his two hands and stroked his hair. For a moment his hand rested on the boy's head.

"I do hope I shall see you again," said Ciske very softly.

The chaplain answered kindly, "Certainly, but not here, my boy."

The woman who had let us in three months before, let us out again to freedom. She smiled at Ciske.

It was spring. A tree in full bloom was the first thing that greeted Ciske outside the prison building.

"ALONE at last," said Aunt Jane in the train.

That was not quite correct, as there was also a young woman in the compartment.

It was very funny how Aunt Jane took over the leadership of our little group. I found it quite appropriate. In two weeks Freimuth was due back from sea and then she would legally become the child's mother.

Aunt Jane knew how one should behave. "Ciske, sit quietly now!" "No, don't lean out the window; it's very dangerous!"

But Ciske could not sit still and had to lean out the window and feel the breath of freedom blowing around his head. Suddenly he turned to Aunt Jane, put both his arms around her neck, and shook her head from side to side so that her hat came off. "Oh, my dearest Aunt Jane," he said.

"Goodness me, child, do stop it!" she protested meekly.

Ciske went back to his corner and then asked, "Where shall we put the picture, Aunt Jane? Next to my bed? Where shall I sleep, Auntie? In the attic, I suppose. Fine! In the little room under the roof on which rain falls so nicely, but where you can keep dry. May I put some begonias on my window sill? I can look after them by myself. . . .

"Teacher, which school will I be going to now? Do Betty and Dorus know that I am coming home today? Will I have to go to school right away tomorrow? May I see your baby on Sunday? I have a present for him, but I won't tell you now what it is."

Ciske prattled on without stopping, speaking very fast with feverishly shining eyes. How differently I had visualized his homecoming. I had thought that I would be bringing back to town a subdued, frightened child, a shadow of the old Ciske the Rat. And here I was, faced with a vivacious boy talking about the future.

I listened to him in silence, while he talked and talked.

And he talked so eagerly! No, my little friend, I said to myself, now I will not interrupt you; now you may happily suck Aunt Jane's candies and behave as you please, but let's wait and see what remains when your intoxication with your freedom has worn off. Then we shall see what has really happened to you.

"The Rhine," exclaimed Ciske when we passed Arnhem, and then he continued like a phonograph record, "It enters Holland near Lobith and at Pannerden it divides into the Issel and the Waal. . . ."

"You silly boy!" I felt I must finally interrupt him.

"Oh no," he corrected himself quickly, "at Westervoort!"

"And when it has split up into the Issel and the Waal, what happens to the Rhine itself, little ass?"

The Rat grinned. "At . . . let me see . . . Oh yes, I've got it now, at Pannerden there is the Rhine and the Waal, the Issel comes in at Westervoort. Westervoort lies east of Arnhem, and west of Arnhem lies Ooesterbeek. We learned it with you, sir!"

"You must take care not to shame me in your new school!" I warned him jokingly.

"Has the boy just come back from a rest home?" piped up the strange lady, who had been listening, highly amused, to our conversation for quite some time.

The Rat made a face and looked embarrassed. What a mistake the good lady was making!

"Would you like a chocolate?" asked our traveling companion next.

The Rat suddenly got up and stood almost at attention, as if he was still in the reform school. I wanted to push him back into his seat.

But the lady was impressed and said, "Very nice, my boy, one can see you can stand firmly on your two feet. One can see it at first sight."

This, too, now!

She got out at the station after Arnhem, giving Ciske a friendly parting wink. As soon as we were alone, I said with slight irritation, "Once and for all—that nonsense is over and done with. In Amsterdam everybody will laugh at you if you stand at attention at every opportunity. Just act naturally, which, with you, is quite stupidly enough. . . ."

The Rat blushed up to the roots of his hair. "What can I do? I've got used to it."

"Get unused, and as soon as possible," I said, taking him by the scruff of the neck and pushing him back into the seat. At the next station I got out and, since this was a festive occasion, bought chocolate éclairs and some lemonade.

Several people had got in by the time I came back and Ciske now sat quite still in his corner, looking out the window and eating his éclair.

"He is either quite wild or sits quite still," said Aunt Jane to me rather anxiously.

Ciske leaned over to me and whispered, "When will Dorus come?"

"Are you longing to see him again?"

"Oh, yes, very much!"

What a good thing that I had had a few quiet words with the Keulemanns. Father Keulemann felt that one should not interfere with friendships between children and was ready to believe that there was some good in Ciske. Hadn't he pushed Dorus to school, day in, day out? And didn't he have the idea that Dorus should be taken on the excursion to the sea?

Sip, Betty, and Dorus were the only ones who knew about Ciske's homecoming. I was curious to see whether they would organize anything of their own accord.

My curiosity did not remain unsatisfied for long; when we arrived in the street where Aunt Jane lived, the first thing I saw was a fair girl's head. Betty, the impulsive, loyal child! Who knows how long she had been waiting there for us?

Ciske, who had been very quiet in the streetcar and in the street, suddenly got very red in the face when he saw his old friend.

Children don't need any greeting ceremonies; they very rarely shake hands. Betty came running up to us and just looked at Ciske, laughing. She greeted him with her eyes, and only after she had looked at him for a long time, said in her high voice, "Morning!"

"Morning," replied the Rat hoarsely.

Betty then produced some candy. "Do you want some?"

"Oh, lovely," exclaimed Ciske. He put his suitcase on the sidewalk and peered into the paper bag.

"Can't you say thank you?" scolded Aunt Jane. "Let the candy wait until we get home. You've already eaten enough candy today anyway. Are you coming up, Betty?"

When the two of them ran on ahead of us, Aunt Jane said, "That Betty is a little darling!"

AUNT Jane's quiet little apartment had become very lively all of a sudden. Children's voices filled the rooms. Ciske had overcome his passing depression now that he could find his old self again in clean surroundings and in Betty's presence. With flushed cheeks he walked all over the apartment.

"Oh, the cat," he cried with joy and stroked its thick fur. "Come, give me your paw, my old friend, or would you like to dance with me?"

Betty laughed shrilly and looked at her friend with admiration because he was behaving so manfully.

Aunt Jane put the kettle on and forced me to stay and have a cup of tea.

Ciske was still exploring his new home. "Oh, a new cushion! Aunt Jane, the curtain has a hole in it. Look there, the lame milkman is still around!"

His tour of inspection continued. He couldn't stop; he had to see everything to be sure that he was really at home and free. He had to enjoy that feeling to the full.

Aunt Jane, who was not used to so much movement in the house, called from the kitchen, "Ciske, you are driving me crazy with all this running around. Come here and sit quietly for a little while."

It had no effect. The Rat had to get it all out of his system. Betty looked at him with surprise. Had she been thinking that she would be able to mother the prodigal son? How self-possessed he was!

Ciske noticed Betty's admiration. In his endeavor to do something out of the ordinary, he began to walk on his hands in the hall, but this was too much for Aunt Jane; just out of reform school, and already acting like a circus clown—that was too much for her feeling of what was right and proper!

"Now that's enough," she called out and pushed him firmly onto the chair near the stove. "Now sit there and don't get up until I tell you you may."

"Are you pleased to be back home?" asked Betty, while Ciske sat in the kitchen, a little subdued. He pulled a long face and stuck out his tongue. That girl with her stupid questions!

When I had had my cup of tea, I prepared to go home at last. "Are you coming too?" I asked Betty. "It's about time you went home to supper."

"May I come with Dorus tomorrow afternoon?" she asked Aunt Jane.

"Yes, of course."

Ciske was by that time sitting, slightly shrunken, by the stove, looking tired and wilted. His pale face was damp with perspiration.

"Well, my boy, I'll look in on you tomorrow."

He just nodded.

"What kind of behavior is this?" grumbled Aunt Jane. "You must thank your teacher nicely for all he has done for you!"

"Thank you," said Ciske.

In the hall Aunt Jane whispered to me, "I won't be a bit surprised if now he starts howling!"

What a sensible woman! How quickly she had seen through the artificiality of Ciske's happiness! What a good thing that the boy was now under her care! She would be firm with him, but kind to him too. Compared with her, I felt like a real bungler.

SUSAN thought it was too much when I told her the next day that I was going to see the Rat. "You should leave the boy to himself for a while. He is being well looked after by this woman."

I agreed with her privately, and yet something drove me to go see my unfortunate ward.

In Aunt Jane's home there was complete peace. The front door was open and I could climb the stairs without ringing the bell. From the kitchen came the noise of dishes being washed, but this was almost drowned out by Aunt Jane's voice singing a song which she must have heard at some Salvation Army meeting. The Rat accompanied her, off key but doggedly.

It was good to hear him sing, because Ciske only did it when he was happy. It meant that the two of them were hitting it off!

"Don't drop the cup. You must sing, 'His loving arms are my refuge where I find all peace and calm.' As you are singing it, it does not make sense."

Yet Ciske went his own sweet way. He didn't care much about edification; he just wanted to sing.

"Do I interrupt a singing lesson?" I asked on entering the kitchen.

"How lucky that you have come! This boy sings so badly that the milk is turning sour," said Aunt Jane. "If you'll sit down for a moment, I'll make a cup of tea."

Aunt Jane and her cups of tea!

"Did you sleep well on your first night here?" I asked Ciske.

"The bed was so soft—I'll have to get used to it again."

"In that case tonight you can sleep on the ironing board," suggested Aunt Jane, laughing. "That, I'm sure, won't be too soft for you."

After a little while, the doorbell rang.

"Dorus and Betty," shouted Ciske and rushed to the door.

I carried Dorus upstairs and sat him on a chair, facing Ciske.

Unlike Betty, Dorus shook hands with the Rat, and Ciske found it so funny that he went on shaking Dorus's hand for a long while, if only to cover his embarrassment.

Dorus smiled indulgently in a slightly patronizing manner. "How are you?" he asked. "You are looking very well."

"And why not?" replied the Rat indifferently.

They looked at each other blankly and didn't know how to re-establish their old contact.

"Look, I cut myself with a knife," said Ciske finally, "I lost a lot of blood."

"You shouldn't play with knives," scolded Betty.

"But you are always so wild. . . ."

"Well, it's all in a day's work!" The Rat shrugged his shoulders, and Betty stuck out the tip of her tongue at him.

Aunt Jane then had to go out on business—to collect some papers "for that wedding performance," as she put it. The children had gone into the adjoining room, but I remained in the kitchen by myself, except for the cat which was purring away on the window sill. Through the open door I could hear every word.

"Wait a minute, I want to show you something," said the Rat.

"Oh!" Betty exclaimed, "A holy picture!"

"A present from the chaplain." Ciske sounded very important.

"For keeps?"

"Of course!"

Betty did not sound very impressed. In her neighbor's home there were whole walls covered with exactly such pictures. Some even nicer than this. The Holy Virgin with a lamb, and the Holy Virgin with a heart in her hand from which a flame was rising.

"Without asking for it, I got the picture and a bowl with holy water in it in my cell," reported Ciske with pride.

"In where? In . . . your cell?" Dorus was painfully surprised. "So you had to sit in a cell?"

"Not all the time."

"Was . . . wasn't it rather hard?"

"Oh, Dorus!"

For a moment there was silence.

"You must not speak about this to the others," said Ciske. "Only you two must know about it."

There was silence again.

"But teacher said that you were being sent to a very strict school. How mean to lock you into a cell! Could you never get out?"

"Oh, yes, twice a day we marched around and around the courtyard. I had to take very long steps, because the other boys were much bigger than I, and I couldn't keep pace." So Ciske had started to tell his story! It obviously did him some good to be able to unburden himself before his friends.

"And do you know what I did when I couldn't sleep at night? I used to repeat geography lessons. I rattled everything off, one after another: Rotterdam, Schiedam, Vlaardingen, Maasluis, Hoek van Holland . . . and so on. When I felt I had something wrong, I made myself repeat it three times more as a punishment. When I made yet another mistake, then five times more. The boy next door could not sleep because I was talking to myself, so he would suddenly start banging on the wall. Goodness, it used to make me jump!"

"How dreadful," whispered Betty with sympathy.

"And what did you do in your cell in the daytime?" Dorus wanted to know.

"I worked! Arithmetic, geography, and writing. I have learned a lot. Have you already done simple equations? I have! Very difficult, I can tell you."

Dorus's curiosity was not yet satisfied. "What other boys were there in that school?"

"Oh, a whole lot of them. All big boys. They had stolen things, broken into stores or houses, or been caught smuggling. But they were forbidden to speak about it, although they did talk in secret. There was another one, you should have heard him talking, Dorus. Come here and I'll whisper in your ear what sort of boy he was. You mustn't listen to this, Betty."

"Then I shall go away! I don't care," said Betty offended, and she came out to the kitchen.

I quickly leaned over a book and pretended to have been reading.

"Oh, teacher!" she exclaimed, most surprised to find me there. "Didn't you go out with Aunt Jane?"

"I don't think so," I replied.

The two boys then joined us.

"Now tell me how things are at school," I encouraged Betty and Dorus, in order to distract them.

"Oh, all right. A few more weeks and then I'll be finished," said Dorus.

"And you, Betty, how do you get on with Mr. Oostra?"

"Oh, quite well. But the boys are so naughty, Piet, Cornel, and Johnny, that Mr. Oostra has to hit them again and again. This week Johnny's mother came to school and made a scene. Do you know what Mr. Oostra said to her?"

"Oh, Betty, you shouldn't repeat this." Dorus tried hard to stop her.

"Why not? 'You are welcome to take your son away,' he said, 'and I have been tired for a long time now of your big mouth.' Yes, really, that is what he said! Johnny's mother was terribly angry and the headmaster had to come out."

Dorus looked at Betty scornfully. These girls! They will always chatter about everything.

Aunt Jane came back at that moment. She had brought with her the documents for the marriage and some cookies. The cookies were very pleasant with the inevitable cup of tea.

WHEN Ciske had been at his new school for a few weeks, I asked him how he liked it. He said he was quite happy there but that he found the other children rather dull. And his teacher? Well, he wasn't too bad; that was all he would say about him.

I suppose one couldn't say much more than that about Dirkzwanger, Ciske's form master at that time. He was a quiet, decent fellow who followed his daily routine with unruffled calm. He was one of those masters who take their jobs very seriously and consider it improper to make jokes!

Every Wednesday afternoon, Ciske used to visit us, sometimes with Betty and sometimes with Sip. I would often leave them alone but sometimes I would listen secretly to their conversation. I found that these were usually quite ordinary children's conversations, about stamps, flying boats, football, and the like. I was therefore rather surprised when Aunt Jane smiled rather wryly when I asked her for her impression of the Rat now that he had been back for some time.

"The boy is not yet his old self," she said. "When I'm alone with him I sometimes can't get a word out of him. At times he seems to have no desire to do anything, and he just sits there and mopes. At night he gets up sometimes, and then his eyes are wide with fear and he is covered with perspiration. But I cannot find out what the trouble is from what he says. Sometimes he talks in his sleep, and it's dreadful to hear him calling aloud in the quiet house. If I get up, go to him, and give him a drink of water, he gradually calms down and remembers where he is. The next morning he does not remember anything about it. No, he is not the old Ciske yet. That will probably take some time."

Aunt Jane and Freimuth got married as soon as he came back from sea. Jane and Ciske went to meet him at the pier.

"He too is a strange character," reported Aunt Jane, laughing. "When he went away he didn't open his mouth, but when he landed he was happy as a child, as if nothing had happened in the meantime. He said to Ciske, 'Well, my little boy, here I am again,' and he embraced him. And to me he said, 'Good, and now quickly to the registry office, then we will have that behind us.' And he laughed like a bridegroom of twenty."

Freimuth had asked me to be a witness at the wedding and I couldn't very well refuse because I had played a part in bringing about this union. So on the appointed morning I went along to the registry office to find Freimuth in a dark blue suit, already smelling of beer. The Rat was all dressed up for the occasion, and looked like the grocer's boy. Aunt Jane was terribly nervous and continually wiped her mouth with her handkerchief. A cousin was the other witness.

Aunt Jane and Freimuth were one of twelve couples who were being married simultaneously. The registrar made a speech, and the Rat burst out laughing when his father had to give Aunt Jane his right hand. She, having a great sense of the solemnity of the occasion, gave him an angry look.

The whole ceremony almost dissolved into chaos when one of the twelve husbands-to-be refused to sign his marriage certificate. "No, damn it," he said firmly, "nothing sensible can come out of this."

The bride went pale and the bride's family blushed scarlet. The registrar walked up to the recalcitrant bridegroom and tried to explain to him that his behavior was not only unseemly but contrary to the law.

"You are already married," he said. "I have just said, 'And I now pronounce you man and wife,' and I have let the gavel fall. Therefore your marriage is already solemnized before the law. You cannot withdraw now."

"And what about my signature?" insisted the reluctant man.

"That is quite unimportant," exaggerated the registrar. "It is enough that I have signed the register."

"Then I have nothing to worry about," laughed the freedom-loving man and prepared to walk away, without giving as much as a look at his bride who had fainted again, having barely recovered from her previous swoon.

But the bride's father rushed after the man and began to belabor him. The two men fought until some officials arrived on the scene and parted them. The bride, who had by then recovered, clung to her husband. This seemed to make an impression on him, and he began to look at her with new respect. Arm in arm the two of them walked away at last, leaving behind the members of their wedding party who were all talking at once in great excitement.

"What a disgraceful performance," said Aunt Jane. "They should be ashamed of themselves."

But the Rat was overcome with delight. In the corner café to which we adjourned for a cup of coffee, he kept talking about the incident. Naturally Ciske got chocolate cream all over his new suit and naturally I had to give in to Freimuth's entreaties to have a drink with him.

So Aunt Jane was now really married to Freimuth and could therefore play the part of Ciske's mother without interference. I was very pleased. . . .

ONE day I asked Ciske, "Don't you ever hear anything from your two brothers?"

He answered with indifference, "No; they are now with my uncle at Deventer and I could go to see them but I don't want to."

My new school kept me very busy. True, we had small classes, but one was not in any way free just because one shut the classroom door at the end of the day. Every week there was a school meeting, and there were endless interviews with parents who were always appearing to inquire about their children. Every mark awarded provoked a whole series of conversations. The parents wanted to be informed of exactly why their Annie had got a grade three and not a three plus in French, and of the reason why their Freddie had not got a star for good behavior. I felt much more responsible to the parents here than in my old school. When you come to think of it, it was quite reasonable. When my own son is old enough to go to school, I will also be interested in knowing what the teachers are doing with him during the time in which he is entrusted to their care.

The change of job had stimulated me. New faces, a new atmosphere, new problems!

I soon grew used to my new class. I came to know the children quickly and I got along with them well. Only when a teacher is fond of the children in his class can he feel at home with them. The memory of my old class was slowly fading, and I supposed that their memory of me was fading also.

I noticed it particularly when one day I met Wanda Bergmann and Frances Klaver. At first they wanted to pass by with only an embarrassed little nod, but I stopped them for a moment. In the past they would at once have taken my arm, but now Wanda replied with a shy little giggle to my question as to whether she still had her lovely singing voice, "I really don't know, Mr. Bruis."

I couldn't think of anything to say to Frances.

"Give my love to all the children," was all I finally managed and we went our several ways.

In six months' time we shall probably just nod to one another, I thought. With Johnny Verkerk it came about just as I had expected. I saw him one day in the street—he saw me too but did not greet me. I was somewhat angry with myself as I had already nodded to him.

And so life went on. Only a few special friends from among the children in my previous class kept in touch with me. After all, not too bad a result when one thinks hard about it.

Then Betty came to me one day and told me of an unfortunate incident. "Ciske was waiting for us today in front of the school. Cornel, Piet, Sip, and I came up to him first, and then Drikus. The last to join us was Johnny Verkerk. Cis asked me if I would go with them to the circus, teacher. And then Johnny said, 'Aha, so he's taking his girl friend to the circus.' Cis told him not to be crazy, as Dorus and Sip were going too. But Johnny would not leave it alone, and took the boys to one side and whispered something dirty to them. It must have been something very naughty, because Sip was furious and slapped his face. He knocked out one of his teeth, teacher. In the end he pushed him too, and Johnny fell against a lamp post. Then Miss Tedema came out of the school and Johnny ran away.

"Sip, Ciske, Cornel and Piet, and I wanted then to go home, but we saw Johnny again. He was standing there with his mother in front of a grocery store and his mother was trying to clean him up a bit—he had blood and dirt all over him. When she saw us, she immediately came over to us. She wanted to scold Sip, but for fun he hid behind Ciske and gave him a little push so that he knocked against her. So then Mrs. Verkerk slapped Ciske's face, although Ciske was completely innocent. It was a shame! But he did not take it lying down—he kicked her in the shin. Then she said she would complain to Mr. Maatsuyker about him, and Piet said that Ciske was not in our school any more. Then suddenly Mrs. Verkerk cried out, 'Oh, so you are that fine boy! I'd take a knife if I were you. You're used to it!' Ciske did not reply at all to this, Mr. Bruis, he just went very red; but Johnny, who was standing beside his mother, began to laugh like mad, so Ciske leaped on him and hit him until his nose began to bleed. Then Sip and Ciske ran away."

Betty told me the whole story with great indignation, and I am convinced that she had presented it with complete truthfulness. I could visualize the incident quite well.

That miserable Johnny and his dreadful mother! Why had this wretched woman had to make an allusion to Ciske's past? The Rat had not encountered a trace of animosity from the other children. How much more tactful children are than grownups!

In the evening Maatsuyker called on me. He used to visit me quite often, and he always followed a routine. First he would gaze for a while at the baby, then he would exchange a few words with Susan, and then finally he would tell me all his news. I could foresee that that night the conversation would be devoted to Ciske. And sure enough, Maatsuyker soon said, "Don't get frightened, but the Rat has done it again."

"How?"

"He kicked Mrs. Verkerk in the shin and bashed her little Johnny on the nose and made it bleed. Ciske is no believer in half measures! I don't have the feeling that reform school has tamed his spirit completely."

"Fortunately not," I replied.

Maatsuyker looked at me over his cup of tea. "Of course," he said, "one cannot expect the boy to have been transformed into a little lamb, but if you had seen the angry face of Mrs. Verkerk . . ."

"I have already heard the full story from an eye-witness," I said. "Believe me, Maatsuyker, I am very pleased that the Rat defended himself. And I'm willing to bet he'll beat up anybody who reminds him of the unfortunate story of the knife."

Maatsuyker agreed that it was quite natural that the Rat should defend himself against juvenile attackers, but he thought he should draw the line where grownups were concerned. After all, a child had no right to kick a woman in the shin.

"Not even when the woman has behaved badly toward him?" Susan said in defense of the Rat.

"As a boy, he must remember that he has to control himself where adults are concerned."

Presently Maatsuyker took his leave. Perhaps he was right, I thought, and as Ciske's guardian I should probably prepare myself for a visit from Mr. or Mrs. Verkerk.

Johnny's father appeared at my apartment exactly an hour later. He came in like a peddler who intended to foist a dozen shirts on me. He told me his version of the story that I already knew, and added, "Before I went to the police, I wanted to speak to you about this matter."

"That was very sensible of you, particularly as the fault lies with your wife and your son."

Verkerk clearly wanted to let fly then, but I gave him no chance.

"Apart from the fact that your wife smacked Ciske without cause, she should not have reminded him of his misdeed, for which he has already been punished enough. Don't go to the police; go home instead and tell your wife and son that they should leave the Rat alone."

Mr. Verkerk went home somewhat deflated.

I summoned Ciske to my apartment and looked at him sternly when he came into the room. Already in the doorway he began to justify himself. This he would never have done at one time. "I did nothing, really nothing, teacher, until they . . ."

His voice became hoarse and uncertain, his face deep red. Now he would have to mention the remarks about the knife, about the matter which he never wanted to mention again.

"Yes, and then Mrs. Verkerk said something about a knife," I made it easier for him, "and afterwards you bashed Johnny on the nose, am I right?"

"Yes!" Ciske threw back his head. He was trembling with rage. "Yes, that's what I did, sir. You can punish me if you like; I don't care. That damned Johnny has nothing to laugh about. I'll never let him get away with it! Never!"

"Did you slap his face really hard?"

"And how!"

"Well, then everything is in order. I was afraid you might not have dealt with him properly!"

Ciske's mouth fell open with surprise. Was I being serious or was I pulling his leg? Caution made him suppress his laughter.

"Listen," I continued, "it was not a good thing to kick Mrs. Verkerk. A boy should not do this to an older person, do you understand? But no one can hold it against you that you hit Johnny on the nose. You don't need to let anybody get the better of you. If a grownup ever drags up this old story again, you must come to me.

But when one of the boys is unkind to you, you can settle it yourself. Grownups against grownups and boys against boys. That is the correct division."

"And what about girls?" asked the Rat, in order to be covered for all eventualities.

"Girls? You can't be serious, Ciske! One does not beat up girls; one can at best shrug one's shoulders and walk away."

Now the Rat really laughed with relief. So that was that.

I FELT that the Rat should go away during summer vacation. Betty was going to an aunt; Sip as usual to the country; and Dorus was going with his parents to stay with friends of theirs —so Ciske would be left all alone, without any friends in town.

"I could take him one day by boat to Zaandam with me," sighed Aunt Jane, "and perhaps once to Aris, but I cannot manage more than that even with the best will in the world. He will just have to run around on his own and be terribly bored. I could willingly kill the person who invented vacations. . . ."

Riemens, my new headmaster, was not the sort of man with whom one had to beat around the bush to ask for a favor. If he could arrange something, he always said yes. If there was nothing to be done, he just said, shortly and succinctly, no. He was a splendid fellow. So I asked him straight out, "Could I take a small friend with me when we go to camp during the first week of vacation?"

"Of course! Who is he?"

"The Rat . . ."

"Oh, that is the boy who . . . Certainly, I have nothing against it."

The next day I informed the Rat about this plan. His reaction was not very encouraging. "Camping?" he asked carefully. "With strange boys?"

"Are you afraid they will eat you?"

He smiled wanly. "No . . . but . . ."

"But what? Are you afraid that you will be out of place with all those decent young gentlemen?"

Ciske nodded.

"Well then, let me tell you that the boys in my new class are every bit as naughty as other boys. They are not conceited, and, like you, have their noses in the center of their faces."

The Rat's interest was aroused then and he began to ask questions. Would we prepare our food ourselves over a campfire, did one put straw under the tents, what did one wear to go swimming? Yes, yes, of *course* it would be wonderful. . . .

The boys who were going camping were excited about the adventure ahead. Some of them had pestered their fathers and mothers so persistently that the planned family vacation trips had been postponed for a week. The boys would not have exchanged a whole month in Switzerland for that one week at Gooi. These boys were a pleasant crowd, not a bit spoiled, and those who went camping were the best of the lot. Wim Norden and Freddie Hylkeman set the tone in my class: two tough boys who always looked you in the eye, even when they were being told off, and who never bullied the weaker ones. They were pure gold—boys of the same type as Sip. I was curious to know how the boys would get on with the Rat, the rough boy from a working-class home, but I wasn't in any way worried about it. And Ciske had finally agreed to come!

On the last day of term, we had a meeting of the camping club to which I invited the Rat. "This is my secretary," I said when I introduced him to the others. "He is coming with us if you approve. If you don't, then he and I will go alone!"

They all grinned at him. Their first impressions could not have been too encouraging, since the Rat just stood quite still, looking rather sad, in the unfamiliar magnificent schoolroom, facing all those boys whom up till now, God knows why, he had always regarded with scorn. He was obviously fighting a hard battle with his class consciousness, but I was convinced that he was bright enough to see things in their true perspective.

On purpose I put him between Freddie and Wim and behind Siets Van der Koey who could recognize sixteen different kinds of fungi and eighty different birds, and who in fact in many ways knew more about nature than I did.

I explained to the meeting that going to camp was not to be considered an excuse for fooling around, although fun would not, of course, be completely banned; that to go camping meant to create in the open air a small world of good comradeship, a community of people thinking more about others than about themselves; that if one person let the group down, then the spirit of the whole camp could be affected; and that whoever intended to behave like that should raise his hand now so that the rest would know about it.

Freddie immediately put his hand up and looked around with a stupid expression on his face. Everybody laughed. The Rat, too, considered Freddie's action a good joke and looked at him admiringly out of the corner of his eye.

"All right," I said, "that has been noted. Freddie can start tomorrow by pumping the water. For such unpleasant boys there is nothing better than hard work."

The meeting continued in the same pleasant mood.

The boys were to report the next day at seven in the morning in front of the school with their bikes.

I suddenly noticed Ciske's frightened face. What a fool I was! I had taken it for granted that every boy had a bicycle. I quickly gave him a wink to indicate that I would arrange about one for him later.

Even if I had to pinch a bicycle from hell, I would see that Ciske had one the next morning.

After the meeting I walked home with the Rat. "You have no bike, I suppose?"

"No, but my father has one. If I fix pieces of wood to the pedals, I can just about reach them," he answered. "My father practically never uses it."

At six o'clock next morning—I was just shaving—Ciske knocked at my door. God Almighty, was he mad? I looked out the window and touched my forehead significantly. He pointed to the pieces of wood which he had fixed to the pedals of his father's bike.

At half-past six I joined him in the street. "Couldn't you get here earlier?" I asked him.

The Rat was carrying a contraption similar to a rucksack, which Aunt Jane had made out of an old piece of carpet. In his bicycle basket he had two blankets and a windbreaker, tied together with a piece of string. Ciske stared at my bare knees, but he said nothing—probably because he approved of them.

And then we started off. Like a pet monkey Ciske balanced himself on the bicycle which was far too high for him.

On our way to the school we met Henry Fabie from the sixth form and a little way further on Siets Van der Koey.

"Your saddle's too high," Siets told the Rat. "You won't be able to manage. Let me fix it a bit lower down."

"We had no wrench at home," said Ciske.

"Siets always has a wrench on him," laughed Henry. "His father is a well-known burglar, you know."

"He must be telling a fib," the Rat said to me uncertainly, and I smiled encouragingly at him.

In front of the school the other boys were already gathered in a noisy group. They were inspecting each other's equipment, but no one said anything about the Rat's carpetbag although they certainly all noticed it. Siets got ready to adjust the Rat's saddle and Henry helped him with it.

"We'll fix this bike up beautifully for you," said Henry, and Uppi Van Laer, who turned up at that moment, asked, "Is the bike your older brother's?"

"No, my father's."

"What does your father do?"

"He's at sea."

"D'you hear, Uppi, his father's also at sea," said Siets.

"My father is with the Netherlands," explained Uppi. "And yours?"

"With the K.N.S.M."

"That's not a very good line," remarked Uppi.

But the Rat did not let this pass. He gave Uppi a devastating look. "The K.N.S.M. has more ships than the Netherlands. They only have a few old crates going to Indonesia."

Freddie rocked with laughter, and the others joined in. But Uppi, who always began to stammer when he was excited, protested, "Old cr-a-aates go-ing to Indonesia? W-hhhat do you mean?"

"That's enough," said Siets. "The score is one to nothing in favor of Ciske. And the seat is now fixed too, my boy."

I was quite pleased that the Rat had won this little battle, because Uppi's father was captain of one of the newest mail boats and Ciske's—a stoker on a broken-down tramp!

Then we started off. Wim, who had won a prize in a road-safety competition, led the procession with me. He rode so exactly in accordance with the highway code that I almost managed to break my neck. I had nominated Siets my aide-de-camp. He rode at the rear and had the special task of keeping an eye on Freddie and Ciske. Our camping site had been excellently chosen. One of the other masters had found for us a piece of meadow by a small pine wood. Close by this lovely spot was a farm, which would give us all a warm meal from time to time.

Everything went off very well.

The wild Freddie became great friends with the Rat. I wondered if he felt a sort of kindred spirit in him? The two of them, with Wim Norden and Uppi Van Laer were the youngest. They were told off by Henry Fabie because they made a mess of opening one of the tents; and so, while Henry fastened the sides of the tent for them, they were put on to cutting the bread.

"But before you start you must wash your dirty paws!" commanded Siets.

I left them all to their own devices. At the end of an hour, three tents had been put up beautifully, and straw laid in them, and we sat down before a mountain of sandwiches on which the boys immediately descended like a pack of wolves.

Ciske sat between Henry and Freddie. He looked very happy. Henry showed his special concern for Ciske in a typically boyish manner: from time to time, he took Ciske by the scruff of the neck or knocked a sandwich out of his hand when he was about to put it into his mouth.

"Well, how do you get on with Ciske?" I asked Henry after supper.

"Very well," replied Henry. "He's an amusing fellow. A little nervous, but he'll have fun here."

Henry had not expressed it at all badly. The Rat fit in very well with the others, insisted on helping to carry water or peel potatoes. In spite of this, Ciske was not really the same boy as the one who had gone on our other school excursion. On that occasion, he felt completely at home among his comrades. The difference this time was not that he did not feel at ease among these boys, but lay much deeper. . . .

Henry had not expressed it badly at all. For the first time Ciske was in the company of boys who knew nothing about his past. That made him dizzy with happiness, but at the same time threw him off balance. He was like a calf which, after a long winter in the shed, comes out at last into the open and expresses its joy at its regained freedom with exaggerated leaps and bounds. But Ciske could not quite cope with this happiness. He ran about with feverishly shining eyes and it would not have surprised me if his loud laughter had suddenly degenerated into bitter sobs. . . .

Poor Rat . . .

One afternoon, we went on a nature ramble under Siets's guidance. He told us what he knew about the various birds and about the types of stones. The Rat followed him like a shadow and listened to every word open-mouthed. He was very annoyed when Wim once interrupted Siets.

Thus Ciske enjoyed the sun, the summer, and the good air. For the first time in his life he was able to feel all their blessings.

During a supper which had been prepared for us by the farmer's wife, he sat very quiet and did not take part in the lively conversations or join in when the others started singing songs. He felt small and lonely when the others sang "*Gentille bâtelière laisse là ton bateau.*" How could he fit in with children who could sing a French song?

Henry, the kind soul, obviously realized how lonely the smaller boy felt and so he put an arm around Ciske's shoulders. I noticed my Rat's face working as he obviously struggled to keep back the tears which, as a tough boy, he must of course not allow himself to shed.

When we all went off to bed and Ciske was standing a little perplexed at the opening of our tent, looking helplessly at the tangle of blankets, sleeping bags, and noisy boys, I drew him to me. "How do you like it here?" I asked softly.

"Oh, it's wonderful, teacher," he whispered. "I am going to make up my bed between Henry and Freddie, but I am not at all sleepy yet."

When everything had quieted down at last, I made my rounds through the tents which shone in the moonlight like small white pagodas. In every tent I heard the deep breathing of healthy sleeping boys. The light of my flashlight wandered over their heads. The Rat was asleep too when I returned.

THE week in camp was over. Tanned brown by the sun, we bicycled home to Amsterdam.

I had expected Ciske to be quiet and sad, but on the way back he chattered incessantly and was one of the wildest boys. I had to restrain him or he would have got quite out of hand.

In front of the school, we said good-bye to one another. All the boys shook hands with me, wishing me a pleasant vacation and thanking me for the "lovely week." They said good-bye to one another with a wave of the hand, making an exception only for Ciske. Siets went very formally up to Ciske, shook him by the hand, and said, "Boys, we must say a particularly nice good-bye to our guest."

So they all crowded around him and then cheered him. "For he's a jolly good fellow," they sang and the Rat himself beat time. It was a real ovation!

I rode home with the Rat. He was now completely silent. In front of my house he said, "Thank you very much, teacher!"

He usually forgot his thank-you's.

All of a sudden he seemed to me once again so small and helpless when he rode away through the sunlit street on his big bike. What would he do now? Tomorrow? And the day after?

I was suddenly overcome by a superstitious fear. Hadn't the Rat been the hero of the day on our school excursion? And how soon afterward had tragedy followed! Would he perhaps again experience something similar? But I decided that this was nonsense and that I must not worry my head about things which lay hidden in the future and over which I had no control.

Oh my goodness! How unpleasant things were at home! Our suitcases were packed, and in my room and indeed everywhere else there was a smell of mothballs. I was already longing for the pure air of the camping site and, with the best will in the world, I couldn't raise any enthusiasm for my vacation in a respectable boarding house by the sea.

AS I HAD expected, at the boarding house we had breakfast every morning at about nine o'clock, consisting of a small dish of butter, an even smaller dish of marmalade, and four almost transparent slices of smoked ham. At midday we had minced meat, roast beef, or chops. Everything as expected and never anything different! Then there was our perpetual anxiety about John William, who was already beginning to wave his arms about. Once he pulled down the tablecloth and upset a vase of flowers. Another time he produced a small lake on the best silk dress of a certain Mrs. Bowens.

Oh, you dreadful, miserable vacation resorts here and everywhere! Vacation prisons where one acquires, for a lot of money, memories of many small irritations!

Well, the three weeks passed. When I got back home, the Rat came to see me.

"Well, how have you been, you little rascal?" I asked him. "Have you set fire to a police station or persuaded a streetcar to leave the rails?"

The Rat laughed and then told me with a certain pride, "I have been to see Mr. Muysken."

"You have not been up to something again?" I asked him, thoroughly alarmed.

"No, I just went to see him," said Ciske. "I helped him clean out his bird cages. When he has a particularly lively canary, he will give it to me."

"Did you yourself have the idea of calling on Mr. Muysken?" I inquired with interest.

"Yes, I hadn't seen him for a long time."

"That was you fault." I tried to make a joke, but it misfired. How sensitive the boy was to any allusion, in whatever form, to his past!

Ciske played with the fringe of the tablecloth. He did not quite know what to do with his hands. I didn't like his expression and wondered if anything was wrong.

"Have you seen anything of Johnny Verkerk during the vacation?"

"N-no . . . yes," he said with some hesitation.

"And?"

At that moment I knew that I had hit the nail on the head.

"He was standing in the street with a crowd of boys."

"And?"

"He again called me names and was horrible to me." His voice had now become stronger, but his fingers still played nervously with the fringe of the tablecloth. I was really frightened when I looked into his face; it was again hard as stone, his eyes were burning, and his cheeks were flushed.

I like you like this, I said to myself.

With tightly pressed lips, he stared straight ahead and his eyes had become narrow slits. "He called me a murderer," he stammered at last.

Good God!

It was not so much the word Johnny had used that horrified me, as the passion with which Ciske spoke. He was boiling with rage, revengefulness, and shame.

"And what did you do?" I asked quietly.

"At first, nothing. I simply went on my way. Then the whole gang began to follow me and Verkerk tried to walk on my heels. The coward! Only because there were so many others around him did he dare to do it. The dirty scoundrel! On his own he is afraid of me, because he knows I will beat him up!"

"Go on with your story. What happened next?"

"I hit him a few times, then I threw him to the pavement, and I was already sitting on his chest when the others attacked me. I kicked one of them in the stomach and he ran away howling."

"But didn't you get hurt, too?"

"Oh, it wasn't too bad. I got a bump on my head and my shirt was torn. A street cleaner came along and dragged the other boys off. He shouted at the cowards because they had all set on me. Aunt Jane was a bit angry at first because of the tear in my shirt, but then she saw that I couldn't have done anything different. And in the afternoon I went to see Mr. Muysken and told him everything."

"And?"

"He just laughed and was not at all angry. 'You beat them up if they come too near you,' he said, 'but only with your bare fists!'

"Look what I have," said Ciske then, suddenly quite calm, and he produced from his coat pocket a picture postcard showing the Matterhorn. "It's from the chaplain!"

In a neat hand the priest had written:

> My dear Ciske, how are you, my boy? You see, your old friend has not forgotten you. When I am next in Amsterdam, I shall most certainly look you up. Does the holy picture still hang over your bed? I am on a walking tour of Switzerland with twelve boys. You would enjoy that, wouldn't you? All best wishes from Father de Goey.

"Excellent," I said, really pleased.

"Yes," said the Rat.

A little later he added as an afterthought, "I would like to push Johnny Verkerk down the side of a mountain as high as the Matterhorn."

Aunt Jane knew more about Ciske than all the rest of us put

together. She could write a long report on the subject of his nervous fears.

"Sometimes he does not know what to do for sheer high spirits," she told me, "and then I hear him, in a moment when he doesn't know I am watching him, whispering to himself, 'Must I go to hell? Please, please, I don't want to go to hell! I am trying so hard and I do regret everything I have done. Please, please, I don't want to go to hell!' Then I feel deep in my soul a terrible pity for the poor little lamb. What remains, in those moments, of the lively little boy, when he sits with me in the kitchen so still, looking into space, as if he did not belong to this world? Who can say what is going on in such a child's heart? I would be most pleased if I could occasionally enter his soul and sweep it all nice and clean. But he is shut in like a box."

I met Dirkzwanger, Ciske's new teacher, one day in the street. "You must keep an eye on Freimuth," he said gravely. "That boy has no inner balance. He laughs and then he cries. At one moment he is working like a demon, and the next he has a spell when one cannot make him work at all, even by force."

Thus I was warned from many sides. Things could not go on like this, I felt certain. But what could I do? The conflict of conscience which was tearing Ciske apart must be resolved one way or another.

NOT long after my talk with the Rat, Sip came running to me in a terrible state of excitement. "An awful thing has happened," he blurted out, "near the malt boat!"

"Near which malt boat? What? Quickly, tell me!"

"Near the malt boat by the brewery. We sometimes play there after school. At lunchtime we were there again, jumping from one boat to another—I, Piet, Cornel, and Gerard. Then Verkerk came along with two boys from his street, and they joined us. And then Ciske came along."

"Hurry up, boy, get to the point," I urged him, but this made Sip even more nervous.

"Well then, Verkerk said that no one can jump as far as the middle of the second boat. . . ."

"Yes, yes, and then!"

"We asked Ciske if he wanted to play with us, because he can jump very far. Farther than any of us, because he is light as a feather. But he said he had to go home. And then Johnny Verkerk said, 'You go away; we don't want you here anyway.' Cornel shouted at him to keep his mouth shut, or he would show him what he thought of him, and he told Ciske, 'Go on, Ciske, show them what you can do.' And Johnny shouted, 'He can't do it!' And then Ciske jumped, and managed it easily. He jumped a whole lot farther than the stick which I had put in the middle of the boat as a mark. He really can jump farthest of us all."

"Hurry up, Sip, get on with the story!" I exclaimed and my hands felt quite clammy. "What did Verkerk do then?"

"At first nothing, sir. . . . That dirty dog! It's his fault what happened to Ciske! That bastard!"

"Now just tell me quietly what happened."

"Verkerk didn't do anything. He's much too much of a coward for that. We went on playing for a little while and he did not join in. He just stood there on the dock and watched us. Then we had to stop because the man from the brewery was tying up a third boat. Then Cornel said, 'Ciske, can you jump over the second boat into the third?' 'I don't know,' answered Ciske. 'I can only try.' He took his shoes off and made a dash for it. When he was in the middle of his run, Johnny tripped him. Ciske hit his head on the edge of the first boat and fell into the water."

"Good God, Sip," I exclaimed in horror. "And then? He didn't drown, did he?"

"No." Sip shook his head. "He didn't drown, but he nearly did. We saw him go under, and I, Piet, and Gerard quickly jumped into one of the boats and lay down on our stomachs and I was able to grab him. Then the three of us pulled him out of the water."

I stared at Sip speechless, while he continued.

"Ciske could hardly breathe, and he was so pale we thought he was dead. So I rushed quickly to the doorman at the brewery, and he called for an ambulance. In the meantime another man came from the brewery, but he did nothing. The doorman then rushed out and started moving Ciske's arms and legs. At last an ambulance came, and took him. . . ."

"To the hospital?"

"I don't know. . . ."

I shot over to see Aunt Jane. She was just seeing a doctor to the door, so I knew the Rat was there.

"How is he?" I asked quickly.

"We must wait and see," replied the doctor gravely. "He has swallowed a lot of muddy water from the canal. Moreover, I think he may have caught pneumonia. I'll look in again tomorrow morning."

On tiptoe I crept into Ciske's room. There he lay, pale as wax, his thin face sharply outlined, his eyes closed. On his forehead he had an ugly bump. He lay motionless, although from time to time his lips trembled. Over his bed the Madonna smiled, on either side of her hung the red ribbons from the reform school, pinned to the wallpaper. Miserable trophies, earned by an iron determination to be good. Poor Rat . . .

Was this the end of his struggle? An ill-treated, worn-out child, sick and vanquished by his adversaries?

I dared not move and stood for a long time by his bed. Only when I heard a slight creaking of the floorboards did I turn to see the frightened face of Betty Van Gemert. Her blue eyes looked anxiously at her friend. She could not understand why Ciske was lying so still. She was very frightened.

I made a sign to her and together we left the room. Outside Betty started to cry bitterly, and Aunt Jane took her on her lap. She too was crying softly. They were two women united in a great grief.

From the very beginning I had the uneasy feeling that this was much more than an ordinary accident. Hadn't I been waiting subconsciously for a great blow to fall for several weeks? I was worried much more about the spiritual than the physical consequences of the accident.

A soft exclamation of Jane's made me jump. I followed her into the bedroom to find that Ciske was throwing himself wildly about his bed. His cries filled the little room.

Aunt Jane sat dejected beside the feverish child. She looked at me imploringly. At that moment there was no barrier between her, Betty, and myself. A helpless sympathy for the dangerously sick boy filled us completely.

"No!" cried the Rat violently. "No! Go away! Go away!"

The thin hands on the blanket were clenched. Lovingly Aunt Jane put an arm around Ciske, but he freed himself with a sudden jerk. Wearily she rose and I took her place, and seized Ciske's hands in mine. They were terribly hot, and his pulse was racing. After a few seconds he freed himself from me too. "Go away!" he shouted. "Go, go away!"

"That boy is dangerously ill," said Susan when she came home after having relieved me at Ciske's bedside. "He is raving. At first I thought that he wanted to drive the picture of the accident from his mind; but there is something else, something much worse which is tormenting him in his feverish dreams. He is afraid of a pair of eyes. A pair of eyes which threaten him."

"His mother's eyes," I said and Susan stared at me unhappily.

"The poor little soul," she said with a sigh and pressed John William's head to her cheek.

When I went to visit Ciske the next day, Aunt Jane said she thought that he would survive his illness. To my astonishment, I found Betty sitting by Ciske's bed. She worried about the boy like a little mother.

The Rat was conscious, but he did not look at me when I came in. His face was very red and his eyes stared into space. "I know when I die I must go to hell," he said to Betty. "In heaven they don't wish to know boys who have killed their own mother. The Almighty God is very powerful. . . ." Ciske laughed shrilly and then this terrible laughter changed into a tormenting cough.

"Now you see, you stupid boy, this is what comes from your silly talk," scolded Betty.

I went up to Ciske's bed and put a cool hand on his forehead. His eyes flitted from Betty to me and from me to Aunt Jane. I said softly to him, "Try to keep calm, my boy. There is nothing for you to be afraid of. In a few days you will be well again."

The Rat shut his eyes. Everything I said was just words, empty words, nothing but words. I was deeply conscious of the inadequacy of my consolation. By chance, I looked at the unchangingly smiling picture of the Holy Virgin. Perhaps some consolation might come from there, I thought. Something had to happen soon. Ciske was in the throes of a crisis which would be decisive for his whole life—I was certain of that. The three of us, Jane, Betty, and myself just could not find the right words to help him. Neither Aunt Jane with her motherly kindness, nor Betty with her pure loving heart, nor I with my warm feeling of sympathy. The three persons who loved Ciske most were unable to help him.

I took my hat and walked away from the house, without saying a word. From a post office a few streets away, I telephoned Nijmegen. Chaplain de Goey came to the phone quickly.

THE young priest had left for Amsterdam immediately. As he walked along the street beside me on the way from the station, I felt a great relief.

"Let's hope I can do something for the boy," he said as we rang the bell of Aunt Jane's house. She was frightened at first when I came up the stairs with a priest, but then she recognized Father de Goey.

"You need not be frightened," De Goey reassured her. "I have only come to visit my dear old friend."

Betty too, who was sitting with Ciske, was frightened when the priest entered the sickroom. She blushed a deep red and ran out, without saying anything. Ciske lay with his eyes closed.

"Good morning, my boy," said De Goey and took the boy's hot head in both his hands. "It doesn't do to be ill, you know. When I heard about it, I came at once."

The Rat opened his eyes and stared at his visitor without speaking. He did not understand yet. I looked at him closely. What would he do? That was the decisive question: everything depended on it, on that and on nothing else.

At last . . . at last the thin hands of the child groped for the protection of the large hand of the priest, and, trembling, came to rest on it. His eyes did not stray from De Goey's face.

It seemed as if something were breaking in Ciske. His eyes filled with tears and then he began to cry bitterly. But it was not hysterical crying, just a continual quiet sobbing. Such crying does a lot of good. I felt I should go out and leave the boy with the priest but, fascinated, I stayed on and watched them.

"You probably think that God does not care for you any more," said De Goey gently. "But then you don't know God. He loves boys such as you. You won't believe me, but that is the truth. God forgave you a long time ago."

Greedily Ciske was absorbing the words which brought solace to his tormented heart. The soothing voice continued: "Graver sins have been forgiven than the one you have committed. Sins of grown-up people who have done evil on purpose."

Ciske lay there with closed eyes and listened. His breathing was still fast, but his face was now calmer.

"And now go to sleep, little boy," said De Goey affectionately and tucked him in. A little later Ciske was fast asleep. . . .

I, sentimental fool that I am, had the greatest difficulty mastering my emotions.

Together with the chaplain I went out into the living room, where we found Aunt Jane dissolved in tears.

"Don't worry any more," the priest comforted her. "I assure you that the boy will sleep quietly tonight once again."

Until the small hours, we discussed Ciske at my home. We had a conversation to which all narrow-minded people in the world should have listened. We spoke of goodness and human kindness, which know no frontiers and which bind people together and foster tolerance.

I lay awake all through that night. But I was calm and happy when I thought of the Rat, of my Ciske, who had found peace at last.

EARLY the following morning Chaplain de Goey accompanied me to Aunt Jane's house. We found that Ciske had had a reasonably good night. I felt sure that something had changed in Ciske, that his illness had reached the critical stage. He had a temperature of more than 103 degrees and was delirious, but now there were no confused cries of distress and remorse. He thought he was fighting Johnny Verkerk. "Take that, you stinker!" he hissed. "Take that and that and that; and now you'll run to your mummy, won't you?"

Later, on that critical day, Maatsuyker arrived at my house just as I was setting out to pay my evening call and we walked along together.

"What do you think of that horrid little Verkerk boy?" Maatsuyker roared. "Of course I knew he had a foul character, but that he knowingly would try to make away with another boy . . . !"

"Come, come," I said. "One could not call it a murderous attempt. It was a dirty trick that almost had fatal consequences."

"I don't agree with you, Bruis!" he replied angrily. "You should not excuse such behavior. To trip a boy when he is running toward the edge of a quay, that surely is a very wicked act. When I heard about it the other morning, my first impulse was to give Verkerk a sound thrashing, but that wasn't necessary. Master Sip Eisma had done it already, and the little fellow did it better than I could have done!"

Personally I felt no desire for revenge. It was strange, but deep in my heart I was even a little grateful to Johnny Verkerk. It was exactly as Aunt Jane had said to me: "It was all meant to happen that way. Really, I am beginning to believe in Providence!"

The crisis over, Ciske lay in bed, miserably thin and deathly pale, but quite quiet. I popped my head around the door and he smiled at me: a touching little smile. Some children look their best when recovering from a serious illness.

"Well, old man," I greeted him, "so you are on the mend, I see."

"Look . . ." he whispered, and I followed his eyes to a great basket of fruit which stood in all its splendor on the table.

"This afternoon Dorus will be allowed to come to see me for a few minutes," he said. "Betty comes every day. Have you heard? Sip has beaten up Verkerk!" These last words he whispered with profound satisfaction.

I happened to overhear the conversation when Sip made his first visit to the Rat. The two of them sat and talked like grown men.

"Boy, I was as sick as hell!" said the Rat importantly. "Look at my arms, they're as thin as sticks, and they were even thinner. Everyone thought I would die."

"People don't die that easily," Sip said. "There's a girl in our street who has had fever of the brain. That's much more dangerous than pneumonia like you had. But she didn't die and already she is running around again."

"Do you ever see Verkerk?"

"Sure! In the classroom. But no one plays with him any more. Boy, oh boy, I beat him to a pulp!"

"When I am better, I'll beat him up too," said the Rat determinedly. "Just tell him that and he'll be scared to death."

"But you'll have to get your strength back first."

"Oh, be quiet! He is no match for me. I'll crush him to pieces with one hand. I'll make mincemeat of him."

The conversation continued in this bloodthirsty way, and it sounded like music in my ears. Ciske was at last speaking quite normally and not in a nervous hysterical voice.

"No more visits today," Aunt Jane declared when Sip had left. "You'll see—your temperature will jump up again any minute. In this way you'll never get better!"

When Betty arrived a little later she was nevertheless allowed in, because Betty was above the law. She had not missed one day. Sometimes she had even come in the afternoon and in the evening.

"What an angel she is," Aunt Jane said. "I never saw anything like it. She, at least, is not a fair-weather friend. Mark my words, she will be his friend for life."

"Do you want them to get married then, Aunt Jane?" I asked, laughing.

Very seriously she replied, "Who knows? Don't laugh at me, but I can tell you those two love each other in their own way. This is not just a whim like children often have—today close friends and tomorrow at each other's throats. It is, of course, foolish to say it now when they are so young, but Ciske could choose a worse wife than that little darling. I am very fond of that girl!"

It was absurd to remain the Rat's guardian, for now Ciske was where he should be. It was unthinkable that he would relapse into his old bad ways. The first part of his childhood was over. During his twelfth and thirteenth years he had gone through more than many a sedate man of sixty had gone through in his whole life. All the dreadful things that had threatened to destroy him had really matured him. I could not say that he had become more serious and less excitable, but somehow he had grown up.

Susan felt the same as I did about it.

"You really should look around for a new protégé," she said mockingly. "Ciske doesn't need help any more. What about paying some attention to John William for a change?"

But I was able to do one more thing for the Rat.

When he was up and about again I asked him if he would like to go back to his school. He pulled a long face as if he had swallowed some bitter medicine. "I don't want to much," he confided to me. "They are so dull, all of them! I wish I could join the boys."

The next day, impulsive fool that I am, I went to Maatsuyker and even succeeded in making him enthusiastic about the idea.

"Damn it, Maatsuyker," I said, "don't you see that this would be just the right finishing touch?"

"But that Verkerk boy . . . ?" he said.

"I'll see to it that he doesn't harm Verkerk," I promised.

A week later everything was arranged. Heavens above, how the Rat jumped and shouted for joy when I told him the news. He rushed at me, calling, "Aunt Jane! Aunt Jane! I'm going to be with the boys again!"

And so Ciske had pulled through.

However, I am human enough to continue to take an interest in him: that boy has become a real friend.

Yes, I want to know how life will treat him from now on. I want to know if Aunt Jane's secret wish will come true—if Ciske will marry Betty.

A boy has grown up. A child has pushed his way through the jungle. He has come out of a dark tunnel and now is standing in the light and the world lies at his feet—a world that needs men of strong character.

He can become a carpenter or an admiral of the fleet, a tramp under God's heaven or a simple shopkeeper—I don't mind which it is as long as he can look me honestly and fearlessly in the eye.

And stand firm.

Like a man!